love where you work

AN OFFICE ROMANCE

ANNA PULLEY

First published by Red Heel Press 2022

Cover design by Lauria: fivver.com/lauria

To Vika, my heart ripens each day in your hands

CLARE KNEW BETTER than to answer the phone. The only person who ever called her at stupid o'clock was her mother, and even though Carole was thousands and thousands of miles away, her mother's presence was so strong she may as well have been standing right there in Clare's tastefully minimalist living room.

Clare hovered over the phone, its singsong chirp like a robotic gnat in her ear. But then something tugged in her—guilt or resignation perhaps, or the singular ache of obligation that comes from being the only child of a widow.

If only she'd act like one, Clare thought unkindly.

Clare answered the video call and her mother's bright, pixelated face flitted onto the screen.

"My lover and I have taken to the alps, darling," Carole said. "You would not believe it. You can even drink the water from the tap!"

"Where are you now?"

Carole conferred with her "lover." That's what her mother called him. Not by his name, god forbid, (which was

1

Simon). "We're in Lugano, Switzerland, in a charming little villa overlooking the lake."

Carole attempted to show Clare the lake, but because she didn't understand how to flip the phone's screen, instead showed Clare a blurry, pink image of what might have been her mother's palm.

"It's pretty," Clare pretended.

Though Clare had heard of midlife crises, she wasn't sure if this could be applied to her mother, who was in her early sixties. A measly 10 months after Clare's father had died, Carole had taken out a new lease on life. Her *mother*, who had never left the United States, who had been with one man her entire life, had suddenly, inexplicably, sold her house to "travel the world," and taken up with "a charming, younger South African man" she met in her senior tour group, Yes We Cane!

"The photos don't do it justice. You must experience it for yourself, darling."

"The tap water's pretty good in Oakland, actually. You'd be surprised."

"Oh, hush now. You know that's not what I meant. They've been working you to the bone over there. Isn't it time to take a vacation, darling? You know, live a little?"

"I live!" Clare retorted, scratching a red, scaly patch of skin at her elbow until it bled.

"Don't do that, darling," Carole said, "and don't scrunch your face up like that, it makes you look 50 years old."

Clare softened her face, then gently dabbed at the small open wound she had just made, attempting to soothe it with spit. Her shoulders tensed with dullness and anti-gravity. "Besides," she said, "I do things. *Lots* of things."

"Oh," Clare's mother replied, pity and tenderness

soaking up her syllables like the sweet German wine she was surely drinking, no matter what time it was. *It's happy hour somewhere* was a quote she was fond of saying. "You aren't referring to that macrame class, are you? Though I will say, the net you sent was very ... nice. It had many ... quaint knots."

"It was an owl, mom."

"Yes, okay, an owl."

As her mother gently berated her, Clare scurried about her apartment. Everything in it was beige or white, with occasional touches of gray, and nothing was out of place. The surfaces were stone and vast and smooth, except for one large off-white living room rug, which Clare often walked around and not directly on, to avoid getting it dirty. No personal items were scattered about—no bills or receipts, no postcards from her mother, no silly tchotchke that a coworker bought for her from their travels abroad. Her refrigerator was polished steel that was so shiny it could almost serve as a mirror, which sometimes it did, when Clare wanted to view her body but not too clearly. She kept the small amount of books she owned—mostly personal finance tomes and *HR Fundamentals,* plus a hardbound copy of *The Old Man and the Sea*, which she'd never read—in her bedroom closet. The erotica collections she kept under lock and key in her desk drawer, lest any guests swing by and judge her for them. Not that anyone came by lately.

She reached for her flats and purse (beige and eggshell-colored, respectively), glancing at the macrame plant holder she had made that summer that drooped near her bedroom window, looking for all the world like a mop that had hung itself. The plant inside of it was most assuredly dead, though Clare couldn't bring herself to check, preferring to think of it as a Shroedinger's cat experiment—it was only dead if she checked. Until then, it might be alive! Besides, she kept meaning to get a new plant—surely it would help offset all the neutral tones in her apartment—but who had the time! It was all too much for Clare to think about.

"I've gotta run, mom. I have to make this doctor's appointment before work."

"Another one?"

"Yes."

"And you've been doing the lukewarm showers?"

Clare grabbed her keys and the brown leather bag that housed her work laptop. "Yes, mom," she lied. "I've gotta go."

"Okay, I'll call you when we get to Austria. My lover got us tickets to the Freud museum. I wonder if they'll mention his love of, you know, frosty flakes."

"What?"

"You know, the devil's Flonase, the Ziggy Stardust, the ol' snow blower."

"Are you talking about cocaine?"

"Yes! My, *some* of us are slow this morning." She tilted her forehead at Clare, to drive the point home further. As she did so, Carole swiveled and Clare finally glimpsed the view behind her mother's head. Glittering through the villa's bay windows was a view of the most beautiful lake Clare had ever seen. It was the kind of blue that made one drop things. That made one question one's life decisions. That made one use the word *sublime* unironically. In the face of such vividness, Clare felt a nip of exhilaration at her neck, a panoramic shock of pleasure she hadn't allowed herself to feel in, well, she wasn't sure how long. Then she blinked, and the melancholy returned.

"I guess some of us haven't had our 'powdered sugar' this morning," Clare said.

Carole ignored Clare's attempt at boomer drug slang. "Oh, that reminds me, darling. Remember Katarina, the Oloffs' daughter?"

"Sure, why?"

"June tells me she's getting married. You should really call her."

"I haven't spoken to Katarina in 20 years, mom. I highly doubt she wants to hear from me."

"Of course she does! Aren't you friends on the Facebook?"

"Yes, but—"

"Such a lovely girl, really. And so ambitious! Vera tells me she's hosting a gala for Ethiopian refugees at the Savon and Bono's hairdresser is going to be there."

Hearing this, Clare couldn't help but put a tiny pinprick in Carole's rosy-hued fantasy balloon.

"Who's she marrying?"

"Well, her partner of course, darling."

"Yes, but which one? Katarina's poly."

"She's double jointed?"

"No, mom. Polyamorous. It means she has relationships with multiple people. She has at least two partners, according to 'the' Facebook."

"Is that so?"

Clare felt as if she could hear the gears in her mother's head turning and felt the tiniest bit of satisfaction in confessing a truth that she had been deeply aware of since childhood: that all children were a disappointment to their parents. And vice versa.

Then Carole said: "How is it that Katarina has two committed, loving partners and you can't even find one?"

Clare's face burned as if she'd been struck.

"Think about what I said, darling," Carole continued in her usual singsong manner. "The days are long but the years are short. I read that in an ad for psoriasis medication in Oprah's magazine. You can always come join my lover and I on our travels. Maybe you could even bring a friend or a ... special someone."

"There are no someones, Mom, special or otherwise. There's only work, which you're going to make me late to again if you don't let me off the phone."

"Work work work. You sound just like your father. Just think about it! Ciao ciao. Or as they say in Austria, auf lederhosen!"

two

IT WAS fall in the San Francisco Bay Area, which felt far more like summer than any other time of year, including actual summer. Clare missed east coast autumns with their somber air, fiery leaves, and muted, tweed coats. That brisk air felt good enough to eat. And while Clare far preferred the mild California winters to the east coast's black-iced roads and devil winds, which had blown her car off the road into a snowbank on more than one terrifying occasion, she still pined for autumns. There was something about them that felt definitive. A changing of the guards. A bright and brilliant stamp of time. Not so much in Northern California, where she needed to carry a jacket in the morning and evenings, but whose doughy, sunshiny middles caused her to sweat and pant and wish that all her dress pants weren't made of wool. It was confusing. To dress for two seasons in one day.

Most days Clare refused to, deciding instead to dress as if it were properly fall and avoiding mid-day entirely. Occasionally she would glance out the fourth story window of her office and see the carefree smiles of people picnicking

7

near Lake Merritt at lunchtime and feel a pang of wistfulness.

But then she'd close the blinds.

If Clare had hoped the dermatologist this morning would be less condescending than her mother, she was wrong. But she so often was wrong these days. She sat on the crinkly white paper in the claustrophobic exam room, placing her hands underneath her so she wouldn't scratch herself for the next few minutes.

While she waited she read the intricate, multi-stepped hand-washing instructions tacked up to the wall. Clare counted them zombily. Eleven steps. Some involved interlacing, others two-fisted lock and turns, and one mildly sexual illustration involving a thumb and a figure-eight that Clare couldn't precisely determine. How was it that she had been doing something as simple as hand-washing wrong her whole life?

Before she could sink into a bout of irrelevant despair, Dr. Laurence Wong knocked on the door. He was short, with broad, beefy shoulders and a relentless chipperness befitting cheerleaders and ads of women eating yogurt. Dr. Wong's professionalism and positivity made it hard for Clare to dislike him, no matter how disappointing his prognosis always was.

"So," he smiled, extending a hand for Clare to shake as he electric-slided his way into the room, his sneakers lighting up as he did so. "Eczema again, huh?"

"The very same."

"Different spots?"

"Yeah, a new patch on my elbow, one between my

breasts, and a big one at the top of my spine." Clare pulled the back of her dress shirt down so Dr. Wong could look at the latest inflamed skin that kept her up at night.

He examined the scaly, itchy skin, which had started to scab over from the last time Clare had picked at it. "Ah, yes, there it is. But on the plus side, that's quite a reach you've got there!"

He swiveled from the exam table to the cart that housed a computer and typed something on the keyboard. "And when did the flare-up start this time?"

"It's been on and off. But it hasn't really let up in a year," Clare said. The smell of disinfectant in the small room made her feel faintly dizzy.

"Since your dad?" he asked.

Clare nodded, but kept her eyes trained on the floor.

Dr. Wong continued: "And I see you've been through two rounds of Prednisone in the last six months. Did the steroids help?"

"Yes, but once I finished, the eczema pretty much came right back."

"I see. And have you given any thought to what I suggested last time?"

"Therapy?"

"Yes."

"Therapy is for Lifetime movie specials."

"No way," he practically sang. "I love Lifetime! Did you see the one last week about the woman who returns to the lake of her childhood to heal from trauma only to realize the lake itself is slowly poisoning her and everyone in the town?"

"*Lake Woebehere*? Yes, I saw it," Clare was ashamed to admit.

He printed out the usual sheet of lotion recommendations and reprimands to take lukewarm showers. *No one takes lukewarm showers*, she thought privately. *Except lizards and masochists.*

"Look, Clare. There's no cure for eczema. And I can't keep giving you steroids or they're going to leech all the calcium from your bones. Stress, particularly stress that's related to traumatic or painful events, can contribute to breakouts. You've tried everything else right? Consider talking to someone."

He stuck his hand out once more for Clare to shake before moonwalking out of the exam room, the red lights on his sneakers flashing like tiny jubilant sirens as he made his way down the hall.

Clare hoped she'd be one of the first ones at the office that morning, despite the doctor's appointment, but she wasn't. She wanted all the extra hours she'd been putting in at W;nkdIn to be noticed. She'd been at the company for almost two years and her performance review was approaching fast. It wasn't that she wanted a promotion so much as that she *needed* one. She needed a win. Something that would excuse the quiet fire of her personal life. Something that would have made her father proud.

Clare rode the elevator to the fourth floor, standing in silence with the other sour-souled workers, their faces creased in perpetual lines of reverse-Botox worry. The doors opened and Clare was deposited into the familiar cavernous space. W;nkdIn's office was no frills and no fuss. Its industrial aesthetic, upcycled wood furniture, and unfinished brickwork surfaces gave the space a raw, utilitarian look that reminded Clare of the former Soviet Union, where her father had fled from 40 years ago. He had only been back once since emigrating to the United States, taking Clare with him when she was 16, and she had been casually depressed by the gray concrete blocks masquerading as museums and the uniform row houses with bars on every window that a well-meaning realtor might refer to as "prison chic." W;nkdIn's open floor plan wasn't quite so grim—it had an Eames' bird, after all. And a black chalkboard on which someone, not Clare, had scrawled the word HAPPY. Clare passed it every day on the way to and from her office. The word wasn't a reminder so much as a reprimand.

HAPPY

Clare forced the corners of her mouth skyward.

Despite its size and an employee count that numbered in the hundreds, W;nkdIn was remarkably quiet. It hummed with the faint clacking of keys, whispered chatter, and the aggressive rustling of protein bars being unwrapped en masse. Paula must've set the morning snack tray out early for the meeting, Clare surmised.

The topic of this morning's all-hands meeting was women. How to attract them, specifically, and how to keep them interested in the startup's services. W;nkdIn was a dating app tailored to busy working professionals, though recently, as the company prepared to go public, they had been trying to break into new markets. W;nkdIn was now offering services in arenas of dating profile help, match-making, sponsored singles events, getaways, and unique luxe experiences for careerists who didn't have the time or inclination to do it themselves.

As someone who spent an inordinate amount of time working for W;nkdIn at the expense of just about everything else in her life, including her love life, the irony that she was perfect for such services was not lost on Clare.

She pushed the thought from her mind as she sat down at the far end of the conference room table in front of a pad of lined stationary emblazoned with the company's winky face logo. She tried to remember the last time a non-inanimate object had winked at her, and couldn't. She crinkled the paper in her fist until its smiley face resembled the way she felt on the inside.

Others at the company began to file in. Sara and Sarah sandwiched themselves on either side of Clare. They were a lesbian couple and the company's founders, who had mostly retired and lived in Marin, but still came to occasional meetings and retreats, making sure to express their opinions and concerns about company affairs. Then came Nikki, whose customary greeting was to glare at Clare and sit as far from her as the circular table allowed. When she walked by, Clare felt the eczema patch on her elbow inflame. She stifled the urge to scratch it.

The C-Suiters came next, then Yolanda, head of sales, and the fall intern—Sofie? Saffron?—who also did the minutes. Clare made a mental note to walk past her desk to find out her name after the meeting was over.

Once everyone was seated, pleasantries were exchanged. Dry bran muffins were handed out, which Sarah had made. Clare sniffed at one—it smelled like an Amazon delivery box. A few polite coughs followed but everyone took a muffin regardless. Since Sara and Sarah went on their heart-health kick, the snacks had become mostly fruit, dense breads with many indigestible seeds involved, and herbal teas hand-dried from their garden. Clare unhappily grabbed a muffin and a banana from the basket.

"Quarterly profits exceeded expectations," the CEO began. His name was Will Williams, but he preferred to be called by his title or his high school nickname, Will Squared. His hair was thinning and reddish brown and he spoke robotically, as if each word had carefully been rehearsed. Membership was up, he said, but the trouble remained. The "trouble," as it was indirectly referred to, was that 79 percent of W;nkdIn's clientele were men. "How can we bridge the gender gap and ensure that women are getting to experience all the company has to offer?

"And not just straight or cisgender women," the CEO went on, pointing with a laser pointer to a rainbow-colored bar graph capped with a sad-face emoji. "There's a sizable market of LGBTQ+ professionals who are languishing in love! How can we find them? How can we reach *them*?"

She may have imagined it, but it seemed to Clare that nearly all the heads in the room swiveled in her direction at that moment. She bit into her banana, pretending not to notice anything, if she had, in fact, noticed anything. Was she imagining the staring? She sank a little lower in her chair.

After the meeting, the Sara/hs handed out individually wrapped homemade tempeh loafs for the board and staff. They also passed around promotional items the company was considering using to lure new potential clients at events, trade shows, and community gatherings. A tiny inflatable donut to hold one's beverages in a swimming pool. Nail clippers (*clever*, Clare thought). A rainbow fris- bee. Clare declined to take any of these items, though she did see a stack of 50% off coupons for psychotherapy services and, when she was sure no one was looking, discreetly pocketed several.

three

BACK IN HER office after the meeting, Clare sighed in relief. The world was chaotic, but here, in this small room, her life was ordered and calm. Outside the sun was shining, not a cloud in the sky. It was Friday and Clare didn't know what she would do for the next 48 hours. The weekends were a struggle, especially in the fall, when the weather turned warm and people began to flout their happiness. They'd go to movies in the park or have barbecues or take their loved ones to the beach. Their bright pink umbrellas and cans of lukewarm beer and smiles flush with sun were all exhausting to Clare. They made her feel guilty, and drove her deeper into her work.

Once alone in her office, her flustered thoughts returned to what her mother had said to her that morning. *Live a little.*

Live a little. *Am I not alive?* She wondered. She placed her hand over her heart, listening to it stutter, like the one person in the drum circle who couldn't keep the beat. Other than that, she felt ... *winded*, which was, she supposed, a kind of aliveness? Or a sign that her pants were too restrictive. Then, realizing she had the answer at her fingertips, she decided to do what any rational, college-educated person would—She typed into the search engine: Am I really living?

Seven trillion hits. *Well, at least I'm not the only one*, she comforted herself. At the top of the search results was a quiz. Clare clicked on it.

Just how alive was Clare Kolikov?

Last year, she had:

- Gone on a road trip, +2 points. (It had been to retrieve her father's ashes, but still!)
- She had fallen in love, +5 points
- She had fallen out of love, -3 points. (*Really? You lose points for that?*)

Clare hadn't, however:

- Lived in a foreign country, - 2 points.
- Nor had she ever fallen asleep on the beach, -1. (*I am not a homeless person, thank you.*)
- And unless they counted the clarinet she played in seventh grade, she did not know how to play a musical instrument, -3.

She had:

- Spent all day in bed, +4. (*Sometimes several days!*)
- But she hadn't, she was embarrassed to admit, had sex outside of her comfort zone, -5.

Not in a long time, at least.

Erik had been rather stodgy in bed. The man thought

15

lube was kinky. There was no way Clare could have admitted to him what she desired, and she certainly couldn't tell him how she often fantasized about her ex-girlfriend in college while they were in bed together. How free Clare had been then! How delicious to say *yes* to her, no matter how uncouth the request. Want to try on this pink rubber thong I found for $4 at the strip mall? Yes. Want to let me go down on you on this roof overlooking the city? Yes! Want to bang in a Gap dressing room to protest sweatshop labor? Dear gods, yes!

The 21-year-old Clare would have thrown her head back and laughed at the 36-year-old Clare asking a search engine to validate her aliveness. But the 21-year-old Clare knew nothing about FSA accounts or the particular joys of organic fruit water. The 36-year-old Clare *did* and she wasn't upset about it. Not exactly.

She clicked and clicked her way through the questions. After 20 minutes, she seemed to have finally reached the last one: "Did you answer every single question in this quiz?" it asked. "-100 points. Get off the computer and go grab a frap!"

Clare shut her laptop in disgust. Shame circled in her like a drain, followed by frustration. *Who needs a life*, she scoffed. Life was messy. Besides, soon she'd be promoted, and no internet quiz could take that away from her.

She did want a frappuccino, though. That would be 500 calories for the 24 ounce version, she justified to herself, but she did skip breakfast this morning, except for the cardboard muffin and banana. And, she knew precisely how many points she needed in her rewards app to get one. Plus, an extra pump of caramel syrup! Clare smiled a little too toothily as she rose from her chair. *This* was the only point system that mattered.

But just then, an intruder.

"Clare! I was hoping I might find you in here," Yolanda said, knocking but then entering anyway before Clare could respond.

"In my office?" Clare glanced around her, as if she might find a portal to another dimension that she had overlooked and could have been escaping from this whole time.

"Yes."

"Well, that was a good guess." At this Yolanda, the head of sales at W;nkdIn, burst into a fit of giggles. Clare didn't realize she had said anything funny. Yolanda was a *presence*—she had big hair and big energy, and a chumminess that made Clare feel like they were friends, even though they were not. Clare tried to recall a solitary fact about Yolanda from their hundreds of conversations. She liked Zumba? She had a husband and a Shar-Pei and one of them was named Brian? Clare couldn't be certain of anything else, even though they'd worked together for a year and a half.

Embarrassed by this, Clare fished for a clue. "How's Brian?"

"Oh, you know, good. A handful at times, but keeps me happy."

Damn, Clare thought. That could apply easily to a spouse or a pure-bred. She'd have to think up better questions, ones that somehow didn't let on that she knew nothing about a woman she saw five days a week.

"Are you free to chat right now?" Yolanda asked.

Clare glanced at her calendar. "I've got 15 minutes before my next call. But I was going to grab a coffee—" She tried once more to rise from her seat.

Yolanda sat down in the chair in front of her. Clare sat back down. "Great! So, remember what the CEO said this morning at the all-hands meeting?" Yolanda asked. "About expanding our clientele?"

Clare felt suddenly sweaty. She ventured a tentative *yes*.

"Well, the marketing team has been working on this new set of experiences, super beta mode right now, but we're hopeful that it's going to have huge ROI in attracting and broadening our client base. And we're looking for volunteers within the company to test it out. We were hoping you'd be one of the volunteers."

Clare swallowed hard. She could already feel the skin at the top of her spine constricting and swelling into an itchy, fiery knot.

"I wish I could, I really do, but—"

"This isn't coming from me, Clare," she said, pointing to the ceiling conspiratorially. "It's coming from the man upstairs."

"Jesus?" Clare pressed the palms of her fingers together roughly, in a kind of anti-prayer.

"No, the CEO! And there's some concern from the Sara/hs that you're not a team player," Yolanda continued.

"The Sara/hs said that?"

"Not in those words exactly. Sara said you were like Fomalhaut, the loneliest star in the constellation Piscis Austrinus. Then Sarah said that was such a Gemini thing to say. You know how she goes on tangents."

"Yes." Clare's voice had taken on a cracked sheen.

"Look, Clare. There's no 'i' in W;nkdIn."

"Technically there is. Two if you count the—"

"You never attend the mixers, or the lunchtime meditations with Meg. You came to the holiday party for 15 minutes before leaving. And you even missed the Smooth Operators concert!"

"I find jazz to be very grating—"

"Let's just say that your absence is *notable* and your contribution to this new effort would not go unnoticed by —" Yolanda pointed to the ceiling again. "You're up for your performance review soon, yeah? I know you've been gunning to head up that ladder. This could be just the thing that gives you an edge."

"I'm not sure how that's true—" Clare tried to interject again, but was swiftly ignored.

"When was the last time you even took a vacation day?" Clare looked toward the ceiling. She honestly couldn't remember, it had been so long. "Listen. This will be perfect for you. You'll be helping the company, you'll be taking a little R&R, and you'll be getting back out there. Plus, I'll be real. You're ... uniquely qualified to test these experiences."

"I am?" Clare had never been uniquely qualified for anything, except Human Resources. Once she'd found HR at 22, she'd never looked back. It was as if the only gift she ever needed had been handed to her. Yolanda's words, however condescending, made her feel oddly special.

"Yes! You're one of the most senior employees at the company, you've been around from almost the beginning, and you're not straight!"

"Well, okay—wait, who told you I'm not straight?" Clare was intensely guarded about her private affairs and her private parts and she wanted to keep it that way. As much as she could, at least. "Not that I am. I'm out and proud. Basically. Not like, swinging-topless-from-the-chandelier proud, but like, waving-a-tiny-rainbow-flag-from-a-moving-car-with-the-windows-rolled-up-while-the-parade-passed-by ... proud." The silence was cavernous. Clare had no choice but to keep talking. "I just ... I didn't realize my sexuality was common office knowledge."

"Oh definitely not. But when we were talking about potential volunteers after the meeting, Nikki mentioned you."

Nikki. Always Nikki.

She and Clare had briefly dated, a two-month period marked hazily by drinking, fighting, and sex. Somehow, during this melee, Nikki had revealed she was desperate for a job, and asked Clare to recommend her at W;nkdIn, which Clare did. Despite their mutual interest in HR, Clare quickly realized how incompatible they were and broke things off, which is when Nikki's true "job" started—making Clare's work life hell. This was a lesson learned the hard way for Clare—to not mix business with pleasure. Except when Yolanda pressured her, apparently.

"So it's settled then?" Yolanda said.

"When would this start exactly?"

Yolanda's eyebrows prickled. "The fun starts next week. Thanks a bunch, Clare Bear!"

Damn that Yolanda, Clare thought. She was good. No wonder she was head of sales.

four

"WHAT SEEMS TO BE THE PROBLEM?" Clare asked. Her 11 a.m. appointment was something of a mystery. The employee had only said that she "needed to talk."

Clare studied the woman sitting across from her desk. She didn't think she'd seen her at the office before—Clare was sure she would remember someone so, well, *creatively* dressed. In a swift, barely perceptible once-over, Clare assessed the woman in her entirety, scanning the parts of her that she could see and guessing at the parts she couldn't.

The woman wore a double-breasted, pin-striped jacket, with multiple colorful pocket squares that seemed to dart off in different directions as if they had a mind of their own. The jacket hugged her contours perfectly, Clare had to admit, as if she'd either had it tailored or had made it herself. The faintest hint of cleavage showed in the rift made by the lapels. And the black trousers she wore might as well have been leggings, they were so form-fitting.

Perhaps they were. Clare couldn't keep up with what

counted as "pants" anymore—though she certainly appreciated them on the woman who sat across from her for all that they revealed—slim, muscled thighs crossed casually, a foot bouncing in tall black riding boots, their worn, buttery leather gleaming in the fluorescent light. Around her neck was a pair of headphones that looked like they were from the '80s. She radiated a kind of effortless confidence that Clare associated with grown men who rollerbladed. Clare also noticed the scent of cinnamon emanating from her—from a recently chewed piece of gum?—which made the woman appear younger somehow than she probably was. Clare guessed in her late twenties.

Though Clare knew absolutely nothing about this woman, she seemed so unlike most of the other people she had encountered in the office. Indeed, Clare thought she belonged somewhere else entirely, perhaps running a small anarchist bookstore or creatively naming new lipstick colors. Angry Birds Red. Mazel-Tov Mauve. That kind of thing.

"It's Joel in Accounting," Julia said. "He keeps making … comments."

"What kind of comments?" Clare asked.

"Sexual," Julia replied, her eyes flashing dark and dangerous at Clare, as if she'd been reading Clare's thoughts and found them prurient. The shame that flared in Clare was enough to force her gaze downward. She felt as if the mere mention of the word sex implicated her somehow. Or had the woman noticed her staring?

Julia was sure she had never encountered a more attractive HR manager in her life. Admittedly, she had known very few—maybe, three?—in her limited stints in 9-5 office culture, but the ones she had were dour, all of them. Priggish. Overly literal. Enforcers of rules and senders of irritating PowerPoint presentations. *We get it, Steve!* She wanted to snap one time. *The deadline for open enrollment ends soon!* No matter how early she complied with their demands, still the PowerPoints came. *Don't wait for the days to fly / or your benefits will go bye-bye,* one particularly ridiculous slide read.

What was *most* surprising to Julia on this particular morning, however, was that she had noticed a beautiful woman at all. She had spent the last six months reeling from Britt's sudden departure, feeling gray and malformed, like a child's piece of playdough that had been left in the sun. Since then, Julia had been far too busy eating Dunkaroos and watching YouTube tutorials about how to dress according to one's *essence* to notice anything or anyone remotely fetching.

Paula Suarez, her platonic office mate, would occasionally point out women she thought Julia might find attractive, but they had barely registered at all.

What about Jet? Paula had asked that very morning, pointing to a stylish woman by the copy machine in pink aviator frames, whose dark eyes seemed to set the wet-sand color of her skin ablaze. *Admit it, she's gorgeous.*

Julia acquiesced that Jet was indeed an attractive woman, because she was, and Julia also sensed that Paula was not one to let up about such things. But the brief agreement did neither of them any good. Julia was too stricken, too dead inside to let beauty in, in any of its forms. Instead, she shut the door on it, as if beauty was a bitter wind, or a racoon. Even the bright-bursting fall leaves, which ordinarily delighted her, felt to Julia like just more garbage in her path. She barely noticed them as she roller skated to work that day, her Walkman silently blasting Ace of Base while she mouthed along.

Since she started at the office a month ago, Julia had seen Clare a few times, but never up close, and had never spoken to her before today. In a company with almost 300 employees, she was still putting faces to names. Mostly Julia knew Clare as the woman who wore neutral tones and paced back and forth past her open office door, making endless phone calls.

But now here they were, face to face, Clare's beauty jarring and irrefutable, like a soft slap in the mouth. She was utterly feminine, somehow made more so by the beige blazer, crisp white shirt, and ballet flats she was wearing. A gold clip held Clare's hair in place—the only color on her, Julia noticed. A few strands had broken free, framing Clare's face in a way that made her seem windswept, like a Victorian heroine pining on the moors, albeit one very properly dressed for the occasion. And who smelled somehow of strawberry shortcake. Mmm, cake.

Her senses suddenly awakened, Julia subtly appraised the woman sitting tall behind the large, crowded, yet meticulously organized desk, the dark hairs that fell in soft waves about her face, the eyes that seemed to change with each shifting of the light—from blue to green to gray and back. Right now they appeared blue, but not the icy kind, the aloof kind. No, to Julia they appeared to be the blue of flame—the hottest part of the fire.

Even though Clare was merely sitting, pen poised to take notes on Julia's claim, she radiated sensuality. A wounded sensuality, to be sure, but a sensuality no less. She seemed both present and not, a shapeshifter who had one foot in this office and the other at a Parisian cafe, cigarette in tow, scribbling maudlin song lyrics in a journal as the world idled by. Perhaps Julia recognized something else in her, too, something she was loath to admit she felt, though it nevertheless snuck in on quiet nights. Sadness. It seemed as if some droopy-eyed beagle had holed up behind Clare's sternum and refused to budge. Julia knew this beagle. It was familiar and it was a bitch she begrudgingly fed. But more than that, she had the urge to reach over the fence of Clare's ribs to pet it. The hairs on Julia's forearms prickled as she allowed herself to wonder briefly what Clare looked like under her beige pantsuit.

But as Julia let her mind wander so, somewhere in her awareness, it registered that Clare had asked her a question. "Hmm?" she said, snapping back to attention and away from her daydream.

"If you don't mind, Ms. Dawes, that is, if you feel comfortable—I'm going to need you to elaborate on the nature of these sexual comments..."

———

Clare felt oddly flustered. She removed the cap from her pen, looked at it as if it was an unruly pet, and then snapped it back on. Clare made sure to keep her face and voice in an expressionless tone, but her hands, which she now folded on her lap, below her desk, were shaking. She couldn't stop herself from noticing again and again the striking brown eyes of the woman before her, which seemed to flash at her like a dare. Clare had never been anything other than the pinnacle of professionalism, so why did she feel as if she was engaging in something *inappropriate* just by talking to this woman?

And why couldn't she figure out what to do with her hands!

"Well," Julia started, suddenly shy to repeat the obscene words that Joel had taunted her with—not in front of this beautiful woman, at least, whose unflappable calm caused Julia's heart to hammer in her throat. "I don't know that I can repeat it out loud."

"I understand this is difficult for you," Clare said. "But you should know that during an investigation like this we keep things as confidential as possible. You will not be punished or retaliated against in any way. Coming forward is a protected activity. We also have a zero-tolerance policy for unwanted sexual contact at this company, and I will do everything in my power to help you. I just need to know exactly what happened."

Comforted though still feeling timid, Julia surprised herself by rising from her chair and leaned forward over the desk, which, Julia noticed, was covered with carefully arranged sticky notes and an inspirational quotes calendar. She glimpsed today's inspiration: "Don't just think about it, *be* about it." Julia felt both embarrassed and endeared by this sudden knowledge of Clare, and nearly retreated, but Clare's mysterious, *tabula rasa* face compelled her forward, so much so that Julia was now leaning entirely over the mammoth desk, inching toward Clare, pressing her elbows against the desk to steady herself. As Clare did not move from her position, and because the desk was bigger than Julia had anticipated, she beckoned Clare forward with a whip of her head. Clare hesitated a beat before placing her manicured hands on the desk and leaning toward Julia's clavicle.

From here, Julia noticed the soft down of Clare's neck, the hair there as white and fine as confectioner's sugar, even though the rest of her hair was black-brown with the faintest wisps of silver threaded through. In a voice barely above a whisper, Julia spoke softly into Clare's ear, her lips so close to Clare's face that the heat of Clare's body sent a thunder clap straight down to Julia's center.

Clare listened to Julia repeat the string of lewd comments that Joel had said to her, struggling to stop the flood of sensation that Julia's lips had awakened in her. *Focus*, she chastised herself, *You have a job to do and it is not ogling a woman in need of your help!* And yet, she could not stop herself from registering the soft peaks of Julia's cleavage as she leaned over the desk—low-hanging fruit, literally!— the impressions of which were now firmly embedded in her mind and would not remove themselves.

The litany of filth continued as Clare warred privately with herself, and when Julia's lip brushed the soft fold of her ear—accidentally?—Clare let slip a brief, throaty "unh."

"I know," Julia replied, still inches from Clare's face. Every hair on the back of Clare's neck stood at upright attention. "Isn't it horrid? I even told him I was gay, which I thought would be a deterrant, but it seems to have only bolstered his advances."

"That *is* horrid," Clare agreed, breaking with her usual, impartial script. Then, she snapped to, remembering herself. "Thank you for telling me. I know it isn't easy to talk about something like this. Openly."

When Julia sat back down in her chair, Clare was relieved, as it allowed her to recover from the warmth and almost unbearable nearness of Julia's body, and a respite from the brief brushing of Julia's lips that had set Clare's particles jostling. "I'm so sorry that happened to you—it's awful," she said, thankful to have enough wits about her to form coherent sentences. "Rest assured that his behavior is entirely unacceptable and will not be tolerated at this company, toward you or anyone else. Is there anything else I need to know?"

———

Julia struggled to come up with something—*anything*—that would allow her to stay in the beguiling woman's presence for a little while longer, but couldn't. She was tongue-tied and more than a little turned on still from the brief glimpse of Clare's long, graceful neck and the sweet, cloying scent of her she had just encountered when she leaned in close to her ear. Definitely cake.

Julia felt twisty and strange. Her skin prickled and her throat felt cloudy as she rose from her chair to bid Clare adieu. As they clasped hands, she allowed hers to linger in Clare's for a fraction of a second longer than necessary.

"It's nice to meet you, formally," Julia said.

"Likewise."

five

THE PLEASURE and heat and memory of this brief encounter stayed with Julia for the rest of the day and well into the evening, where she freely allowed her mind to wander over and over again the details, the scents, and sights that so suddenly and shockingly bewitched her.

Her daydreaming was interrupted by her sister's ringtone, "It's a Small World After All," which was unquestionably the most annoying song in the world and which Julia had chosen to match her feelings toward her sister.

It was rare for Candace to call her. They weren't close as children and as adults the chasm seemed only to widen and widen with each passing year. Eventually the birthday parties became birthday phone calls and then birthday texts. Then even that became too much for Candace, who had missed Julia's last two birthdays entirely. Julia felt more hurt by this than she thought she should and almost didn't pick up the phone when Candace called. Until guilt or obligation or perhaps an ordinary devotion drove her to answer.

"Hello?"

"How fast could you get to Fruitvale?"

"Uh, maybe 30 minutes? Why?"

"Mom locked the keys in the car while we were getting gas. We're at the Shell off the 880. You need to come down and do … your thing."

Julia could picture her sister waving her hands in the air as she said your *thing*, as if popping locks was something she thought came about by magic. Julia knew just how non-magical it was, having worked for almost a year as a locksmith for Jimmy-In-A-Shimmy, an emergency car unlocking service where she was on call 24 hours a day. She took the job right after she had graduated high school. Candace had just aced her MCATs and was interviewing at high profile hospitals. All her life, Julia had been told she was the "pretty" one. Candace was the "smart" one. The driven one. She was voted Most Likely to Succeed in high school, whereas Julia had barely graduated at all, preferring instead to read books and create performance art pieces about ending the heteropatriarchy (which mostly involved a lot of Barbie doll smashing) rather than attend classes. And though Julia had ambitions of her own, their mother never pushed her.

Julia didn't fault her mother for this. Rosa had been a single mom, raising two girls on her modest social worker salary. Their father, Julian, had skipped town before Julia was in kindergarten. Occasionally he sent postcards, always from different places—the Poconos mountains, Oklahoma, Memphis—never a return address. As if he was afraid Julia might track him down or they were playing some perverse game of *Where in the World Is Carmen Sandiego?*

She used to keep the postcards and their strange missives, thinking perhaps they were clues to under-standing him or why he left, but when she turned 21 and he'd still made no attempt to contact her, she threw them all away, refusing to stay connected to a past that barely concerned her.

Still, she missed him. Or at least the idea of him. He had a legacy for leaving that reared up in Julia often. She never knew when it might come about. One day she'd be fine and happy and the next she felt claustrophobic, as if she had to get out—to do something, change something. Gigs. Girlfriends. Cities.

Aside from this tendency to slip and slide from place to place or gig to gig, Julian left Julia with little else except his light skin and his name, which seemed to follow her about, casting a ghostly pale shadow upon her wherever she went. In a white world, Julia knew her light skin was a kind of dowry. She recognized it and was grateful for it. Especially when she saw the way people responded to her sister and mother. It was often subtle but always there, a thumb pressed to the neck, ready to dig in, if provoked.

Candace took after their mother, dark skin and hair, their faces both round and freckled. The only trait that seemed to bind them all together were the matching small but noticeable gaps between their front teeth. Once Candace could afford it, she'd paid good money to fix her diastema, and urged Julia to do the same, but Julia refused. To most, it was a "flaw," but to Julia, it was belonging. Communion.

In her more morose moments, Julia sometimes wondered if her mother felt Julian's absence each time she looked at Julia. She wondered if perhaps she was always already a disappointment, which was why Rosa never pushed her to succeed in her endeavors. Or to even try. Then again, perhaps Rosa had merely been tired. Julia knew it was hard enough for Rosa to send Candace to college on her salary. She didn't remember how exactly—surely there must have been a conversation—but somehow it was conveyed that if Julia wanted to go to college, she would have to pay for it herself. And as that was entirely too daunting for Julia at 17, instead she shimmied over to Jimmy-In-A-Shimmy. Breaking into cars was not a career by any stretch of the imagination, but it was nevertheless a skillset that had proved to be useful to her many times throughout the years, and continued to impress a certain kind of woman. Candace was not one of those women.

"Are you saying you need my help?" Julia asked.

There was silence on the line so Julia waited. She so rarely got to gloat in front of her sister, who was more together than Julia in every conceivable way.

"Don't be a dick."

"If you want my services you're going to have to try a little harder than that."

Julia could hear Candace talking over her shoulder to their mother. "I told you she'd be a dick about it."

"I am not!" she shouted back, though she was sure her mother couldn't hear her. To Candace she said, "Just one word, big sis, and I'm there."

Julia heard a grumbling and some faint crunching, as if Candace was walking over gravel, perhaps to avoid being overheard by their mother before she whispered, "Please."

"Thank you. Was that so hard? What were you doing in Fruitvale, anyway?"

"Getting pupusas from that little place on 27th."

Julia's heart sank a little. "Why didn't you invite me? You know I love that place."

Julia swore she could hear her sister's eyes rolling. "You're so possessive."

"Fuck you. I'll be there in 30."

Julia hung up the phone, her face hot with an acid feeling bubbling in her throat, the kind that occurs right before a cry. She shook her head violently to stymie the tears. When that didn't work, she tried the trick of repeating the word *cripes!* over and over again, hoping the ridiculousness would sufficiently distract her. By the time she hit the freeway, she was as emotionless as a Pottery Barn throw pillow.

———

After Julia rescued her mother and sister, which took almost an hour, (she was rusty!) her prize was two soggy pupusas and some cortida in a zip-top bag.

"Can't I have these in a regular Tupperware container?" Julia asked.

"As soon as you return the countless other ones I've already given you," Rosa said.

"Oh, come on, mom."

"You can't be trusted to give them back. I'm waiting patiently to be proved wrong."

The accusation was entirely true, but still grated on Julia at times. "Do you know how difficult it is to explain to my coworkers why I'm eating enchiladas out of a plastic bag?"

"Probably not as difficult as returning my Tupperware." Rosa cocked her head to the side just as Candace burst out laughing.

Julia kept meaning to return her mother's Tupperware, along with the glass baking dish and the decorative towels from last Thanksgiving and the springform cake pan. And one day she would! But today was not that day.

She sat on her mother's green formica kitchen counter,

the way she had when she was a teenager. There was something about being in her childhood home that made her revert instantly to a childish state. And much like her teen years, when Rosa asked how Julia was doing, she lied outlandishly.

A few of the things Julia was currently lying about were:

- That she was over Britt, her ex-girlfriend
- That she was not drowning in debt from the business Britt had started, (an essential oils aromatherapy subscription service that turned out to be a Ponzi scheme) and then left Julia shackled with when she took off
- That she was also not literally drowning in aromatherapy oils, thousands of vials that filled her studio apartment but ironically only made her stress levels worse
- That she was not about to default on her student loan repayments

And that, because of all these debts, she could barely afford the studio she once shared with Britt on her own

"How's the job going anyway? Or have you quit already?" Candace asked. The job at W;nkdIn was keeping Julia afloat for now, if she could stick with it, something she'd never once managed to do in her decade of employment, aside from her years in the Peace Corps, which she decided didn't count, as it was the antithesis of corporate.

Julia shot her sister a look. "It's going fine, thank you, and no I haven't quit. In fact, they just put me in charge of this new initiative of LGBTQ+ date experiences. Mostly singles nights, but I'll be putting together a bunch of different outings for queer people."

"That sounds perfect for you," Rosa said.

"Better not fuck it up—for once," Candace said.

Julia's breath quickened. For a moment she thought Candace had somehow found out about her money woes, which she'd worked hard to hide from them. But if Candace knew something, she didn't let on any further. Instead, she began unloading her mother's dishwasher.

"Oh, that reminds me," Rosa said. "I finished Suzana's quinceañera dress." She pulled a white sequined princess dress out of the hall closet to show them. "Isn't it darling?"

"Wow, mom," Candace said, admiring the intricacy of the lace work. "This must've taken weeks."

"It's really beautiful," Julia said. "How did you find the time, what with work and all?"

Rosa waved her away. "Family comes first."

Julia once thought about asking her mother for a temporary loan, but found she couldn't. Her mother was always doing everything for other people. She barely had the resources for herself.

So, Julia lied. She did it to protect her mother, who was a worrier. She lied to keep her disapproving sister off of her back. And she lied because for the first time in her life, Julia had a real job—with benefits! And an HSA account! Julia still didn't know what that meant exactly, but it was *hers*, nonetheless. She wanted to prove to her family that she could be *something*, to prove that she was responsible and trustworthy and every bit as capable of success as Candace.

But as these lies made up the bulk of Julia's life, there was not much left to discuss, outside of fabric, the weather, and food. Hence, they "caught up" quickly and Julia found herself back at her studio in El Cerrito before the sky had fully darkened.

On her way in, she checked the mail, glancing at yet

another bill that had come in the mail, its envelopes had been changing colors like an ominous sunset, from white to pink to blue. Thankfully she got paid on Friday.

And the rest? She'd figure it out on her own. She always had.

six

"JOHN, GOTTA MINUTE?"

Clare jog-walked up to the Director of Finance. He was almost never in his office, preferring to take his meetings in motion at the nearby Lake Merritt. Power meetings, he called them.

Clare was winded already. The pencil skirt she wore severely restricted her range of motion, and as such, she had to take three tiny steps for every one of John's unimpeded ones. She hoped this unpleasant task would be over quickly.

"Clare! Talk to me." He paused the music he had been listening to, which Clare tried not to notice was Beyoncé's "All the Single Ladies," but left his earbuds in. Sweat dotted the sides of his face, though otherwise he seemed nonplussed.

"It's about Joel," Clare said, continuing her clipped gallop. She dodged a man on a Segway holding a terrified shiba inu.

"Joel! Good kid. A Phi Beta Kappa man. What's he up to?"

"Well," Clare said slowly. "It's not good, John. An employee brought a sexual harassment claim against him."

"What? Against Joel? Who?"

Clare felt the sweat beginning to pool near her lower back. They were rounding the part of the man-made lake that smelled like hot garbage. She chose the wrong moment to catch her breath, inhaling sulphuric rot and algae, and coughed. "That's confidential, but what I can tell you is that, when an allegation is made we conduct a thorough investigation. And in this case, it's in the company's best interests to let him go."

John stopped power-walking and looked at Clare for the first time. "Can't you just give him a warning or something?"

Clare stiffened. She had anticipated pushback, but it never failed to rile her. She lowered her voice to an almost robotic lull. "It wasn't a singular incident, John. During the investigation, several other women at the company came forward with complaints. I also found a note in his onboarding file about a prior complaint made against him at his previous company. Frankly, things should not have escalated this far."

He ran his hands through his thinning hair. "I don't know, Clare. He's young. I mean, think of his future."

"His future?" Clare felt the muscles in her throat tighten, her blood pressure rising. She steeled herself. A bitter taste coated her tongue and she swallowed it. John's reaction didn't shock her; she'd worked too long in HR and had encountered this kind of dismissiveness many times before, but it still disgusted her. She tried another approach. "The only future I care about is ... the future of this company, which would be compromised if Joel continued here."

He began to walk again, though, thankfully for Clare, more slowly this time. "I don't know. It was thanks to Joel that we got the Bancroft account. Do you know how long we've been trying to land them? Clients rave about him!"

Clare felt the conversation veering and slipping beyond her grasp. Then she realized that John was a numbers guy and switched tracks. "Let me be frank. A lawsuit of this magnitude would cost the company hundreds of thousands of dollars, and that's best-case scenario, assuming it's settled out of court. Not to mention the PR nightmare and how that would impact our bottom line."

"Shit, Clare. All right. Set up a meeting with Steve and Rob. If you can convince them, we'll do it your way. Poor kid. Make sure he gets a decent severance, yeah?" He began to punch buttons into his phone. Clare couldn't tell if he was checking his calendar or had turned Beyoncé back on. "Hey, you want a smoothie from the truck up ahead? The acai berry blast will knock you on your fucking ass. Antioxidants up the wazoo."

seven

THE FOLLOWING WEEK, when Julia walked past Joel's desk on the way to her own, she was startled to find it empty. Even his nameplate had been removed, only a ghostly, sun-stained outline of it remained on the outside of the gray cubicle divider.

She wore a swirly green zebra-striped sundress, lace-up white sneakers, and tiny beaded taco earrings that she'd made herself. Though perfectly work appropriate, the dress showed off her curves and contours, and she had anticipated further comments from Joel.

Had her harassment complaint actually worked? Was she finally going to be free and able to do her job in peace? A thrilling lightness moved through her as she sat down at her desk, placing today's coffee cup next to three other half-drunk coffees, which sat in varying stages of congealment, like a science project she had enthusiastically forgotten about.

As she waited for her laptop to load, she dug through her purse, searching for chapstick. When she couldn't find it amid the receipts, the student loan bills, the dried out wet wipes, journals, notebooks, and expired mascaras, she nearly gave up in defeat. But then she pulled out a loose Mentos, and, after brushing the lint off of it, popped it eagerly in her mouth instead. Glory restored.

The first message in her inbox was a company-wide email from the CEO. It was about Joel's departure, though there were scant few details as to why. Julia scanned the email " ... blah blah ... thankful for his service and dedication ... blah blah ... wish him luck on his next enterprise..."

Horse shit! She thought, wanting real answers, and knowing precisely the woman who could provide them.

Julia peered her head over her cubicle wall, craning her neck down the hall to the office Clare occupied. Her door was open again and Julia could see that she was once again talking on the phone. She paced while she talked, her crisp, pressed shirt buttoned all the way to her throat. Her face placid and indecipherable. There was something about Clare, something mysterious, unreadable. Her life was a hieroglyph, a locked car that she desperately wanted to crack. Julia's breath quickened. She felt faint, loopy. Her insides soup.

When Clare glanced up briefly from her pacing and saw Julia's eyes upon her, Julia swore she saw the corners of her mouth flicker into a smile before looking away. Julia smiled in kind, almost involuntarily. She typed a message to Clare.

Subject: Case Update

Does this mean what I think it does?

—J

Ten minutes later, Clare responded:

. . .

RE: Case Update
Unable to discuss details at present. Tonight? At 1221?

Julia's eyes widened. 1221 was the queer bar near their office. Was Clare suggesting it to convey her sexuality to Julia? Or did she choose it because she knew no one at the office would likely be there, and hence, they could talk more openly? Regardless, Julia was thrilled, both to learn more about what had happened with Joel and to spend time out of the office with Clare. She did a little dance in her seat, hoping no one would inopportunely walk by, as she typed: "I'll be there at 6pm."

Then she texted Paula. **On a scale of 1 to 10, how dumb would it be to hit on the HR manager?**

Paula: **Steve?! I didn't know you liked thin, judgmental mustaches**

Julia: **OMG, no. I'm talking about Clare**

Julia: **You know what? Just come here**

Half a minute later, Paula sulked up to Julia's desk, clad in all black, matching her hair and general surliness. Paula had once described herself as a "recovering goth," which Julia respected, having been in her own misfit group in high school, albeit the kind that dyed their eyebrows and wore enormous pants that could accommodate a family of five with room to spare.

Julia thought Paula might be grateful for a reprieve in her current task of relabeling all the W;nkdIn member files to comply with the newly agreed-upon naming convention. She'd been working on it on and off for the last 47 days and the task showed no signs of abating anytime soon.

"Girl, you know it's September, right?" Paula pointed with her nose to the calendar on Julia's wall, which was two months behind. It had been a gift from Britt's mother last Christmas, involving anthropomorphic fruits getting into shenanigans.

"I know," Julia sighed. "I just really enjoy seeing these two tiny pumpkins sitting on a beach, reading a fashion magazine that claims to teach them '47 ways to be GOURDgeous.'"

Paula considered this. "They really are living their best lives, aren't they?"

"We should all be so lucky," Julia said. "But come, sit. Tell me the hot goss on Clare. Spill dat tea. And more importantly, why have you kept her from me?"

"Oh, girl, no. Do not pursue Clare. You'd have a better chance of seducing an espresso machine."

"But why?"

"Clare is ... well, she's the least interested person in dating I've ever met."

Julia's face fell. It would be fitting for her to fall for someone entirely uninterested in dating when she herself had been uninterested in dating ... up until a week ago when she met Clare.

She pressed on. "Really? Do you know her well?"

"That's kind of my point. No one does. She's unknowable. Like the position and momentum of a subatomic particle. Or what's really in Taco Bell 'beef.'" Paula sniffed at one of Julia's week-old coffee cups, and made a face. "Besides, Clare's an order muppet."

"A what?"

"You know, an order muppet! Have I not told you my theory?"

"Um, no."

"There are two kinds of muppets: order and chaos. And most people fit into these categories as well. Kermit the Frog, Fozzie Bear, Dr. Bunsen Honeydew—these are examples of order muppets, as they're the ones who are always trying to keep things together and play by the rules. Miss Piggy, Animal, and Gonzo are examples of chaos muppets. They do what they want and generally cause mayhem that the order muppets then have to clean up."

"Oh my god, you're right. Which am I?"

"Seriously? You're such a chaos muppet. Remember when you told me you snorted pepper because *Cosmopolitan* said it was similar to an orgasm?"

Julia did remember, unfortunately. She couldn't stop sneezing or crying for hours. It was not her finest moment.

"I'm guessing you're an order muppet then?"

"With a chaos heart," Paula added, confusingly.

"But order muppets and chaos muppets can work! Look at Miss Piggy and Kermit."

"Um, Piggy tricked Kermit into marrying her and beats the crap out of him not infrequently. He's terrified of her! Is that really the example you want to use?"

Julia sighed, considering this intel despondently. If Paula, of all people—who was so keen to set Julia up with anyone who breathed and wore plaid—was a no-go on Clare, then Julia would be silly to not listen.

But still, something stirred in her when she thought of Clare. Something bent and blurred and went a little wobbly at the elbows. She decided to push the thought of Clare from her mind for the time being. Besides, she'd see Clare tonight.

If Clare had no interest in her, she'd be able to suss it out. Julia had a sixth sense for sniffing out rejection. The way dogs are trained to find narcotics in unmarked packages, Julia could always tell when someone was about to give her the ol' heave ho. It was a curse, but also a curse. Occasionally Julia would try to prove herself wrong after she detected it, but inevitably the rejection would come. Sometimes it took a few days or weeks—and with Britt, a whopping two months—but the results were always the same.

She dreaded this Spidey sense as much as she felt relieved by it. There would be no barking up the wrong tree for Julia. No. Though occasionally, the tree fell on her anyway.

eight

IT WAS ONLY as Clare walked into the bar that evening that she realized she was nervous. As she pushed the bar's saloon door open, she looked down at her hands and saw that they were shaking again. She shoved them in her coat pockets and out of view, making her way to the end of the small, dark bar and ordering a vodka gimlet.

She turned back to the bartender. "Make it a double, actually. I'm living! A little." The bartender looked at her blankly and rinsed a glass.

Clare cracked her neck from side to side, hopping a little on the balls of her feet, as if she was not about to meet a colleague for drinks, but instead readying herself for a UFC cage match.

To steady her nerves, she took out her phone, hoping a stream of corgis, bunnies, and cats knocking things off of tables would calm her. Instead, when she opened the app, the first thing she saw was Erik. Not just Erik, but Erik and his wife, who held a black and white sonogram, smiling into the camera as he kissed her cheek from behind.

A wave of nausea hit Clare like a brick. Her hands had

stopped shaking, replaced just as suddenly by the tight fists that formed in their wake. She dug her nails into the flesh of her palms, the soft sharp of them gradually releasing her anger and pain.

Of course she's pregnant, Clare thought. *Of course she is. She has no idea what happened or what kind of man Erik really is.*

She shoved the memories from her mind and told herself she was over it. She was moving on! Wasn't she?

The place was filling up fast, as the after-work crowd streamed in, removing blazers and backpacks, loosening neckties and replacing laptop cases with pints of beer. Clare managed to carve a space out at the bar that could just fit two people as she waited for Julia to arrive.

Why was she nervous? *There is nothing improper about meeting a coworker,* she told herself. And yet, she felt as if she was getting away with something. It didn't take long for Clare to remember the wild charge of Julia's lips against her ear a week ago, an unsettling current coursing down and down and down. Clare shook off the memory and stood up straighter, telling herself, *It's just a drink. She's just a coworker. It's fine. I'm fine!*

When Julia entered the bar at 6:19pm, the sight of Clare struck her again like a volt of electricity. When she found Clare's face among the crowd of bar-goers, tucked beneath a slew of bears and queens and flannel femmes, Julia felt stunned, unable to take even a single step forward. But then she saw Clare smile, and found the resolve to make her limbs obey her. Clare wore light gray pants that showed off her long legs and small waist, plus another white dress shirt, crisp, with the sleeves rolled to the elbows. The rolled-up sleeves might have conveyed a breezy casualness if it hadn't been for the buttons on her shirt that fastened all the way to the top, the last a small silver diamond guarding her throat. Clare's dark hair was down, its shiny waves loose and giving off an air of disarray that contrasted with her perfectly set posture and features.

Julia pushed her way through the throng of happy-hour bodies and wedged herself in the small space next to Clare. They were close enough to kiss and Julia found she did not know where to look. She focused on the side of Clare's neck, inhaling once again her brisk biology, a musk that smelled like September this time, something ripe and red and warm. Julia was feeling intoxicated already, though she hadn't had a single drink.

"Sorry I'm late," Julia said, breathless, cheeks flushed. "I've been up to my tits in expense reports."

Clare's mouth opened slightly, but nothing came out. She shut it.

"Am I allowed to say *tits*?" Julia said, interpreting the silence and mouth agape-ness on Clare's face as shock. "You won't report me?"

———

Clare couldn't tell if Julia was joking or not, so responded earnestly, "I'm not on the clock now. Please feel free to discuss breasts as much as you'd like." Then thought, *Christ, did I just say that?*

Thankfully, Julia laughed. "My kinda gal," she said. "Speaking of tits, gonna try and fail to get the gay male bartender's attention for a drink. You good?"

"I am, actually," Clare said, surprised at how much she

meant it. She did feel *good*. In spite of her nerves and the news about Erik. Maybe the vodka was doing its job. Or maybe it was something else.

Clare's foot toed Julia's tote bag under the table, surprised at how heavy it felt. Curious, she opened the flap and the top of a roller skate peeked out. No wonder she had rollerblade confidence.

As Julia chased after the bartender a few feet away, Clare watched her. There was a wildness to her, a wilderness. Something dangerous and expansive, as if she was getting a drink with wolves. She wore green plaid pants with a matching vest and what appeared to be a pocket watch, though perhaps it was only a chain. On her feet were black engineer boots. The scuffed leather toe looked like it had some stories to tell. Clare wanted to hear them. There was something so young about her, too, Clare thought, vivacious even. Her movements and gestures. She did not walk, but rather, bounced. And unlike Clare's guarded demeanor, Julia seemed so open, so undisguised. An innocence emanated from her, which is possibly why her casual swearing felt so jarring to Clare. When Julia came back with a manhattan, three cherries skewered on a bamboo pick, Clare smiled again.

"What?" Julia asked, wedging herself once more into the space. Clare registered the nearness of Julia's body to her own and felt herself flush with heat.

"Three cherries? Greedy."

"A bonus from the bartender for making me wait so damn long. Plus," Julia winked, "I once heard that things should always come in threes, for good luck."

"I'm pretty sure that's death—deaths come in threes."

"Is it? Fuck! Quick, take one then."

Julia held the skewer up to Clare's mouth. Clare paused

for the slightest moment before parting her full lips, which circled, then vanished the soft, whiskey-soaked fruit.

As she chewed, tasting the sweet, subtle burn of the cherry, the sudden intimacy of the moment made Clare demure. She tried to change the subject to something she hoped would be more neutral, realizing only after she said it that it was both a signal and an invitation. "All of my ex-girlfriends are whiskey drinkers."

"Are they now?" Julia delighted in this information, even though she didn't know what to do with it. At least she knew that Clare *did* like women. But she heard Paula's words in her head, reminding her that Clare was off limits. Clare was an order muppet in a chaotic world. No wonder she was so tight-lipped.

Plus, she couldn't casually hit on the HR manager, could she? And when she herself had just submitted a harassment claim! This was going to be trickier than she anticipated. And all the while there was Clare's sweet scent, casually debilitating her while they stood, the soft fabric of their elbows touching on the bar. How was it that just last week, Julia hadn't even been able to notice the small pleasure of fall leaves and now—in Clare's hands, she had become a season. She had no idea, but decided for once to tune into it, to relish every sensation.

Julia attempted to distract herself from her confusion. "Why do you think this place is called 1221?"

"I was wondering that, too," Clare said, placing her foot on the rung of the bar stool near Julia's thigh. Julia noticed it painfully, wishing she could lay her hand upon the muscled contours of it. The allure of Clare drew her like a magnet. She clutched tighter to her drink. Julia had never felt so exhausted from *not* touching someone! *What is going on with me?* She wondered.

"I bet the internet knows," Julia said, punching the question into her phone. "Aha ... it's, oh, that's disappointing. It's just the address."

"Not a very good story."

"No, I was hoping it'd be something like: In 1221, the first glory hole was invented. And today, at 1221, we honor that hole and every hole that has found a similar path to glory."

Clare placed her hand over her mouth, stifling a chuckle. "Let's definitely tell people that. It's a *hole* lot better."

Unlike Clare, there was nothing delicate or demure about Julia's laugh. She *chortled*. She *brayed*. "You did not."

"I did."

Julia tuned into her Spidey rejection sense just then and detected nothing. This was a relief. Even though she probably shouldn't hit on Clare, the door hadn't been entirely shut. She raised her glass to Clare's and together they cheered. "So," Julia flashed her darkly shining eyes at Clare once more, "tell me. Tell me everything. I'm dying to know."

———

Clare considered Julia's words and felt for a fraction of a moment that she *could* tell Julia everything, the darkest contents of Clare's soul, the triumphant and brilliant and strange recesses of her grim, untidy heart—but then she blinked and the urge was gone. The wall she had erected around herself stood firm. She touched the rough bricks of it in her mind, seeing the wall clearly for what it was, not a fortress but a prison. Dark but familiar. It was only when Clare realized Julia was expecting her to say something that she snapped to.

"Oh! Joel. Yes. Turns out he had a rap sheet a mile long. Not just at this company but several priors. I can't give you gory details, but let's just say the man has an appalling history."

"So it wasn't just me?"

"Far from it. W;nkdIn was smart to let him go. He was a lawsuit waiting to happen, or several lawsuits."

Julia squeezed Clare's hand suddenly, in a fit of excitement. "Well, that's both the worst and best news I've heard all day!"

The pressure and warmth of Julia's hand sent another wave of unsettling through Clare. She sipped her drink to steady herself, feeling like a spider web that Julia had just walked through.

"I can't believe it," Julia continued, whether she was aware that she was still holding Clare's hand, Clare didn't know. But then, Julia let it drop. Clare took a sip of her drink reluctantly. "In the past, whenever I've complained, either nothing happened or the harassment got *worse*! Like, they knew they could punish me for speaking up. You're a goddamn hero, Clare Kolikov."

Clare's cheeks burned bright at the sound of her name on Julia's lips, but all she said was, "Just doing my job."

"And a damn fine one at that," Julia said. "You seem surprised though. Are you?"

"That a beautiful woman like you would get harassed? Sadly, no."

It was Julia's turn to blush now. "I meant, are you surprised that men like Joel are trash?" Clare tucked a wave of brown-black hair behind her ear and looked down at Julia's engineer boots.

Clare stammered. "Well, no, I can't say I'm surprised by *that* either. Forgive the assumption—"

"There's nothing to forgive," Julia said, no longer looking at Clare's neck, but staring straight into her eyes. "You are very attractive yourself. But surely you must hear that all the time."

The blood pulsed in Clare's temples. This was quickly veering in a direction that was entirely out of her control. She didn't know if she liked it. She didn't know if she liked anything. She scanned her inner filing system, trying to remember every code and bylaw from her extensive career at the company, to make sure she wasn't doing something improper. Yet, the alcohol coursing through her had its own ideas of what was *proper*.

Still, Clare was unsure how to proceed, and the slight buzz from the gimlet only confused her further. She decided to restrain herself. She must not let Julia's allure get in the way of her professionalism.

And then Julia kissed her.

Julia's hand wove its way to the back of Clare's neck and pulled her face to hers. Clare's lips parted in surrender, her body's gates opening to whatever flood Julia threatened to release in her. Clare surprised herself by taking Julia's face in her hand and kissing her back.

As Clare reeled from the surprise and shock of Julia's softly probing mouth, a man precariously holding four beers elbowed her on his way past, spilling some of the amber liquid on her shoes, releasing its yeasty perfume into her nostrils, and forcing her body even closer to Julia's. The clash was enough to jar Clare back into remembering herself. She pulled away from Julia, gently pressing Julia's shoulders back. She had been too caught up, too beside herself, and now the authoritative part of her brain tugged at her.

The bar was packed now, the air dense and thick, conversations pulsing and roaring, an animal scent emanating from so many bodies releasing the tensions and anxieties of the work day.

"We shouldn't," Clare managed to whisper, turning her head away from Julia's lips. But Julia then found her neck, kissing along the line of her jaw, her ear, the muscle leading to her shoulder. Clare's hands trembled. She struggled to find the part of herself capable of saying no in this moment, in the face of this enormous, unending wave of yes.

"Wait," she tried again, gripping the sides of Julia's face in her hands. "It's not—"

But Clare's words lost themselves in the labyrinth of Julia's mouth, which had found her lower lip once more and gently nibbled on it.

Clare groaned again. The lustful side of her said, *She has a point.*

But the responsible side countered, *Think of your job. The promotion you want. Your integrity. You're playing with fire, Clare.*

The lustful side shot back: *Yes, but I'm also taking a keen interest in the ... welfare of my colleagues!*

She warred thusly with herself, until finally, achingly, responsibility won out. She'd worked too hard to let anything or anyone interfere with all she'd put in at W;nkdIn. She grabbed Julia's wrists and held them away from her body. And then, when even *that* gesture of restraint felt unbearably hot to her, she let go of Julia entirely and moved herself as far away as she could.

"I can't," Clare said. "We shouldn't." Clare's throat

constricted. Her words were puny and lacked conviction. But they would have to do.

"I'm sorry," Julia said, "I thought we ... I was ... my signals must have gotten crossed."

"No, it's ... it's just that your claim was so recent and I ... it would look very bad if I ... if we—"

"Oh god, I'm so sorry. It's not like that with you—at all!"

"No, I know, but it *looks* ... *I* would look—" Clare stumbled over her words. In her distress, she felt the spilled beer squishing in her leather shoes and shuddered to think about what they would smell like later. "It would be extremely inappropriate of me to—"

"You don't have to explain, it's okay. Let's ... let's talk about something else."

Clare's mind darted in 18 directions. The silence between them yawned into a space that may as well have spanned years. She took a long sip of her gimlet, finishing it, wishing for all the world that there had been more left in the glass. Then she straightened her spine and crossed her long legs, as she had done countless times during employee interviews and first dates, and said, "So what do you do at W;nkdIn, anyway?"

<hr>

Julia's heart pounded. Her stomach sank to somewhere in the vicinity of her knees. Her embarrassment was so intense she didn't know if she could recover. What would happen if she just turned and walked out of this bar? *No, that wouldn't work. You'd just see her at work tomorrow.* She berated herself. *You should have waited. You should've known better. Or listened to Paula! Now you've ruined it.*

"I'm an Experience Coordinator," she said, surprised the words did not come out in a whispered chirp.

"Oh, right. What does that mean again?"

Julia forced herself to continue speaking. "You know those romantic outings we set up for clients—the wine tastings, the picnics, the concerts, the yoga with goats, and so on? I'm the one who researches the dates, books venues, schedules the experiences, that kind of thing. I make the magic happen, basically." *Good god, the magic? Really? Why do I let myself out of the house?*

"Oh no."

"What?"

"Well, I suppose you'll be working on, um, me soon. I seem to have just been volunteered by the company to try the new beta LGBTQ+ experiences."

The look on Julia's face was a cross between stomach upset and taking a pie in the face.

"I'm sorry, what? *You're* the new case study?"

"Starting Monday, Clare said. "Yolanda said it'd be good for me. My career, I mean. To show that I'm a 'team player.'" A sudden concern filled Clare's face. "Are you going to throw up? Because I have a beer-filled shoe you can use."

"Oh no no no no, I'm ... fine," Julia backpedaled. "You're ... I'm just ... surprised. I ... they didn't tell me it was you."

"Would that have mattered?"

Julia's stomach knotted. She definitely couldn't pursue her attraction to Clare now, which was difficult enough, but on top of that she'd have to set up magical experiences for her *with other people*! The world felt small and cruel and the manhattan did little to alleviate her disappointment.

As Julia tried to ignore her embarrassment and the maddening closeness of Clare's body, she couldn't help but notice a thin sheen of sweat glistening on Clare's neck. She longed to trace the line of it with her tongue. But she didn't, of course. In spite of the sting of Clare's rejection, Julia could feel Clare pulling her in like a celestial body in orbit.

"No," Julia blinked, her eyes suddenly heavy. "I suppose it wouldn't have."

She downed the rest of her drink in one long gulp and ordered another. By the time she was half way through the second one, her head began to swim in a mischievous downward stream. She couldn't pursue Clare, though she very much wanted to—fates be damned!—but she *did* have the power to ensure that Clare's dates were a little less *magical*, as it were, than the ones she usually arranged. She wouldn't orchestrate dates to the local sewage treatment plant or anything overtly terrible, as that would not bode well for the company and would certainly raise some red flags about her abilities and/or sanity. Plus, she didn't want to inflict any needless suffering upon Clare. But Julia could create the exact wrong kind of dates for a woman like Clare. The kind that might frustrate, provoke, or bring about mild discomfort, and hence, Julia hoped, hinder any potential romantic connections. Who could fall in love in such circumstances? Former prisoners of war, perhaps, or those dealing with chronic gastrointestinal upset, but few others.

The more she thought about it, the more convinced she became. It was a horrible, wonderful idea, like in *How the Grinch Stole Christmas*. It was wrong, yes, in a sense. It wasn't giving Clare much benefit of the doubt or even acknowledging that she was perfectly capable of making her own romantic choices. Julia knew this. And yet, her scheme also seemed right, in a sense, in that it bought Julia more time to get to know Clare and to see if there was a potential connection between the two of them, aside from lust. Plus, maybe these kinds of experiences would work for other people down the road. Just because Clare might not have the most fun on these dates didn't mean other people wouldn't. This was her job, after all. To bring new experiences to people. It's research!

The only problem with her plan, as Julia saw it, was that she didn't know what kind of "woman" Clare was so that she might create these Bizarro World opposite dates on her behalf. But, well, the night was young.

"So, Clare," Julia smiled crookedly, a slight twitch in her lip. "Enough about me. Tell me about you."

nine

THE FOLLOWING DAY AT WORK, Clare felt flummoxed. She ordered a large caramel macchiato, instead of her usual small, as she had slept fitfully. The night with Julia had been such a surprise, the kiss beautiful and unexpected and strange and she felt hopelessly conflicted. She didn't know what to do with the beast that had been unleashed inside of her when Julia's lips found hers, and so she did what she did with other emotionally confusing endeavors—she locked it away, promising herself she would maybe possibly deal with it. Later.

But how refreshing it was for someone to be so interested in her! She could barely get in a question of her own before Julia had asked three more. And though Clare had not mentioned Erik or her father or the fact that she had no close friends to speak of, Julia seemed to really listen, almost as if she had been mentally cataloging everything Clare was saying.

She felt for the first time in ages like an *interesting* person. The thought buoyed her all the way to the office, until she glimpsed Nikki on an overstuffed couch near the breakroom. Clare wondered if there would come a time when she would stop bristling at Nikki's presence. She hoped she would, but Nikki went out of her way to make Clare's job harder as often as she could, which made Clare's attempts at neutrality next to impossible.

This was why people said not to date where you work, wasn't it? To keep your romantic life and your professional life separate, otherwise you ran the risk of having to see your poor choices 40 hours a week, every week. When Clare ended things with Nikki, she had no idea it would get this bad, and she did not want to make the same mistake again, not even with Julia, whom she was intrigued and slightly intimidated by, and who seemed as different from Nikki as night was to day. As much as she couldn't deny Julia's allure, Clare decided the best course of action was no action.

Thankfully, she didn't have too much time to dwell on it, because as soon as she sat down, she also remembered what she had signed up for.

"Clare, hi! So good to meet you!" Rodrigo air-kissed Clare on each cheek before she could even register what had happened. She pursed her lips to air-kiss back but he had moved on to more pressing matters.

"I'll be your Virtual Dating Assistant," he said. "Today we'll be creating your profile for the site. Follow me."

Before Clare could object, Rodrigo had whisked her away to his cubicle and sat her on an orange bean bag, which folded around and sunk her body in its spongy grip, until only her head, feet and one arm were visible. She felt like a shrimp cocktail.

Rodrigo parked himself on a blue yoga ball, opened his laptop, and smoothed his black pompadour, which, Clare noticed, did not move at all. "Okay! Let's get your vitals first."

"Like, my blood pressure?"

Rodrigo laughed, though Clare's question had been in earnest. She decided to laugh along with him. "No, honey, like age/height/pronouns."

"Oh, right. I'm 36. I'm 5'7"."

"So 5'5" in reality, got it. Go on."

Clare wondered if she should protest, but he said it so authoritatively that she couldn't. "And she/her are my pronouns."

"Fabulous," Rodrigo said, typing her answers into a spreadsheet without looking at her. "And what are your interests or hobbies?"

Clare raised both eyebrows, considering. The buoyancy from her evening with Julia had waned to a blip. "I took a macrame class recently?"

"Crafty! So spicy. Got it." His typing was so fast and plentiful, it seemed to Clare there was no way he was writing down what she said. "What about fitness, recreation?"

"Uh, pass?"

"You can't pass. This is the Bay Area. You have to be into rock climbing, yoga, or beach camping."

"Beach camping? That's not even exercise."

"Look, I don't make the rules." He looked at her, an aggrieved smile spreading across his face. Clare tried to sit up straighter in the bean bag but it only made her sink deeper into its squishy maw. "What about walking? Do you like that?"

"Sure, okay."

"Great, 'loves to hike.'"

"*Love* is a strong word," she interjected, but Rodrigo kept on going.

"Okay, and what are you looking for in a relationship?"

This one Clare knew. She had known it for a long time, even when she couldn't admit it to herself. "I'm looking for a partner. Someone interested in a forever-type situation." Saying the words made Clare feel instantly vulnerable. She was grateful suddenly that the bean bag was clutching her in a kind of trap hug.

"Too needy. Let's say, 'casually looking for something more serious.'" After he finished typing, he bounced on the yoga ball a few times, then did a few crunches before continuing. "Okay, and now for some fun questions. What's the best compliment you've been given?"

Clare tried gamely to think of something nice her mother might have said about her, but drew a blank. Rodrigo fidgeted impatiently. "My dentist once told me I had great incisors."

Rodrigo swiveled, cast her a grim look, but then something akin to respect crossed his bushy, manicured eyebrows. "Really? Show me."

Clare bared her teeth at him.

"Damn, no wonder you never smile. Those are some heart-breakers."

"I ... I smile."

Rodrigo cocked his head at Clare. If she had been a child or a pet, he might have patted her just then. "What're some things you want in a partner?"

"Um, smart? Not terrified of spiders?"

Rodrigo's hands hovered over his ergonomic keyboard, waiting. "Is that it?"

"You got the spiders part?" Clare asked. "It didn't look like you were typing. Oh, but they shouldn't *kill* the spiders.

It should be a catch-and-release situation. If possible." Clare realized she was bad at this. Why was she so bad at this? And why couldn't she think of what to say?

"Any deal breakers?" Rodrigo asked.

Here, Clare had lots to say. "Smokers. People who clap on airplanes when the plane lands. People who wash their lights with their darks. People who put 30 hashtags on a social media post of a danish. People who post breakfast pictures on social media at all, maybe. Oh, people who refuse the freshly grated parmesan at Olive Garden. People who tell you how many times they've been to Burning Man within five minutes of talking—"

"Clare! That last one eliminates three-fourths of the dating pool. How about, 'No smokers or heavy drug users."

Clare's blood pressure began to rise. "That's it?" Isn't this supposed to be about what I want? How am I going to find someone compatible if you keep editing out whole swathes of my answers?"

Rodrigo swiveled on his ball, leaned forward, palm on chin, and looked at Clare like a concerned parent. "Oh honey, you got it all wrong. What we're doing is high-lighting the *most* attractive parts of you and leaving ... the rest to be found out on the dates themselves. It's all about putting your best Louboutin forward, sugar shoes."

"Sugar shoes?"

"You've only got one chance to make a first impression!" He continued. "Plus, I don't want to limit you. There's lots of fish in the sea but less in a puddle, am I right?" He didn't wait for Clare to answer. "W;nkdIn is all about expanding your comfort level, yeah? Broadening your horizons with experiences that will blow your mind and then put it back together again. My job is to gently nudge you toward those horizons. Your job is to keep walking and try not to get in your own way. You just have to leave a tiny amount of room for possibility, okay hon-bun? W;nkdIn: Find your passion! It's not just a catch-phrase. It's a lifestyle."

He resumed his typing, whistling a hook from a Lady Gaga song.

"Okay," Clare said, feeling a little indignant but quite sure she had lost the fight. "But no beach camping."

He swiveled back toward her once more. "Girl, have you tried it? It's divine!"

ten

JULIA WAS HOPELESSLY DISTRACTED at work. Each time she tried to make eye contact or catch a glimpse of Clare, Clare looked away. And when they happened upon each other at the break room, Clare actually turned and ran from her! Well, walked briskly, but Julia got the message. She knew Clare was avoiding her and she hated it. Maybe her rejection sense had been off after all. Or maybe Clare really was the epitome of responsibility. But that kiss! There was no way Clare didn't feel it too, Julia was sure of that.

Back at her cubicle, Julia noticed that Clare's office door was shut, and spent an inordinate amount of time staring into it, willing it to open.

In an attempt to distract herself from her longing and the debt that threatened to topple her life at any moment, she logged into the blog she ran, where her goal was to write 17 syllable film reviews of every Kristen Stewart movie ever made, also known as: The K Stew Haiku Review.

She typed in the following title: *Twilight: New Moon.*

Tongue tapping against her front teeth, she thought,

puzzling over how to say in three lines everything she was feeling in this moment. After typing, deleting, and typing again, she settled on:

Bella! How on earth
could you possibly choose the
vampire? He sucks!

#Feelz #NeverSettle #TeamJacob

She posted the review just as Paula walked by her cube, peeking her head over the wall before Julia was able to log off.

"Rough night?" Paula asked.

"Something like that."

"Britt stuff again? Want to come over later? We can drink our feelings while you help me with this Twi'lek costume I'm working on."

"What feelings are you numbing this time?"

"Oh you know, the usual—dead-end admin assistant job, the garbage fire that is online dating, etcetera."

"I thought things were going better. What happened with that one girl, the super-cute sci-fi writer?"

"Yeah, she stopped texting. She got back with her ex maybe? Or she moved? I don't know. That was a long time ago," Paula said, her mouth scrunched in displeasure.

"In a galaxy far, far away?" Julia asked. Paula smiled tightly in spite of herself. They weren't each other's romantic types at all, but Julia was grateful that she had someone like Paula, who knew Julia so well and so easily. It was a rare and beautiful friendship.

Paula leaned her elbows on top of the gray divider wall.

"What's up with you? Must be pretty bad if you're writing *Twilight* haikus."

"My love for K. Stew has no bounds, Paula. I'll watch her moody, French existentialist work just as gleefully as I'll watch her seduce a sparkling, anemic boy."

"Uh huh. Well, let me know when you tire of *that* and want to join us over here in the real world."

"Says the woman who spends every vacation at cosplay conventions."

"Hey, at least it gets me laid. I can't say the same for your ... hobby."

"Fair point," Julia said. "I'll fill you in on everything tonight, tequila in tow."

"Great!" Paula clapped excitedly. She ran her hands through her short cropped black hair and straightened her spine. "Also, while we're on the subject—Bella? Total chaos muppet."

Julia inhaled sharply. She had the sense that Paula was onto something profound and now Julia was in on it, too. Maybe she'd go home after work and read Susan Sontag's theory and understand more than one-quarter of it.

"Now if you'll excuse me," Paula said, "there are very important copies to be made and coffees to be fetched."

Finally, after hours of stewing (and K. Stewing), slightly before 3pm, Clare's door opened. As two of their colleagues exited Clare's office, without thinking, Julia leapt from her desk and ran down the hall before the door could close on her.

Flushed and a little breathless from running in heels, even low ones, Julia entered Clare's office, shutting the door behind her. Startled, Clare greeted her by standing up from her chair.

"Oh—hi," Clare exclaimed. "Do we have an appointment?"

"No, um—"

Julia realized too late that she didn't have a plan, aside from forcing her way into Clare's office. She looked down at Clare's inspirational calendar for help. *Wine is what happens when you're busy making other plans.*

"I have a few questions ... about your intake plan," Julia said, hoping her lie was convincing.

Clare sat back down, her face mildly perturbed. "Are you also here to sell me on the unsung merits of beach camping?"

"What? No. Who wants sand in their clam casino?"

Clare's smile emboldened Julia. She stepped closer, more tentatively than her brassy entrance, but still purposeful. She strode around Clare's desk and sat on its corner. Their bodies were, once more, mere inches from each other. The familiar heat knocked against Julia's ribs. Her heart pounded; she felt as if at any moment, her limbs would detach and float away from her body. *I'm not imagining this,* she thought to herself, almost accusatory.

"But tell me," Julia had already gleaned that Clare hated any events with forced participation and mingling, and that she was, at least on the surface, quite reserved. She had plenty of fodder to plan Clare's bizarro dates, but what she really wanted to know was less tangible. Not the facts but the in-betweens, the tangents, the scruff and circumstance that made up her life. "What movie can you watch over and over without ever getting tired of it?"

"Hmm, *Labyrinth*, maybe?"

"I love that movie. I'm pretty sure David Bowie's Big Femme Energy in that turned me a little gay."

"You and me both," Clare smiled.

"Okay, coffee or tea?"

"Coffee."

"Me too."

"Who do you go out of your way to be nice to?"

"Baristas. And my mother, though she doesn't extend the same courtesy to me."

Julia noticed a weariness in Clare's face. She paused her questioning, hoping Clare would say more about it. Hoping to learn, perhaps, the reason Clare seemed to be so guarded, so tense, and so fearful of the unknown.

Clare opened her mouth to speak, but just then, a knock. As loud and as unwelcome as a fart in an elevator. It appeared to Julia, however, that Clare found the intrusion to be a welcome relief.

"That's Benjamin," Clare said. "My 3 o'clock."

She searched Clare's eyes, not realizing what she hoped to find exactly. But the windows had been boarded up. She looked at Clare's unreadable face, the slight slump in her spine, and made her way back to her desk.

eleven

AFTER JULIA HAD LEFT her office, Clare's body wouldn't stop vibrating. She kept smoothing her skirt, getting up to pace, then sitting back down. Seeing her coffee from that morning, she took a long sip from it, relishing the cold, creamy sweetness. It must have been simple nerves, she told herself, not wanting to admit the effect Julia had on her. Her first "experience" was to begin that night, after all.

Outside her office, she heard the low hum of voices and shuffling of tennis shoes—"casual" attire was permitted at W;nkdIn, but Clare wore tailored suits and heels, mostly out of habit. The women in her family had always been meticulously dressed. Even her grandmother, who lived to 90, refused to check the mail without proper attire and a full face of makeup. The other reason was that Clare didn't know who she would be in a hoodie, and she didn't care to find out.

Rodrigo had told her to dress casually for the experience tonight. "It's not a date-date, but a group event with many other singles. It'll give you the opportunity to meet a lot of people at once!" He'd said enthusiastically, as if this was a perk.

When Clare asked what she was going to be doing with this group of strangers exactly, he went coy. "You'll just have to see, won't you, Clare Bear?"

Remembering this, Clare's eczema tingled and burned. A new patch had appeared between the web of her thumb and index finger. She pressed on it hard, hoping this would be enough to calm it. It worked, but then the spot between her breasts flamed anew. It was further agitated by her underwire, and by the fact that she couldn't relieve the itch unless she removed the bra entirely, which she would never do at work.

She opened her desk drawer and pulled out the stack of therapy coupons she'd snatched from the last all-hands meeting. She counted them—eight. She could be cured of her eczema in eight sessions, right? And if not, then she could at least tell Dr. Wong that she'd tried and he'd been wrong. Her eczema was not related to her father or her grief or anything emotional, Clare felt sure of that.

She stacked the coupons neatly and placed them back into her desk drawer. Not today. First she had to get through tonight.

twelve

"SHE NEEDS A HOBBY."

"Nobody asked you, Simon!" Clare shouted at her mother's "lover." She still couldn't say the word without sarcasm or dry-heaving.

Carole had accidentally video butt-dialed her. Before Carole had figured out that the video had started, however, Clare overheard them talking about her. A rustling ensued and then a pinkish blur entered the screen. "Hold the phone away from your ear, mom, ... farther, yes, it's a video call. Down now ... no, that's the floor ... there."

Simon's face appeared behind Carole's on the small screen. He waved. "I've cocked it up, haven't I? Sorry, love. I didn't mean anything by it," Simon said in what Clare had to admit was a delightful British accent.

"No, darling, no. She does need a new hobby," Carole said to Simon. "Maybe something physical, like spin class? Or tai chi?"

"I took tai chi once years ago," Simon said to Carole. They were having an entire conversation without Clare's involvement. She felt annoyed by this, yet also somewhat relieved. "The class was taught by two lesbians."

"Lesbians?" Carole glanced at Clare now. What did the look mean? Was it a warning? A reproach? Clare wondered.

"Yes," Simon said. "They were very masculine. More than me even! With their help, I got swole in about 12 weeks."

"They gave you edema?" Carole gasped.

Clare buried her face in her hands. Maybe if she hung up, they wouldn't notice.

"Honestly, I don't understand what two women even *do* together in bed!" Carole laughed a little too forcefully. Was she being coquettish for Simon's benefit? Clare's face burned. She was at a point of exasperation with her mother.

"We try on each other's shoes, obviously," Clare interjected.

"Don't take that tone, darling," Carole said. "It's unbecoming."

"You should mail her some Turkish delight!" Simon non-sequitured, and Clare noticed the gelatinous dessert on the nightstand next to her mother.

She welcomed the change of subject. Clare's sexuality was not a topic that she and her mother discussed openly since Clare had come out at 21. Carole promptly dismissed Clare's bisexuality as "a phase" and alternately became pouty and sullen when Clare dated women and euphoric and righteous when Clare dated men. Once, when Clare dated a trans man, an archaeologist with statuesque features and bon-bon eyes who passed easily, Carole was so beside herself with conflicting emotions that she refused Clare's calls for two months, claiming she was too busy propagating hydrangeas and listening to Bonnie Raitt to call Clare back.

Clare didn't mind this shunning exactly. She preferred to talk to her father anyway, who had always been supportive of her. He had even attended a few PFLAG meetings and bought a t-shirt that said, "No one knows my daughter's a lesbian." He never wore it, a fact that Clare was eternally thankful for, as it was both embarrassing and not even accurate—no one made shirts for bisexuals, it seemed—but her father's gesture touched her nevertheless.

"That's a marvelous idea, Simon." Carole turned back to Clare, "Though you are looking a bit ... wide in the face, darling. Are you watching your carb intake?"

Clare chose to ignore her mother's barb. She had enough to worry about without inheriting more of her mother's neuroses about food. "Where are you now?"

"We're in Istanbul. Today I had my fortune told from the grounds in my coffee."

Carole swiveled the phone around to show Clare the view from their hotel room. The sun was setting and glowed orange and pink, silhouetting the buildings. The water beneath glinted pink as well, reflecting bright flashes of city lights in its small waves. In the distance were several mosques, their colorful domes and towering minarets jutting proudly into the sky. Clare's heart caught in her throat at the view. At the wonder that such beauty existed and that her mother was the one who was seeing it. It felt wrong, backwards. Her mother couldn't appreciate such beauty. But could Clare?

She shook herself out of her reverie and fixed her eyes on the rain-splattered window of her own life. The drops hit the pane and trickled down, sometimes joining others on the way. Outside the window's ledge was gray with brown sludge. She needed a ladder to clean it properly, and made a mental note to herself.

"And? What did she say?" Clare asked.

"Well, she said I was at a crossroads—and that something from my past was interfering with the present. She said I needed to get rid of the obstacle before I could find transformation."

Clare's stomach dropped. She knew where this was going and she wasn't pleased. Her bones felt heavy, and so did her tongue. She wished she had a glass of water. Or someone who would bring her one.

"This is, well, this is partly why I booty called," Carole said.

"Butt-dialed, mom. There's a diff—you know what, never mind. The call was an accident."

"Accidentally on purpose, darling. Just like the coffee fortune teller lady said."

Simon piped in again, "Tell her, love!"

The air around Clare's face diminished, replaced, it seemed, by tiny paper cuts. "You want me to get rid of him," Clare said.

"Darling, ashes are not a *him*. They aren't your father. And yes, it's time to scatter them, isn't it?"

"Without you? I can't. Let's wait until you get back—"

"Oh, Clare. I don't know when I'll be back." Carole sighed. "You know more than anyone how much I loved your father. But that plastic box full of dust is not Yuri. At least, I can't see him as that. It's time for me—for us—to let him rest. In peace. It's time to get him off your shelf in the closet and back to nature where he wanted to be."

Clare considered this. It had been more than a year since her father died. She had intended to scatter the ashes; she really had. But then Erik happened and she was dealing with *that*, and then her mother left the country, and then, things with work and then, life! This life that everyone insisted she was not living. How was it that it kept getting in the way?

"Hang on a sec," Clare said.

She took down the black plastic box full of her father's ashes and set him on the kitchen table. It was true, she thought, he probably wasn't very happy "living" in Clare's closet—as far as Clare could envision cremains having feelings. He loved to hike and camp and read mystery novels in the sunshine on the deck. So what exactly was she holding onto? She couldn't say. Perhaps she kept his ashes because it made her feel close to him. Perhaps it had become, like so many other things in her life of late, a burdensome task she felt ill-equipped (and ill-prepared) to deal with. Like Julia. Perhaps she was waiting for a Turkish fortune teller to read it in her future. Or, perhaps it was simple avoidance.

Carole had not been the most nurturing mother. She was quick with her judgments and slow to praise. And yet, she had been devoted to Clare's father. She cooked, she washed his clothes, she made sure Clare got to school on time. Yuri had been unwavering in his acceptance and support of Clare, which made him easy to love, but Clare had to admit that her mother bore the brunt of the parenting and caretaking. Carole also asked for precious few things. In the whole of Clare's life, she could recall only a handful of times her mother asked for anything. Sure, she had not been shy about making her opinion known when it came to Clare's life choices. But could Clare really deny her this? Especially when it was actually her father's request?

"Well, darling?"

Clare searched her mother's face, her blue, hopeful eyes, which were creased by years of hardship, and now, mirth. The corners of Carole's eyes crinkled. Clare thought her mother might be on the verge of tears, which caused her own eyes to water.

And then Simon shouted from the background. "I've got it! She should try the ancient Japanese art of kintsugi!"

thirteen

CLARE WASN'T sure how to dress for her first mystery beta date, so she wore dress slacks, a white turtleneck, and low heels. She checked the address for the bar several times but the GPS kept leading her to an ordinary-looking Irish pub.

She stepped inside to find that it was indeed an Irish pub, replete with shamrocks, Guinness on tap, and several old men who were either shouting at the TV screens or asleep. Clare thought she must have gotten the address wrong. But then she saw a queer-looking person—an androgynous sporty type with a square chin and an ultimate-frisbee vibe—and decided to follow them.

Clare followed them past the worn wooden booths and black and white photos of rolling green hills and Irish immigrants. Toward the back of the bar was a set of stairs that couldn't be seen from the main entrance. Down the stairs they went. Once they reached the bottom, to the left Clare saw a sign for the bathroom, and to the right was a floor-to-ceiling bookcase loaded with books.

Clare was about to give up, not willing to follow a

stranger into the toilets, but then the stranger instead went to the right towards the bookcase. The stranger turned the knob and Clare realized it was, in fact, a door that led to another room entirely. A secret bar within a bar.

She pushed her way inside nervously. The bar was cavernous and dark, with a speakeasy vibe. On the far end was a stage with thick, red curtains and gold ropes holding them back. A lone microphone stood at its center. The rest of the room was set up with what appeared to be activity stations. Clare saw an enormous version of Jenga, the blocks reaching Clare's torso. She saw twinkle lights dangling from the ceiling with little cards attached to them. She saw a detachable dance floor lit up with colored squares. Another table held silver trays covered with silver lids, similar to a banquet. All of these things caused Clare's throat to catch. She squeezed it, hoping to relieve some of the pressure, but nothing happened. *Think of your promotion.* She repeated to herself silently. *Think of your promotion.*

About 50 people milled about inside, a few of whom she recognized as W;nkdIn staff, wearing dark blue t-shirts with the ubiquitous ;). Feeling like the kid in school who eats lunch with the teacher, she headed toward her own, asking if they needed any help setting up.

"We're good, Clare," they dismissed her. "You enjoy yourself!"

Thus rejected, she headed instead for the bar. The lights flashed and dimmed as she went to order her drink, of which there were only two options, lite beer and white wine spritzer. She chose the latter, wishing a flask would have fit into her pants. Alas, it had no pockets.

"Welcome to 50 First Dates! An LGBTQ speed dating event that combines games, activities, and a heaping dose of fun.

Tonight's event is sponsored by W;nkdIn, the dating app for busy professionals. Lean in ... to love." The emcee for the night was a squat, amply tattooed man in a Hawaiian shirt, whose age seemed impossible to gauge with numbers. His high-pitched voice didn't match his burly biker vibe, but Clare barely noticed. She was too aghast that such an event could combine seemingly every activity she hated into one giant nightmare scenario. She pinched herself to ensure she wasn't dreaming.

Sweat began to drip down the sides of the emcee's face. Perhaps, Clare wondered, he was exhausted by his own exuberance. He began going over the rules.

"You have 5 minutes at each station. The games and activities include icebreaker questions and fun dares to keep things interesting! When you hear the bell ring, move on to the next station and the next person. At the end of the night, you'll fill out a card with the names of the people you'd like to see again. If it's a match, you'll both be emailed. Let the fun begin!"

A bell dinged and Clare was ushered to the giant game of Jenga. Her first date introduced himself as trans, with he/they pronouns. He wore a dark suit and a bluetooth earpiece with a small blue light that blinked intermittently at her, like a lonely Christmas ornament. He was short, bespectacled, and soft-spoken. So much so that Clare barely heard him when he offered her the first move.

Clare pushed a Jenga block out of the tower and read the prompt. "What did you want to be when you grew up?"

Clare looked at her date, who was looking at his phone. She nudged him in the knee with the Jenga block and he glanced up, irritated. She read the question aloud again.

When he still didn't answer, Clare said, "I work in HR."

"Okay," he said, still looking at his phone.

Clare pressed on. "I didn't want to *be* that when I grew up or anything, because what child would dream that? I didn't even know what HR was until I was in my twenties. It's pretty bizarre to even ask that of children, don't you think? Why are we pushing capitalism before kindergarten? Playing with blocks is hardly an exercise in career skills assessment. If it was, then I guess the kids who fought all the time would turn out to be lawyers."

Winded, Clare glanced up from her monologue and noticed he was still on his phone, the glow of the small screen highlighting the dark circles under his eyes and thinning hair. "And what do you do?"

"Lawyer," he said, without looking up. "Patents."

The night only got worse from there.

No matter how many spritzers Clare drank, she couldn't seem to get drunk, which she desperately wanted to, and realized too slowly that the drinks were designed to keep everyone mostly sober. Clare supposed this made sense. Clare could see the potential for rage at events like these, and with enormous board game pieces at the ready, who knew what riots could ensue?

At the icebreaker Twister station, Clare contorted herself with a non-binary Filipina aerial silks teacher, who was voluptuous, lithe, and obviously winning the game. "Right hand red," Clare called out, watching in awe as they moved from a crouch to a backbend, without so much as a grunt. The prompt was: What's something that's been occupying your mental energy?

"Hmm," Jasmine said, pushing their arms against the mat into a full wheel pose. "I've been thinking a lot about energy. Like right now, I can tell straight away that there's way too much wind in your meridians."

"What?" Clare had not expected that. "What's wrong with my meridians?"

Jasmine spun the spinner. "Left foot blue," they said. Clare placed her foot between Jasmine's legs, her thigh muscles shaking with strain. Their bodies were uncomfortably close. The smell of palo santo emanated from Jasmine's crotch. "The wind ... it's really interfering with your abundance. I think fixing it would help—" they waved their hand in Clare's face, "—all this aggressive energy."

The bell dinged.

Clare moved from station to station, performing interpretive dances with Avry, the social worker. She confessed her hidden talent (finding the silverware drawer in people's houses) to Jen, the pastry chef with the pixie haircut, whose job started at 3am, which was why she claimed she couldn't stop yawning at everything Clare said. At the banquet table, where Clare was meant to learn how to "broaden her culinary horizons," with various, unique delicacies from around the world, she found she was too squeamish to eat the ants on the tray she uncovered, no matter how much chocolate they were dipped in. Addison, a beautiful, pale trans woman who reminded Clare of a goth ballerina, happily ate all of Clare's ants. But the conversation stalled there.

No matter which station and which person Clare was paired with, Clare seemed to disappoint them all in some way or another. It wasn't so dissimilar, she thought, from interactions with her mother, but was nevertheless draining and unpleasant. Finally, after what seemed like hours, she appeared to have reached the last station. But no one joined her. She looked around, taking this as a sign, and began to make her way toward the exit, when Julia appeared before her in acid-washed jeans, the end of the large W;nkdIn shirt tied in a knot at her waist.

Julia gestured toward the two pillows that sat on the floor. "We're unevenly numbered tonight. Do you mind if I step in for this one?" Clare shook her head in welcome relief and sat herself down cross-legged on a pillow.

She saw Julia's eyes widen as she read the card. "Okay, this one is called the two-minute touch game. It's a way for partners to give and receive consensual, non-threatening, non-sexual touch. You and your partner will take turns. The first person tells the other how they want to be touched (such as head scratching, skin stroking, light massage, still pressure, etcetera), for two minutes. And then you switch and the other person gets to be touched the way they want."

Clare tensed her shoulders. She hadn't been touched by anyone in a non-sexual context, aside from her doctor, in a long time. She wasn't sure she could do it. Not easily anyway. She struggled to think of where she might even *want* to be touched. Holding hands? That felt so intimate. So did spooning or hugging. They could play patty-cake maybe? No, that would be absurd.

Julia, however, looked entirely at ease, as if she'd played this game hundreds of times and knew precisely what she wanted and how she wanted it. "Want me to go first?" Julia asked.

"Yes."

"Okay, let's see. Want to braid my hair? It's something my sister and I used to do for each other and reminds me of childhood."

"I don't know how to braid hair."

"Really? Your mom never did? Your sisters?"

"No. And I don't have any siblings."

"Well, that's okay, braid it badly. It doesn't matter. I'll take it out anyway." Julia turned her back to Clare and flipped a small hourglass over. The sand began to spill. "Just don't, like, tie it in square knots."

"Okay." Clare looked at the wave of coppery brown before her. From this distance, she smelled the coconut of Julia's shampoo. Grateful that Julia couldn't see her, she picked up a section of Julia's hair, feeling the softness of it thread through her fingers. With her other hand, she took hold of another section and with a child's sense of inexperience and determination, began to weave the strands this way and that, pausing to run her hands along the fine short hairs at Julia's neck, which stood at attention with each caress.

Julia seemed to sink a little lower into Clare's hands as she wound her fingers through Julia's hair. Clare took this as a sign of pleasure and relaxation and pressed a little harder, trailing her nails against Julia's scalp. Slow music filtered softly through the loudspeakers, and just as Clare herself was reaching a calm, almost meditative state, the hourglass emptied and the time was up.

"That was really nice," Julia said.

"Your hair is soft," Clare replied. Even in the dark, Clare could see Julia blush.

"What can I do for you?"

"I'm not sure. No one has ever asked me something like this."

"No one's asked you how you like to be touched?"

"No." Julia looked a little shocked and then a little saddened by this information. "Okay, well, your shoulders look pretty tense. Would you like a massage?"

"Okay." She turned her back to Julia and moved her hair off to one side. The feel of Julia's hands on each side of her neck caused her to stiffen and then relax at the gentle pressure.

"Tell me if this is too much," Julia said, kneading her fingers into the knots near Clare's shoulder blades.

"No, it's ... it's nice."

Clare closed her eyes to the warmth of Julia's hands. She felt the low, faint murmur of Julia's breath at her ear as Julia worked at her stubborn, resistant muscles. Her own breath rose and fell in quiet symmetry, the tension and anxiety and weight of the day and evening slowly dissipating with each firm grasp of Julia's fingers.

When the hourglass ran out, Clare was not ready for the two minutes to be up. She hoped Julia would keep going when the infernal date bell dinged, but instead Julia released her, removing her hands unceremoniously and rising from the pillows.

"Okay, my work is done here!" she said, retreating.

Before Clare could say anything, she noticed a few W;nkdln staffers staring in their direction. When Clare caught them, they swiftly looked away and began busying themselves.

Clare rose up off the floor. When the emcee asked everyone to turn their date cards in with the names of the people they wanted to see again, Clare left hers blank.

She drove home, tired and weary, with the faintest heat and impressions of Julia's fingers embedded in her skin.

fourteen

"YOU DID WHAT?" Paula stood in the bathtub, with Julia behind her. With a small canister of blue body paint in one hand, Julia painted the parts of Paula's back that Paula couldn't reach herself.

"Is speed dating really so bad?" Julia asked. She was glad, however, that Paula wasn't facing her. She couldn't bear to see the reprimand in her friend's face.

"Um, yes."

"Aren't you always saying we should try everything once?"

"There are exceptions, Julia. Murder is one, and speed dating is another."

"I'm trying to broaden Clare's horizons, is all. She's so buttoned up. And at W;nkdIn, we pride ourselves on our diversity of experiences. *It's the journey not the date-stination*, as we like to say."

"Oh god, when did you start believing this bullshit?" Paula swiveled around and Julia shot her a pleading smile. "Wait, what was that even? You *don't* believe this bullshit. You're up to something."

"Turn back around so I can get your shoulder blades."

Paula did so reluctantly.

Julia didn't quite know where to begin about Clare, but somehow Paula managed to get a confession out of her, even with her back turned. Julia found herself telling Paula everything—about her crush on Clare and the bar kiss and the flirting and Julia's not very benevolent plan to send Clare on dates tailored to her personal hells.

"Girl, that is all kinds of fucked up."

"How many kinds?"

"Like seven at least."

Julia had known she wasn't going to win any humanitarian awards with this scheme, but she hadn't expected to be judged quite so harshly by her best friend.

Paula's phone vibrated on the counter next to them. "Can you reach that for me?" Paula asked.

"Yeah. Don't move, you're not dry yet."

Julia picked up the phone. "It's from ... a couple? Abby and Tod. They want to know if you're ready for them to meet ... Juicy? Paula, what is this? Since when do you date men?"

"You're one to judge, Scheming Sandra." Paula tried to snatch the phone away but couldn't without stepping out of the tub. "Besides, I'm not sure I'll meet them. I'm just ... I don't know ... I thought maybe if the girl liked me I could ... get used to the guy."

"No. Really? No."

"We're just talking!"

"Who's Juicy?"

"That's what they call my—"

Julia waved her arms frantically. "Don't even say it. Do not. I'm serious. A threesome that only two of you want will not go well. Plus, have you *seen* balls?"

"I saw my high school boyfriend's briefly once—"

Julia felt flustered on behalf of her friend. "Why are you always going on dates with people who don't want what you want?"

"Why are *you* sending the woman you like on shitty dates?"

"Because it's my job!" Paula rolled her eyes. "Besides, you know I need the money." Paula, perhaps seeing Julia's pained, pitiful expression, softened some. "You can come out of the tub now. The paint should be set." Julia set the canister of body paint on the bathtub's ledge and stepped out to face Paula.

"At least you're not bitching and moaning about Britt, I guess."

"No." Julia's eyebrows tilted upward hopefully.

"And these dates for Clare are all W;nkdIn-approved and not, like dangerous or harmful?"

"Of course they're not harmful!"

"And you like her?"

Julia nodded.

"Then why not just ask her out the old-fashioned way?"

"You mean, swiping 8,000 times on apps until I find her, messaging back and forth for months, and then never meeting?"

"No dummy! Ask her out for dinner."

"I can't! The HR thing is a problem for her. Plus, she's in the beta dating program."

"Oh."

"You're the one who told me not to ask her out!" Julia protested. "In a way, this is entirely your fault."

Paula snorted. "Well, that was before I knew you were gonna get all sneaky-House-of-Slytherin up in here."

Paula secured the light blue headpiece to her head, its

two-pronged extensions falling to her waist. As she stepped out of the tub to look at herself in the mirror, she said, "You're gonna have to tell her, you know."

Julia looked at her friend sternly, waving Paula's phone at her. "Please do not have sex with someone you don't want to because the attention is nice."

Paula sighed. "Fine. I won't. Just let me flirt. And tell me about the other wicked dates you have planned for Clare."

The next few weeks were strange for Clare. After the disastrous speed dating night, W;nkdIn had lined up a pole dancing meet n' greet, an erotic figure drawing class with a nude model, a cuddle party, and an astrological plant healing workshop. The latter was led by a white woman named Brenda. She introduced herself as a "flora medium."

Clare sat in a large circle on a plastic chair with the others in Brenda's living room, which doubled as her daughter's playroom. Unicorns and Pokemon stuffies lined the dresser facing Clare, their plush, shroomy eyes glittering mockingly.

In the center of the circle sat several varieties of plants, succulents, and cacti. After an opening chant, a compassion mantra, and a 10-minute speech from Brenda about the healing power of plants, the participants were supposed to choose one from the pile that "most called to them."

Clare chose a cactus. Not because it called to her but because it was closest. She studied the knobby fruit of its green head and the pale yellow spines that slumped out of it. The spines, though meant to protect the plant, looked so harmless that Clare felt compelled to touch them. And so she did, running the pad of her index finger along its prickly exterior. It didn't hurt. Indeed, it felt almost nice, like touching the bristles of a hairbrush.

"Close your eyes," Brenda said, and the room vanished, along with the cactus Clare held and the tiny bangs that clung to Brenda's forehead. "Become one with your plant. *Connect* with it. *Commune* with it. *Learn* from it. Plants have existed—and thrived!—on this earth long before humans ever came along to muck things up. What does your plant have to tell you? Why do you refuse to listen?"

Brenda's voice had a soothing urgency to it, particularly with the room and the world blotted out. Clare clutched her tiny cactus, gingerly petting its fuzzy spines, and listened.

"Love is intangible but the plant is real. Just like your body in space is real, waiting for you to pay attention to it, to heed its warnings and enjoy its many pleasures."

Clare admitted to herself that she was not great at listening to her body's cues. She slept poorly and ate swiftly and often at her desk, typing one handed while the other dipped into her limp Pad Thai noodles. The onus of food had never been *enjoyment* or pleasure, but on sustaining her blood sugar levels until the next meeting. Perhaps this was why she ate as if, at any moment, someone might come along and snatch the food out of her hand.

She breathed deeply, a calm stillness filling her. Perhaps she had misjudged Brenda after all. Perhaps she had a real gift!

"You may open your eyes now."

Clare did, hoping to be transformed, hoping to have opened her eyes and be in an entirely new place—or perhaps even a new dimension. But no, she was still in Brenda's living room with 15 other thirty-somethings on a Sunday afternoon, all holding plants on their laps like children or tiny dogs. The woman across from Clare still had her eyes closed, possibly in a state of ecstatic union with her plant. Or maybe she was sleeping. It was hard to tell without staring.

"Plants aren't just vegetation," Brenda said. "They are *instinctual*. Tune into them. Tell the plant what you want. What you *really* want. If you're true in your intentions, the plant will grant it."

Brenda struck a ceremonial gong. She burned nag champa. In the middle of the circle she sat cross-legged with a recorder and played a D#, then an A, then another D#. This meant the partner work had begun.

Clare glanced to her right and was struck immediately by a mop of dark curly hair that grayed at the temples. They had a distinct yet genderless dominatrix vibe, even though they wore a sweater and loose cargo pants. Clare wasn't sure what it was exactly that gave her the impression of toppiness. The pout? The unwavering gaze? The posture and sense of surety?

They stuck out their hand, their voice as slow and thick as sap. "I'm Azure. Azure St. Clair."

Clare grasped the hand. She felt as if she might melt under the syrup of that deep voice. "I'm Clare. Saint of nothing."

"Funny," Azure said, while neither laughing nor smiling. Clare's palm began to sweat in Azure's hand. She hoped they didn't notice. "So what does your plant say about you?"

Clare looked down at her tiny, innocuous cactus. "Oh, well, I suppose that I'm ... prickly."

"Are you?"

"Yes," Clare admitted, and then blushed. She felt scrutinized by Azure but in a way she distinctly enjoyed.

"What was the last thing you dreamed?" Azure asked.

Their gaze was unwavering and penetrating. Clare tried to hold it but could not, instead waffling and pitching her head downward to the gray metal chair she was sitting on.

"I don't," Clare said. "Dream much."

"How sad." Again Azure said this without vocal inflection. It was unnerving and mildly intoxicating.

"The only one I can remember of late is where I tried to take a selfie with Jodie Sweetin."

"Stephanie from *Full House*?"

"Yeah. Except she kept cropping me out of the frame." Clare laughed uneasily.

"Hmm," Azure said, as if genuinely interested in Clare's silly dream. "What do you think it means?"

"That Jodie Sweetin is bad at selfies?" Clare ventured.

"I think Jodie Sweetin is you, Clare. So the real question is: Why are you cropping yourself out of your life?"

The blunt edge of Azure's words shocked Clare in its truthfulness. "I ... I don't know." She really didn't. Her palms sweat even more. "What does your plant say about you?" she deflected.

Azure considered her plant. "It's a calathea. Tropical and rare. I grew up on a small island in the Pacific. One that Kim Jong Il was always threatening to bomb out of existence."

"Oh," Clare said. "I grew up in Sacramento." She struggled to think of something interesting about Sacramento. "Elon Musk launched a SpaceX rocket from there once."

"Hm."

Azure looked around not just the room, but it seemed, around the world. Assessing the known universe. Clare was losing them, this intriguing person. She was boring! She tried to bring Azure's attention back. "What's something you've done that other people think is crazy?"

That did it. Azure's penetrating gaze returned to Clare, causing Clare to blush. "You first," they said.

Clare hesitated, unsure of what to share that wouldn't be too vulnerable. "One time, when I was in college, I drove to a city three-and-a-half hours away to meet a girl for a first date."

"Really," Azure said.

"Really."

"Do you generally lack impulse control?"

"What? No ... I'm very responsible. I just ... at the time, well, I thought it was ... I really wanted to meet her."

"Hm," Azure said, a glazed look in their blue-gray eyes. "It was nice talking to you, Clare."

As Azure turned away, shame hit Clare with the force of a brick. She'd shared something about herself and they had found it distasteful. Something that wasn't even true any longer! Clare was nothing if not pragmatic and practical. And yet she'd wanted to impress them. And failed. Clearly. The shame came up in waves, stronger, then weaker, then strong again. It twisted in her stomach. Her face felt hot. She could feel the ivy of her walls shrouding her, closing her in, keeping her safe. *This was what happened when you were vulnerable*, she told herself. *You get shot down. You get seen.*

She shuddered, closing her eyes tight as if it might make everything disappear.

When she opened them again, Clare looked down at her cactus and saw herself for what she was—spiny, insubstantial, and full of drought. Then the person sitting on the other side of her in the circle stuck her hand out. Her name was Heidi and she wore pigtails, a pale green mechanic jumpsuit, and had red-rimmed eyes that made it appear as if she had just stopped crying. Perhaps she had, but this felt too intimate a question to ask a stranger.

Brenda instructed the group to clasp palms with their next partner. Clare held her palm up to Heidi's, with the other hand cupping her cactus. Heidi's palm was both sweaty and cold, both foreign and familiar. And when she closed her eyes again she could picture the hand as not Heidi's but belonging to anyone Clare wanted. She was startled to discover it was Julia's hand that popped into her mind.

Clare flushed the thought and focused instead on wishing upon the plant. In between bouts of wishing she asked Heidi noncommittal questions about herself, which Heidi responded to perfunctorily. Eventually Clare gave up speaking and closed her eyes to commune more intensely with her cactus.

The smoke from the incense reached her nostrils and she realized it wasn't nag champa after all. It was marijuana. Brenda was getting high in between bouts of tooting out the two mournful notes on the recorder.

She wished harder on the plant, squinting and straining her muscles. Perhaps her intentions were not true. Perhaps they never had been. She clutched Heidi's hand harder, as if the exercise was an endurance contest and she intended to win. And just as she was about to give up, her wish came true. The gong chimed again. She was allowed to leave.

On the way out, Clare left the circle of folding chairs holding her cactus, whom she named Darlene. It looked like a Darlene. Brenda called out to her. "Ma'am, stop. The plant stays here."

"Oh. We don't get to keep them?"

"No."

"But what about the connection? The sacred communion between flora and fauna?"

Brenda reached for Darlene but Clare held on tight.

"That's a metaphor, ma'am." She reached again, taking hold of the lip of Darlene's little plastic pot. There was a scuffle, a silent, dignified scuffle, in which the two women wrestled using only their forearms, thumbs, and the penetrating gaze of their irises, which expanded and contracted from the effort.

In the end Brenda won. She was much stronger than she looked, possibly from wearing all those heavy beaded necklaces. As Clare walked to her car, squinting in the bright fall sunlight, she vowed to find another Darlene and to bring her home to her macrame plant hammock. But as soon as she pulled the door of her car closed, a forest fire erupted on her skin. She scratched and scratched, leaving white streaks on her skin that soon became raised beds, and then pink, and then broke open, relief pouring out of her just as much as the red did.

Shame quickly followed the relief as Clare dug in her purse for hydrocortisone cream, blood blooming on the surface of her forearms. But as she searched for the cream, one of the therapy coupons fell out onto the floor. She picked it up, dialed the number, and sent an inquiry message before she could change her mind.

Luca Portinoy was the therapist who emailed Clare back and scheduled her first appointment. Technically, he was not a therapist, but *studying* to be one, he said, and Clare was his first client, which was why he was on the coupon roster.

When she arrived in the small windowless office for her appointment, it smelled faintly of peanut butter and dust. Luca told her to make the check out to his mentor, the man whose framed degree hung on the wall behind Clare's head. She glanced back several times to get the spelling right, as it had a lot of z's and c's in it. Perhaps he was Czech or Polish, but Luca did not share any more information about him and Clare did not ask.

Next to the chair was a small white noise machine, which he turned on, and then a three-foot-tall floor fan set to high speed. Behind Luca's head, Clare noticed two framed artworks, one that said, "It's OK to not be OK," in a scripty font, and the other a colorful profile of a human head that was dissolving into birds flying away.

The office held a small love seat with a southwestern design facing a gray, curved, velvet armchair in the shape of a baseball mitt or a half-womb with skinny metal legs. It was a nice chair, a therapy-looking chair, yet it didn't match the room at all. Plus, Luca was too big for it—he was somehow lanky and stocky at once, or, as Clare's mother might have called him, *meaty of bone*. Strands of dark hair fell into his eyes, and he brushed them away repeatedly. Clare noticed that his cheeks were dotted with uneven stubble and acne, which, coupled with his other boyish features, made him seem barely legal. He looked pained as he folded himself into the small chair, then rested his hands in his lap and smiled placidly.

"Are you comfortable?" Luca asked.

The fan blew Clare's hair around when the rotating face of it whooshed by her. "Not really."

He tipped the fan over on its side so that now the air was blowing at her knees. She decided this would do.

"What brings you in?"

Clare told Luca about her worsening eczema, and how she had tried everything to rid herself of it, but nothing seemed to work. He asked her if she knew what her triggers might be.

"Dating?"

"Are you dating someone?"

"No, like dating as a concept. I think that might be a trigger."

He looked at her blanky and then scribbled something on a yellow legal pad. By the shape of the marks, though, Clare thought it might be a game of tic-tac-toe that he was playing against himself.

"Anything else?"

Clare didn't feel especially inclined to tell Luca about her father's death, as that was intimate and personal, so instead she talked about work and the terrible dates her work was sending her on.

He shifted forward in his seat, his tic-tac-toe game suddenly abandoned. "What exactly goes on at a pole dancing meet n' greet?"

"Oh, um, a bunch of really nice former strippers teach you some sultry moves and then you imitate those moves on a pole while asking perfect strangers about how they minored in Communications in college."

"Fascinating. What kind of moves?"

Clare winced at the memory. "Well, one of the teachers told me to clap my ass like I was salting a chicken."

"And did you?"

"No. My chicken remained woefully under-seasoned." Clare began to grow weary. What did this have to do with her eczema? Or anything?

"And your job is making you go on these dates?"

"Technically I volunteered."

"You did?"

"No, but also yes. It's complicated."

"So you never said, 'I don't want to do this?'"

"Correct."

"And you plan to go on more of these dates that you hate? Because you don't want to disappoint the people at your job."

"Also yes."

Luca was quiet. He tilted his head slightly up and to the left, like a dog transfixed by something on YouTube. "Have you thought about saying no sometime—to someone, or anyone?"

"No," Clare said, then smiled awkwardly. "Ahh, I see what you did there!"

"It wasn't a trick question."

"Oh."

"Just kidding, it was. A little therapy humor." Luca sat back in his chair once more. He couldn't stop fidgeting. "Here's another one. Why did Freud decide not to hit on the woman of his dreams?"

"Because of the devil's Flonase?"

"Because she was too Jung!"

Clare pinched her face into a smile. She could feel the nerves beneath her skin beginning to itch and swell. Luca crossed and uncrossed his legs, then leaned into the padded expanse of the armrest, then thought better of it and sat upright once more.

"New chair? Does it need to be broken in?" Clare asked. She was deflecting but also genuinely curious.

Luca elbowed the wide shell-shaped padding at his back. "Maybe. It was a present from the 'rents."

"For your new therapy practice?"

"More like a 'sorry we called you an animal and said you belong in an institution or prison' gift."

Clare's mouth opened, a slurry of questions turning to

sludge in her throat. But she said nothing and he said nothing.

After a long silence, in which the discomfort in Clare coiled so tightly she felt she might wring herself to death, she finally spoke. "Looks like our time is just about up."

Luca looked at his watch. "There's 20 minutes left."

"Right, but what is time, even? Time is soup. An arbitrary constraint we impose upon the relentless present." Clare babbled as she stepped in her coat.

"Are you sure you're all right? You seem ... flushed."

"Oh yes, well, I blush when healing thoroughly from trauma, so, job well done!" She rushed to gather her things, stepping over the still-on floor fan, whose air rushed right up her skirt. She clamped her legs together as she made her way to the door of the small room.

Over her shoulder, Luca shouted, "Same time next week?"

fifteen

JULIA BLEW a bright red bubble with her gum, savoring one last burst of cinnamon-y goodness before tossing it in the trash in the office breakroom. She had decided to stay home from the next batch of Clare's dates, after a few of the other experience coordinators had made snickering remarks about Julia's behavior at 50 First Dates.

She knew she wasn't supposed to "interfere" in the dates that way, but seeing Clare look so confused, lost, and miserable had an effect on her. Julia couldn't just stand by and let it happen. So she stepped in.

Let them laugh, she thought about her colleagues, who had begun asking Julia for her massage rates. She didn't regret anything. Especially not the chance to loosen the knots in Clare's broad, muscled back. But, just to be on the safe side, she stayed away from Clare's experiences the last few weeks, even though she was dying to know how Clare fared, especially on the stripper pole. What if she didn't have a bad time? Or worse, what if she *connected* with someone and actually started dating them? Julia already felt bereft at the thought, as she swore she overheard Clare mentioning someone named Darlene to Rodrigo when he did Clare's R&R, recap and reassessment.

She didn't have too much time to wonder, however, as Clare and Rodrigo walked into the break room arguing.

"I told you to wear black today!" Rodrigo huffed.

"Why? Am I going to a funeral? Because honestly, it'd be an improvement to the dates you've been sending me on."

He looked at Julia imploringly. "This one is about to make me permanently lose my Netflix and chill!"

Rodrigo opened the fridge door and took out a probiotic cannabis-infused yogurt, a reefer keifer, which he then pressed against his forehead like a cold compress and closed his eyes.

"Why don't Clare and I get a coffee from the cafe next door to chat a bit and give you some time to cool off?" Julia said.

"Yes," Rodrigo said, eyes still closed, forehead raised to the ceiling. "It is best this way. Leave me here. Save yourselves. But bring me back an oat milk matcha latte, por favor."

Julia steered Clare out of the break room. Once out of earshot, she said to Clare, "He can be a little dramatic sometimes. It's part of his drag queen persona."

"He does drag?" Clare asked, a surprised look on her face mixed with ennui, as if drag queens were a more advanced species of humans that Clare was sad not to be born into.

"Yeah. You should see him perform actually. He's really sultry. His stage name is Lana Del Gay."

"That's a great name."

Julia beamed. "I helped him come up with it."

"I love puns," Clare said. "I tried to enter a pun-off

when I was in high school, but my mother forbade it. She said it wasn't ladylike."

Julia made a sour face. "I hope you did it anyway."

"Alas," she said, pace quickening, "I didn't. I remained *a lass*."

At this, Julia couldn't help but laugh. Julia felt so goofy and *sincere* around Clare, so hopelessly Midwestern, even though Julia was born and raised in California. In any minute, she'd be baking Clare Hot Dish and inquiring about the local hockey team.

Once seated at a table on the cafe patio with their drinks, Julia questioned Clare about her date experiences. Clare had, predictably, not had a grand time at any of the events, but, perhaps because Clare knew Julia was behind their orchestration, she made sure to throw in several compliments about the experiences. Of the pole class, she said, "It really worked my deltoids!" Of the cuddle party, "I wanted to vomit several times, but thankfully kept it in." Of the plant healing workshop, "I may indeed get a succulent now."

But of the people Clare had met? Julia was happy to note that Clare didn't mention anyone of interest. Not even anyone named Darlene. This relieved Julia, who relaxed into a more casual demeanor, which seemed to relax Clare in kind. She took a sip of her matcha latte.

"Mm, you really oughta try this."

"What is it?" Clare asked. "I try not to eat anything ... green."

"Even salad?"

"Especially salad!"

"It's matcha! It's nutty and delicious. You've really never tried it?"

Clare turned up her nose distrustfully. "No."

"Well, come on then." She pushed the drink across the table in Clare's direction. Even Clare's stubbornness was attractive. How did she do it? "In the spirit of trying new things."

Clare closed her eyes and took the tiniest mouse sip of Julia's latte. Then she took a slightly bigger one. Foam coated her upper lip when she smiled at Julia, whose eyebrows peaked expectantly.

"All right, all right, you win. It's delicious."

"See?" Julia reached for the drink but Clare slid it just beyond her reach, then took another sip. Julia realized there was a playful side to Clare that probably almost never saw the light of day. She smiled to herself, feeling privileged to have witnessed even this small glimpse.

"Do I really need to wear black for today's date?" Clare asked.

"It's optional."

"Are you going to tell me what I'll be doing?"

"And ruin the fun? No way."

"Am I allowed to guess at least?"

"Sure," Julia smiled. "But you never will."

"But what if I do?"

"You won't."

"If you're so sure, why don't we make it interesting."

"Interesting?"

"Yeah," Clare said, pausing to take a sip of her iced coffee. Julia noticed that she had put four sugars in it and was trying not to judge her. "If I guess what the next date is, you have to do it with me."

Julia gulped. While she was more outgoing and adventurous than Clare, she didn't exactly relish the idea of this next experience. But she did relish the thought of spending more time with Clare, so, "I'm in," she said.

Clare tapped her lip with her index finger, as if deep in thought. "You're making me write feelings poetry and then performing it in front of a live audience while wearing a black turtleneck?"

"No!" Julia laughed. "I'm not a sadist."

"You're making me ... do a reenactment of *Waiting for Godot*?"

"Not even close."

Clare clasped her hands in front of her. Underneath the table, her foot bounced in its beige leather flat. "You're making me ..."

Before Clare could finish, a middle-aged man in a tweed blazer and white loafers came up to their table, pulling up a metal chair right next to Julia. Its heavy legs dragged loudly against the asphalt, screeching in her ears. His hands were slim and manicured, as if the only manual labor he'd performed was lifting books. His hair was uncombed. An order muppet disguised as a chaos muppet. "Um, hi," Julia said, a bit nervously. "Can we help you?"

"Are you Julia? Julia Dawes."

"Yes?" Julia said.

"Of the K Stew Haiku Review? I'm such a fan!"

"Oh, thank you!"

"Do you mind if I get your autograph?" He thrust a piece of paper in front of her.

"No, not at all." She signed the paper.

"Thank you again," he said. "Sorry to disturb you."

Clare's eyes widened as the man walked back to his table. "Um, what was that?"

"Oh, nothing."

"Nothing?"

"I write this blog. It has fans. Rabid fans. That guy was one."

"And what's this blog about?"

Julia smiled sheepishly. Her fingers gripped the holes in the metal table. "It's silly."

"It can't be that silly."

"Well."

"Do you review pet costumes?"

Julia snorted. "No."

"Do you write recipes for savory cheesecakes?"

"No, but that's ... intriguing actually. If I get fired, that's my new plan B," Julia said. She took a long breath. "I write Kristen Stewart film reviews in haiku. Get it? The K Stew Haiku Review."

"Kristen Stewart? The actress who did the vampire movies?"

"It's—She's so much more—" Julia opened her mouth to defend herself, but against what, she wasn't entirely sure.

"Wow, okay, so you're famous. That's neat! I guess I should watch one of her movies then?"

"I'm sorry, did you just say you've never seen a Kristen Stewart movie?"

"Oh my god, I've got it." Clare gasped. "The date you planned next—you're making me attend a mime class, aren't you?"

sixteen

IT WAS A GOOD GUESS. It was the correct guess. Julia had to give Clare that, even in her shock. Even as she grumbled to herself while putting on a face of white makeup. The moment for interrogations about Clare's questionable movie viewing habits had passed quickly and unceremoniously, so Julia asked nothing. Instead she went back to work, then went home, showered, dashed off a K Stew haiku that encapsulated her shock, denial, and eventual acceptance of Clare's pop culture shortcomings.

Spencer
They wanted you to
be perfect. They didn't know
you already are.

And then she found herself in a clown school studio.

It was in a dilapidated, red-and-yellow-painted warehouse in a not-great part of town, which only made the whole place seem more whimsical and fitting. Someone had painted bushy, quizzical eyebrows over the two largest windows that faced the freeway, giving the building a Big Brother quality. In the photos online, it looked like a Fun House, but in person it took on a decidedly *House of Leaves*, bigger-on-the-inside-than-it-is-on-the-outside vibe.

The inside was better, less cannibal-y. Trampolines lined the halls. An enormous trapeze bar hung 50 feet in the air. Next to it was a ladder that Julia shuddered to even think of climbing. The air in the studio smelled damp, yet chalky. In one corner sat a miserable looking person counting foam noses and deflating whoopee cushions to put away in storage.

Bob and Midge were the instructors at Mime Time. It was a small class, with only 10 or so people. Everyone was handed sponges, along with white, red, and black face makeup. "Draw the essence you wish to portray," Midge said. "As Shakespeare once wrote, 'To mime own self be true."

Julia drew in a single tear on her left cheek, then donned a black beret. She had made her bed, so she might as well cry in it. Clare, on the other hand, appeared to be in excellent spirits. She applied the white face paint with flourish, gave herself a rosy, cupid's bow mouth, and turned her eyebrows into bushy, Charlie Chaplin-esque parentheses.

Julia had never seen Clare in non-muted colors before, and was surprised how transformed she looked in the white-and-blue-striped sailor shirt and red suspenders.

"To be able to communicate without words," Bob said, "*this* is the mime's goal. His singular task ... or hers ... or theirs! Mimes see no gender!" The deflating whoopee cushions in the distance punctuated his speech with sad tooting sounds. But Bob was not deterred. He marched on like a general who had lost all of his soldiers but retained a single trombone player from the cavalry band. "To accomplish this we'll use a number of techniques, mirroring exercises, and, to encourage interaction," here he winked, "we'll also have a little getting-to-know-you portion of the evening."

A tall, stocky woman with red hair and a gummy smile raised her hand. "We're supposed to get to know people without speaking to them?"

"It worked in *The Little Mermaid*, didn't it?" Midge chimed in. She had painted over her eyebrows, so that all the skin from eye socket to hairline was white. This made everything she said seem both alarming and irrefutable.

The class exchanged looks, but no one could exactly poke a hole in Midge's argument, so nothing further was said.

"Precisely!" Midge said, looking from face to face and widening her eyes. Julia noticed that her forehead didn't wrinkle and wondered if she'd had Botox done. Midge, as if reading Julia's thoughts, smiled a manic, red smile. "So, for the rest of the class, Bob and I will be the only ones talking. You, my lovelies, will be *expressing*. You will *gesture*. You will *emote*. And, if you leave a five-star review on Yelp, you'll receive 10% off the next class. Are we ready?"

Julia felt suddenly nervous. And like a hypocrite. These were the kinds of experiences she was foisting upon people and expecting them to fall in love! Julia did not feel romantic. She felt awkward and performative. She'd never been on the other side of the fence before in these experiences. And hadn't been on a date herself in ages.

Britt didn't believe in "dating" once you were a couple. She'd considered it unnecessary hoop-jumping. She had been happy to do it in the early stages, to perform the rituals of courtship, but once Julia had moved in with her, she stopped, hung a metaphorical "mission accomplished" sign, and stopped trying. And so their relationship had settled, like a fine sheen of dust on a neglected surface. Julia noticed it slowly and tried to rouse Britt from her complacent slumber. Tickets to comedy nights, sake tastings, mystery picnic scavenger hunts, new vegan restaurants she thought Britt might enjoy—Britt wasn't having any of it. She preferred to stay at home. She preferred not to be bothered.

In hindsight, Julia was far more devastated by this than she let on. Eventually, the routine and malaise of their unrelenting sameness led Julia to start begging. With considerable effort, she managed to drag Britt to the Grand Lake Farmers Market one Saturday, where Britt met the potato farmer she eventually left Julia for.

The memory still singed. The pain was less of a blow now, and more like a bruise, a tender soreness she tried not to brush up against too often. Julia had never been left before, and certainly not for a woman who recited Adrienne Rich's poetry to her fingerlings. No. Julia was the one who did the leaving. Julia was the restless one, the wanderer, the one whose possessions could all easily fit in the bed of her truck. Until Britt domesticated her. Britt with her competent, bike mechanic hands and terrible tattoos. Britt with her ability to decipher Ikea furniture instructions. Britt with her 18 different sizes of allen wrenches. Julia had loved all of these things. But more than that she loved that Britt had made her want to stay put. To build something and make it beautiful. It still sometimes shocked Julia to think of Britt leaving. But, in spite of everything, Julia couldn't help but be grateful. All the date research she'd done for Britt had prepared and led her to her current role at W;nkdIn. Led her to Clare.

Julia knew the mime class was pretty out there, even by

her standards, which were niche and weirder than average. She wasn't certain if she would be recommending it for future dates at W;nkdIn. But then Clare looked at Julia, wiggling her drawn-in, bushy black brows in Julia's direction, and she became more convinced that she'd chosen well. Julia didn't know how Clare did it, how she managed to become the bright, molten center of every room she entered.

The class had begun. Bob and Midge pointed to a woman with pink John Lennon glasses and unicorn-colored hair. "You," Bob said. "How might you show us that you're annoyed?"

The woman rolled her eyes and Bob and Midge applauded thunderously. They worked their way through several other emotions, picking people at random—boredom, joy, anger, sadness, hopelessness, defeat, and whiff-of-death. The last one was a real challenge, but Clare wowed them all by taking a giant sniff in Bob's general direction and then keeling over, half-fainting, then stumbling up on her knees, then falling again, ending in a corpse pose with her arms in a cross over her chest.

Julia did not think she could be more attracted to anyone as she was attracted to Clare at that moment, and yet she was. Perhaps she would give Mime Time a five-star review on Yelp during the intermission.

Next came the mirroring. They stood in a circle in pairs. The people on the inside of the circle would mime something and the person on the outside would try to imitate their movements. "There's nothing wrong with the classic poses, my pretties," Midge said, "but we strongly encourage you to think outside the box."

Julia's first partner, a dirty-blonde with a pinched, bird-like face, took Midge's words a little too literally and mimed that she was trapped ... outside of a box. Julia struggled to follow along, moving her hands wildly and frantically in order to mirror her partner's faux panic.

The next several were easier. One mimed drinking a hot beverage. Another mimed a singer belting out a tune. And one curled herself into a ball on the floor and cried. Julia was not sure if this was a performance or if she needed real help—it was hard to tell from her position on the floor. When Bob and Midge told the class to rotate, she left the circle. This miming was a serious business, Julia thought to herself. It unleashed emotions. It dramatized the air. It gave each pair of strangers an invisible string and tethered them together, in silent, wordless embrace.

When Clare finally appeared before Julia, she paused, thinking about what she would enact. A slow smile spread across Julia's face when she figured it out. First, she placed her hand in a stiff shelf near her eyes, as if surveying the scene. Clare mirrored her. Then, finding the thing she sought, Julia did a happy little dance. Clare also did the happy dance. Then Julia bent down and plucked an invisible flower from the earth, and Clare did so, too. Julia smelled the flower, scrunching her shoulders up at this ornamental bouquet of delight. And when she handed the flower to Clare, who momentarily forgot what she was doing and took the flower, clutching it to her heart.

Bob shot Clare a look then that was so expressive, it managed to convey, "Hey now! You're supposed to be mirroring, but also that is an excellent back-and-forth partner dialogue and you've come so far in 35 minutes!" He *is* good, Julia thought, then handed another imaginary flower to Clare, who "blushed" and mirrored the gesture back to her.

Now they both had imaginary flowers in their hands

and sheepish grins. The next step would be for them to kiss, wouldn't it? Julia thought. This was where their imaginary courtship was clearly headed. And yet, they could not kiss. They were in mime school. Julia was used to making bold gestures in her romantic life, but even if they had been in an imaginary bar in mime school, it seemed to Julia that a kiss would be inappropriate. The thought of kissing Clare, however, made Julia blush non-imaginarily.

"Rotate!" Midge yelled. And there was no more time to imagine. She hopped to the next person, the red spreading across her neck and down her chest. She wondered if Clare had noticed.

seventeen

"THAT'S the most fun I've had in years," Clare told Julia at the wine bar they went to after class was over. Julia had said she needed something to wash the mime off of her, but Clare secretly thought Julia had enjoyed herself. Clare certainly had! She could practically feel her mother sighing into her Gewürztraminer wine several time zones over. She felt like a rebellious teenager.

They didn't have to go far, it turned out, as the giant loft warehouse that held the clown school also housed a small wine bar on the ground floor called EKG. "Like the machine that tests your heart?" Clare asked the bartender, a middle-aged man whose short hair stood straight up, as if he'd been electrocuted and then come into work instead of going to the hospital. "Yeah," he said, touching the sides of his hair. "We owe our lives to so many machines and they never get any credit. I decided to honor the true, unsung heroes at my bar."

"How interesting," Clare lied. "But why a medical device and not something related to owning a bar?"

"I thought of that," he said, thoughtfully. "But, like, Credit Card Reader just didn't resonate with people."

Julia and Clare moved to the far end of the bar, drinks in tow. They were still in full mime makeup, a fact that ordinarily would have horrified Clare (or more precisely, Clare's mother), but because Julia seemed so fine with it, and because she felt so loose and free after the class, she decided not to let it bother her.

"I never thought I'd say this to a person," Julia said, raising her glass, "but if you ever decide to pivot in an entirely new direction, I think you'd make an excellent mime."

Clare raised her glass too, clinking their thin, shiny lips together. "You know what's funny? I wanted to minor in theater in college. But my mother wouldn't hear of it. She said it was 'impractical.'"

"And you listened?"

"Yep." Clare took a long sip of her merlot.

"Do you have a hard time saying no to your mother?"

"Not just her—but most people."

"Really?"

"Really."

"Do you want to try it, like, for practice?"

"What, saying no to you?"

"Yes."

"I don't know."

"Come on, try it. Here, I'll ask you to do something and you tell me no."

Clare pursed her lips. She wasn't sure if she could say no to Julia, or if she even *wanted* to, regardless of the ask. But Julia was looking at her with those hopeful, childlike eyes. She couldn't say no. Damn it! She was already failing this exercise.

"Say, Clare, do you want to hop on this here bar, take your top off, and dance like no one's watching?"

Clare cleared her throat. Her words came out just shy of a whisper. "No ... thank you." She shouldn't have thanked her, she realized too late. But Julia didn't reprimand her. She kept going.

"Do you want to try one of those pickled eggs sitting in the jar over there?"

Her voice gained in volume this time. "No."

"Do you want to pat the bartender on the bottom?"

"Emphatically not." It was her loudest no yet. The more absurd questions Julia asked her, the easier it became for Clare to exert her opinions. Opinions she was surprised she had. It turned out she had strong feelings about a great many things, both trivial and pressing. By the time Julia had asked her about fifteen questions, Clare was practically bellowing. Her no's reverberated frantically around the industrially designed space. Her no's bounced and buoyed. Her no's grew in size and dimension, garnering the attention of the few other patrons in the place and the bartender. But Clare didn't care! She no'd with abandon. She no'd with aplomb. She no'd jollily, clutching her belly, like a slightly drunk Santa Claus. *No no no! Merry Christmas!* By the time she'd ended the last chain of no's, she was actually laughing, a chorus of ha's filling the dark space. Julia joined her.

The bartender came up to them and asked Clare if she wanted another drink.

"No!" Clare shouted. She was on a roll; it was hard to stop. "Wait, actually yes. Another merlot ... please."

He nodded slowly, backing away from Clare as if her mouth was a loaded gun.

This made Clare and Julia laugh even harder. Though Clare didn't smoke and never had, she felt like she finally understood the impulse. She wanted very much to light a cigar, lean back, and watch the smoke curl and twist and engulf her pale features.

Once the bartender was out of earshot, Julia said, "That was so good, Clare! And you clearly have a calling for the dramatic arts. Though I guess I should thank your mom, since our paths never would have crossed if you'd become the next Great Mime."

"Don't put me in a box, Julia."

Julia laughed again.

"You were pretty good yourself," Clare said.

"I have a confession. That wasn't my first time."

"It wasn't?"

"When I was in the Peace Corps I taught a little bit of everything—math, drama, literacy, even P.E."

"You were in the Peace Corps?"

"In Guyana, yep."

"Developing world P.E. teacher, amateur mime, and matchmaker—your career trajectory has been very ... untraditional."

"I was also a locksmith and, briefly, a wedding planner."

"Really?"

"What?" Julia smirked. "I take direction well."

"So you can break into things?"

"Yeah."

Heat radiated up and down Clare's spine. She looked at Julia's fingers, which were short, square, and lightly calloused. She pictured briefly what else they might be good at. "You've lived so many lives."

Clare felt both in awe of Julia and also a little jealous. What had she been doing all these years? What would her tombstone even read? Here lies Clare. She worked and made wall hangings that her mother didn't know were owls.

Julia stretched her neck, cracking it to the right and left, interrupting Clare's pity party. "I really loved teaching. I would've stayed on after my stint with the Peace Corps was up, supporting the NGO that worked with the kids I was teaching. But it didn't work out."

"How come?"

"They fired me. Because I wouldn't have sex with my boss," Julia said, almost nonchalantly. Clare felt indignant on Julia's behalf, and conflicted by her own desire for Julia. Was she no different than these men? "I would babysit my boss's kids sometimes," Julia continued. "We had a cordial relationship. No one was more shocked than me when he 'reported' me to the Ministry of Education after I turned him down."

"I'm so sorry. That's terrible."

"It's okay," Julia shrugged. "It was a long time ago." She wouldn't look at Clare, staring instead at some unfixed place on the back wall.

"Still. It's bullshit. And even more so that a similar thing happened to you at W;nkdIn, too."

"But you put a stop to it," Julia said, smiling now. "My knight in shining ... ballet flats." Clare tried not to laugh too hard at the thought of being anyone's knight in shining anything.

Julia continued, "I know that I can come off as kind of a bimbo—"

"Not at all—"

"No, I do. I accept it. But I thought if I worked hard enough I could convince people to take me seriously, which is all I've ever wanted."

Clare closed the distance between them, taking one of Julia's hands. "I take you seriously."

Their eyes met and Clare felt herself move to Julia like a magnet once more. Julia was a cymbal crashing. She was a winking garden gnome in a pristine church yard. A tiger's soft chin. A tumbleweed rolling perfectly past an unmarred desert sky. Clare leaned forward, drawn by some perverse other gravity, some alternate force that led her ever back to the soft O of Julia's mouth. Julia leaned toward Clare in kind, their movements as slow as tectonic plates shifting, and then Clare awakened from her trance and stiffened, dropping Julia's hand and sitting bolt upright on the stool once more.

"Thank you, by the way," Clare said. "This has been, by far, the funnest date I've been on yet."

Clare noticed that Julia's eyes seemed to widen at the word *date*.

They sipped their wine in silence for a moment. Was this a date? Clare wondered. She knew it had been set up to be a date, of course. But she also knew it would be wrong to date Julia. She remembered their kiss at 1221, its brief, tumbling tenacity. And then she remembered pulling away. The memory hit her slowly and painfully. Her heart had been too ripe then. Too at war with itself. But now?

Now here they were at a wine bar. A strange wine bar, but a wine bar no less. Talk was occurring. Alcoholic beverages were being consumed. This was very datey territory. And it felt good and right and easy.

Clare traced a circular stain on the reclaimed wood of the bar with her finger. With Julia, it was all so muddled. She was a coworker. She was Clare's junior. Before, when Julia had kissed her, Clare's no had felt so certain, and now she felt herself slipping. Because W;nkdIn was a relatively new startup, Clare wasn't even sure if there was language on employee dating in the handbook. She had never received any complaints or fielded any questions about the matter.

She pondered such quandaries as Julia finished her drink and ordered another round. When her wine came, Julia scooted her stool a little closer to Clare's, causing their elbows to touch momentarily and sending a trail of nerves in Clare's lower back to shoot up to the base of her skull and back down. She heard Brenda the flora medium's voice in her head—*Tune into your body*—and was startled to realize she was trembling. Not in fear, but in anticipation. And more so than that, her skin felt entirely calm. She hadn't had the urge to scratch herself all evening. Perhaps Luca, her therapist, had been right after all. Standing up for herself, saying no, even in practice, appeared to have a calming effect on her. So did Julia, if it was possible to feel both at ease and aflame at the same time. Around Julia, Clare felt as if every kind of beauty imaginable had been tossed at her at once, like too many juggling balls. She held out her hands dumbly, knowing she couldn't possibly catch them all, and yet desperate to try any way.

The air was thick and staticky in the wine bar, charged with possibility. Clare felt the downed power lines of her heart sparking, knowing a storm was on the horizon. She decided at that moment to listen to her body's wants. She would live *a little*, the tiniest amount, in fact. If her life were under a microscope, only then would scientists be able to see Clare's version of living just then. But to Clare it was huge. She let her legs fall open so that the fabric of her black, wide-legged pants was touching the fabric of Julia's tight denim jeans.

A curious half-smile appeared on Clare's lips. Her heart

raced. She'd done it! And Julia had not moved away from her touch. Indeed, she had leaned into it. Surely this was a sign that Julia still wanted her? Clare decided to be a little bolder, to press, as she had wanted to earlier, her knee and a part of her thigh against Julia's. Again, Julia did not move away. Far from it, her leg pushed back against her own, the muscle and bone and skin softly sighing together now, nodding their perfect, wordless approval.

"By the way, you forgot something in class," Julia said.

"I did?" Clare patted her pockets, looking to see that her purse was still resting under the bar at her feet.

"You did."

Julia set her wine glass down on the bar, and began to glance across the room, as if searching for something.

Clare swiveled around with a confused look on her face, but when Julia then plucked an imaginary flower from the floor and smelled it with delight, Julia knew that Clare understood. But instead of offering Clare the flower, Julia reached for Clare's face, tucking a wave of Clare's hair behind her ear to make room for its imaginary stem. In this small gesture, something was unleashed inside Julia. Her insides performed some kind of acrobatics, with tigers, hoops, tight-ropes, and a unicycle. The pleasure was so acute it was almost painful. It was so acute, in fact, that she couldn't help but do it *again*.

Julia grazed Clare's hair and ear with the tips of her fingers, smoothing and tucking the flower into its proper place. Clare closed her eyes as Julia did this, a dreamy calm overtaking her face. Clare kept them closed as Julia's fingers reached the arc of her lower earlobe, where they rested now against Julia's neck and cheek, and still closed when Julia leaned in and kissed her long and full and hard on the mouth.

For a moment, Julia kept her eyes open, wanting to watch Clare's face register the sensation, the intimacy, the *intentionality* of the kiss. Clare's mouth was softer than Julia had remembered, yet more insistent. Julia felt the wet press of Clare's lips starting little bonfires in different places around her body—on her hip bones and threaded through her vertebrae and the fleshy part of her calf. The room grew both louder and muted, the air full and drenched in the shrewd storm of Clare's mouth capsizing her past, present, future.

Julia had never been kissed like this. She felt the uncomfortable sensation that she was buoying and sinking, drowning and desperate to drink every last drop. The kiss was a homecoming and a departure, a grounding and a spiriting away. Kissing Clare saturated her senses. She was watching the sunrise over a Moroccan desert. She was eating her grandmother's posole. She was listening to a swell of violins in a Tchaikovsky overture. Kissing Clare dropped a beautiful anchor into Julia's center, where Julia knew it would stay, whether she wanted it to or not.

As the kiss Tetris'd inside of her, Julia swore she could feel Clare's pleasure in her own body, the soft sigh of it radiating along her spine, her hips, and down into her soft center, which pulsed intently and rhythmically, like the hammering of her own wildly beating heart.

Momentarily stunned, Clare's mouth twitched slightly, as if it had encountered flame. She let out a low moan before kissing Julia back, the force of her lips and tongue sending wild pulsations down the length of Clare's body, down to the tips of her toes and back. Her hands went to Julia's breasts, almost unconsciously, cupping them firmly in her palms before she realized she was doing it, feeling the soft pull of Julia's nipples against her thumbs.

The force of the pressure now unleashed sent their bodies closer together, every part of them touching that could—knees and thighs and hands and breasts and lips— each woman forgetting where they were or even *who* they were, responding only to this hunger, the indelible ache of connection, of grasping, of a need so raw and pure and true it didn't have or require a name.

And then, in the span of no more than a minute or two, Clare remembered her usual rules, her sense of responsibility, and the catastrophe of breaking up with and then working with Nikki. And she ignored it. And kissed Julia anyway.

eighteen

PAULA LOOKED AT JULIA SLANT-WISE. "INTERESTING."

"Don't look at me like that," Julia said.

Paula continued to stare blankly at her friend. Julia had brought them both coffees and scones that morning. She thought Paula was going to debrief her on yet another lackluster date she'd had, but then Julia looked at Paula like a startled raccoon and her friend sensed something was up. "Interesting," Paula said again. "Something happened." It wasn't a question.

"What? No."

Paula began to inhale the air around Julia in small bursts. "Then why," she sniffed, "do I feel like I need a shower?"

Julia instinctually glanced in the direction of Clare's office, which caused Paula to gasp. "You didn't! You hooked up with Clare!"

"Shhhh," Julia said, taking Paula by the arm and dragging her closer to her ear. "Okay, okay, we kissed last night. After the mime class date."

"You kissed Clare!" Paula clapped, hopping a little as she did so. "The ice queen! Did she break into a thousand tiny frozen pieces, like in *Terminator 2*?" Julia made a face of rumpled protest. "Wait, are you upset? Tell me. What did she do? Do I need to sharpen my Shuriken blades?"

"You made those 'blades' from cardboard and aluminum. I was there, remember?"

"True, but I can still cut a bitch."

Julia smiled faintly imagining Paula getting in a fight with anyone. She presented a tough veneer with her black-on-black attire and menacing eye makeup and shit-kicker boots, but inside, Paula was a pile of puppies.

"We kissed and it was magical and now I don't know what to do. I mean, the first time we kissed she kind of ran away."

"That happened to me once," Paula said wistfully, "in third grade. Allison Duran. I never shared my Capri Sun with her again."

Julia picked at a dried bit of food stuck to the surface of her desk. It was hard and revolting, and smelled like cheese. "I was so confused before and then we had this amazing night and I ... I just don't want to fuck it up. I really really like her."

"Valid," Paula smiled. "Don't fuck it up then."

Julia sighed.

"Also, aren't you supposed to *not* be mackin' on the clients you're ostensibly helping to find love?"

Despite herself, Julia laughed. She covered her face with her hands to hide the irrepressible smile that erupted thinking of kissing Clare. Even in full mime makeup, it was the best first kiss she'd ever experienced. "So what do I do now? Help me, Obi Wan Kenobi."

"Hmm, I think the ball might be in her court now.

Maybe give her a chance to sort herself and her feelings out. Give her some breathing room. Don't go all chaos muppet on her."

"I am not—" Julia huffed.

"You're a fucking catch, Jules. I mean, don't tell her your credit score, but aside from that, a fucking *catch*." Paula became strangely angelic when she was spouting her know-it-all truths. It would infuriate Julia if it wasn't so endearing. "Just give her a little space. She probably needs to freak out a little bit. The way, you know, you're freaking out. But don't, like, cancel your future joint Costco account or anything."

nineteen

CLARE WAS FREAKING OUT. She could not quite believe what had happened—that she had *allowed* it to happen, and enjoyed it so thoroughly. This behavior was so unlike her. Perhaps that's why she liked it. This last year she'd felt frozen, always playing it safe, hoping to not make another mistake the way she had with Erik, and then Julia came along and here she was, not merely playing with fire, but looking for a condo on the sun. That's how it felt to be around Julia. She was radiance, exuberance. She lived fully in each moment, reaching her hand out, begging Clare to join her, to do the same, to, as her mother had put it, "live a little."

Julia's voice echoed in her ear as Clare drove to her next appointment with Luca. He was not a good listener and technically not even a real therapist, and yet he had been right. What he had said to Clare had worked. Clare felt lighter and freer, even though the buoyancy was punctuated by jabs of confusion at breaking her own rules around dating and work. Had she learned nothing from the saga of Nikki? And what about her focus on her promotion? Where had that gone? Vanished in the heart-breaking gap between Julia's two front teeth, apparently.

He wasn't sitting in the womb chair this time. Clare thought perhaps Luca had sent it back to his parents, but then she noticed its shiny, upturned legs in the corner. The chair was upside down and half-buried in manila file folders, like a beetle that had met an unfortunate bureaucratic demise.

The right side of Luca's face was red and bore the pattern of the throw pillow on the couch, a sort of fleur de lis swirl. Clare sat on the pillow, and as she suspected, it was warm. She hoped he hadn't drooled on it, but it was too late to check now.

He smiled at her groggily. "Hi Chloe."

"Clare."

"Right, Clare." He rubbed his eyes. "How's things?"

"I'm so glad you asked!" She slid off the pillow—it was overstuffed and not at all comfortable. Plus, it made her tower over Luca. She felt that in this moment she needed to be humble. "I took your advice and practiced saying no, and it worked! It felt great, even though I kind of yelled at a bartender accidentally. But my skin has been itch-free for 24 hours! And it's all thanks to you."

He nodded but said nothing. Perhaps he knew there was more to the story. Or perhaps he was asleep with his eyes open. She decided to try a little test.

"Also, I discovered that I have a preternatural talent for miming and my coworker kissed me."

That seemed to do the trick. He sat up straighter, trying to tame the hair that stuck out at odd angles from his nap on the couch. "And how did that feel?" He licked his fingers and smoothed the hair down, like a cat.

"Which? The miming or the frenching?"

Lick, lick, smooth, smooth. "The frenching."

"It felt incredible."

"Yeah?"

"Yeah! Except dating Julia would go against everything I've been working toward this year. It's not ... ideal, to say the least, and kind of makes me want to run for the hills."

"Because you've been running away from real intimacy since your father died?"

Clare's mouth hung open. An expressionless staring contest ensued. Until finally Clare broke it. "How did you know about my father?"

"You mentioned it in the in-take survey you filled out on the website. I finally got around to reading it."

"Oh."

"I don't see what my father has to do with Julia."

"Then why do you want to run away?"

"Because she's my colleague. It's *inappropriate*!"

"I thought you said she kissed *you*."

"She did!"

"And you enjoyed it?"

"Yes!" Clare didn't know why she was shouting. She hated confrontation, but was this a confrontation if she was essentially agreeing with everything he said?"

"So what's inappropriate, Clare? Is it against your company's policy or something?"

———

When Clare returned to W;nkdIn, she shut herself in her office and canceled the rest of her afternoon meetings. She glanced down at her inspirational calendar. Today's said, *Go ahead, buy the good cheese.* She didn't think that applied to her situation per se, but she added a pricey camembert to her online grocery cart, then she settled in to read the Employee Operations Manual cover to cover. Afterward, she cross-referenced it against local, state, and even federal laws to be as thorough and precise as possible. Lucky for her, Clare loved to nerd out on this precise kind of data. When the last bylaw was checked with the company's core values, she shut her laptop triumphantly, her smile as long as her slender legs, which were still fatigued from sexual tension and all the miming. She picked up her phone.

Julia answered on the first ring, and Clare became suddenly tongue-tied.

"Are you calling me from your office?" Julia said.

"Yes."

"Do you want me to come—"

"No!" Clare was still incapable of vocalizing her no's at a normal volume. "I mean, it's not necessary. And I don't want to attract ... unwanted attention from anyone. But I do have news that's ... relevant ... to our ... situation. Can we meet at yours? If you'll have me?" She hadn't meant for the last question to come out quite so pleading.

In the silence, Clare hoped Julia hadn't changed her mind about her. Old insecurities began to loom. Why would Julia want to date someone so unsure? So work-obsessed? So reluctant to try even a different colored tea? Of course, Julia would be over Clare by now. Or what if Julia was dating other people? She was blog famous! She clearly had suitors lining up the block, and not just coffee shop professors who made love nightly to their thesauruses. Thesauri? That Clare didn't even know the plural of thesaurus was further proof of her inadequacy.

"I have something to tell you, too, actually," is what Julia finally said. "How's 8?"

"Perfect. Let me get a pen to write down the address."

"Also, an enormous cheese wheel arrived for you. I signed for it and set it against your door."

"Oh, yes. Well, I'll bring the cheese then."

When Julia got home, she was surprised to find her landlord standing at her doorstep. In a cosmic Freudian joke, her landlord shared the same name with her mother, Rosa, which rendered the pain of disappointing her more acute. It wasn't that her landlord was terrible—she'd had far worse over the years. It was that her niceness was so forced. Landlord Rosa demanded that her niceness be *noticed*. Recognized. Plus, she hated confrontation, Julia could tell, so she disguised every blow with compliments and diversions, which made their conversations excessively polite and irritating. The shit-sandwich method of conversing.

"Julia, hi! You're still roller skating to work? You're so good about exercising. I wish I had your discipline."

She started to unlace her skates to take them off, but decided she liked the idea of having them as an escape route—so kept them on. Her happiness about Clare coming over began to flag a little in the face of what was sure to be a "nice" lecture.

"You should try it," Julia said half-heartedly. She tried to picture Landlord Rosa on skates, her face a grim line, her top-heavy frame swaying like a palm tree in the wind.

"Yeaaaah." Rosa looked down at the pile of mail she was clutching.

"Is that my mail?"

"Oh, yes, it is. The box was overflowing. The mail

carrier complained." She thrust the pile of bills and junk mail in Julia's direction.

"Oh, okay, thanks." Her face was flushed with sweat from skating home and she teetered a little with the envelopes and laminated mailers. The bills were getting brighter and the fonts bigger. It was as if they were shouting at her. PAST DUE. FINAL NOTICE. THIRD WARNING. There was no way her landlord hadn't seen them. Julia felt a flush of shame rise to her neck. She desperately wanted a shower.

"Speaking of mail, your rent check is late again. That's three times, so I'm gonna have to charge you the late fee, which you know I really don't want to do."

"Yeah, okay. I get paid Friday, so I was gonna cut you a check then but since you're here, why don't I do it now?"

Julia quickly ran some calculations in her head. If her landlord read between the lines and didn't cash the check for a few days, then it wouldn't bounce. She could cover some other bills with the new credit card she'd signed up for, which would tide her over for a little while.

"That'll be great, thanks! I'll wait out here and admire your ... garden."

There was no such garden. The November rains had finally started and the weeds were happy for it. Their bright spiky leaves seemed to grow several feet overnight, chaotic and bold, as if they had something to prove. One such weed, which grew out of a crack in the driveway, turned out to not be a weed at all, but a tomato plant. Julia had never noticed it and had certainly never watered it. Then one day there it was, plump, round fruit practically bursting from its stems.

She couldn't help but be impressed by it, its tenacity and

grit. Its defiance of the odds. Its stubbornness. If the world was a "ruthless furnace," as poet Jack Gilbert had written, then this plant had jammed its gears, halted production. Once the fruit had reddened, Julia plucked its offerings and made a small salad with it. It wasn't very good, which was perhaps not surprising, given its growing environment. Still, Julia began to tend to it. She watered it and fed it nutrients. She began to see it as a small version of herself.

Grabbing her checkbook and a small plastic watering can inside, Julia cut her landlord a check and watered the tomatoes. They were looking well today, Julia noticed, full and tender. She told herself this was a good sign.

Once alone and back inside, she began to madly tidy up her studio apartment, throwing her skates and shoes in the closet, kicking her Hitachi Magic Wand under the bed, and scrambling to clean the remnants of the tofu chorizo scramble off the skillet she'd left on the stove that morning. She hadn't had a woman in her apartment—aside from Paula, who didn't count—since Britt had moved out.

Britt had been a bit OCD about cleaning—she claimed she couldn't have sex if the house was dirty or disorderly, that it interfered with the "vibe"—so Julia had kept the place spotless. It was only after Britt left her for a gazelle-like creature who ran an all-womxn farming commune in Florida that Julia began to slacken, and then outright rebel against cleaning, to spite her ex. *Let the place turn into a pig sty, what do I care!* she choke-laughed, tossing a few cheesy poofs in the air like deranged confetti. *It's still better than fucking in an actual pig sty. Good luck with that, farmer Britt!*

As the months passed and Julia's depression turned to ordinary sadness and then eventually acceptance, she also returned to a satisfactory, non-sad-human level of tidying. But with Clare coming over, Julia suddenly felt panicky.

Clare liked order, didn't she? Wasn't that kind of the whole HR shtick? Rules and such? And so, Julia *dashed*. She wiped and sprayed and scrubbed until her apartment resembled a state that would not elicit passive-aggressive comments from her gay male friends. She couldn't hide all the aromatherapy oils from the failed business, but hoped Clare would see them and simply think she was THE MOST RELAXED.

Once finished, she had just enough time to shower, run a brush through her hair, reapply mascara and lip gloss, and change out of her work clothes and into jeans and a tight red shirt with fire licking up the hem that showed just enough cleavage to be inappropriate for work. But they weren't at work now, were they? Julia could be as inappropriate as she wanted in her own home, and oh how she hoped Clare wanted to be similarly inappropriate with her.

Five minutes before Clare was due to arrive, Julia practiced seeming casual. She placed her arm on the wall, arcing her body away in a pose she saw regularly on Instagram, and nodded at no one. No, too obvious. She crossed her arms over her stomach and leaned against the door frame blankly. No, too cold! As she attempted a third pose, which involved hooking her thumbs into the belt loops of her jeans, the doorbell rang.

Clare didn't expect to be as nervous as she was when she walked up to Julia's apartment, but her hand shook as she pressed the small white button. When Julia answered immediately, Clare's hand still hung in the air, not having had the chance to return to her side.

"Hi," Julia said, her voice causing Clare's heart rate to quicken to a punk tempo.

She noticed Julia's plunging neckline immediately, the two perfect half-moons rising and falling with her breath, and bit her lip. Had Julia been exercising? Her golden skin seemed to shimmer in the soft light.

"Hi," Clare said.

Julia stepped aside to usher Clare past the doorway, apologizing for the mess.

Clare stiffened only a little at the clothes slung over the armchair, the crooked hallway rug, and the smell of burnt onions that emanated from the kitchen. "What mess?" she smiled.

Julia plucked a pair of balled-up socks from the floor of the landing and threw them into a drawer that wouldn't quite shut. "Drink?" Julia asked.

"Sure."

Julia trotted off down the hall to the kitchen and began to rummage through a cupboard. Clare took advantage of her back being turned to shove the socks deeper into the drawer so it would close correctly.

"I have sauvignon blanc and … peach Schnapps? Why?" Julia shouted from the kitchen.

"Sauv blanc is perfect," Clare laughed. She placed the enormous block of cheese on the kitchen counter, next to a stack of unopened bills with bold red fonts, mailers, and several Bed, Bath & Beyond coupons. She wondered about the bills, but decided to file it away for now. It felt intimate to be sharing so small a space with Julia and to get such a personal glimpse into her life. Erik had only invited her over a few times, and even then she never slept over, a fact which now struck her as so obvious she could have kicked herself.

As Julia poured them wine, Clare surveyed the studio apartment, taking in the boho-chic aesthetic, admiring the white lacy curtains, the photos of Julia with people she didn't know, and the mahogany bookshelf that took up an entire wall. Scattered throughout were dozens of tiny vials of aromatherapy oils. Maybe these were the reasons Julia seemed so calm. She picked up a vial that was labeled Release and took a whiff. It smelled a little like pee, which was a kind of release, but possibly not the one the oil was trying to conjure. She set the vial down and picked up a librarian action figure from the bookshelf, whose hair was in a severe bun. She wore cat-eye glasses, and her finger was poised in a perpetual *shush*.

Julia came back into the room holding two wine glasses as Clare put the action figure back in its place. "I was a library science major in college," Julia said.

"Were you?"

She drew her finger up to her face, as if Clare might not believe her without a pertinent demonstration. "Shhhhh," she said.

At this, Clare laughed. "I can totally see it." Because there was nowhere else to sit, she sat down on the bed's bright red duvet cover and, noticing the brown plastic eyeglasses on the nightstand, picked them up and put them on Julia's face. "You would've been the hottest librarian."

Julia sat down next to her on the bed, pushed the glasses down on her nose, and gave Clare a stern wink. "I would have waived all your overdue book fees."

Clare felt a familiar warmth wash over her, heat and light radiating up and down her spine. She hadn't felt this way in, well, she didn't even know how long. Her breakup with Erik, had been shortly after her father died, about a year ago. But she'd been wracked with guilt almost the entire time. Three months into their budding romance, Clare discovered that Erik was married. He was not "traveling for work," as he had told her. He was traveling to his real life. The life he did not share with her. Clare was devastated, and spent the next several months trying to break it off, only to be wooed back with lofty, empty promises, lavish gifts, and trips. Once she finally, mercifully, freed herself from his clutches, she swore that she would never ask the rules to bend for her again—that she would never be illicit, a secret, something to be hidden and tucked away out of sight.

Thinking of him, almost as if on cue, Clare absentmindedly began to trace the scar next to her lower lip.

"How'd you get that?" Julia asked.

"Pardon?"

"That scar. The one shaped like a backward 7."

"Oh." She moved her hand away and rested it in her lap. "It's stupid really."

"Tell me. I have lots of stupid stories."

Clare thought about lying, about telling the usual story she told people whom she didn't want to know—that she had fought an Ikea lamp during assembly, and lost—but faced with the quiet fact of Julia, Clare realized she didn't want to lie. Clare wanted Julia to know her, for better or worse.

She took a deep breath and began the saga of Erik. "Ever hear the expression, 'Don't let the door hit you on the way out'?"

"Of course."

Clare went quiet for a moment, gathering up her nerves before telling Julia about the ill-fated day she discovered Erik was married. It was the one of the few times he'd invited her to his house. She remembered it was raining, the thunder so loud it seemed the floor was splitting each time the storm cracked its whip at the night sky.

The thunder was also the reason they hadn't heard her open the door. It was only as his wife called to him from the stairs that Erik heard and began to panic, urging Clare out of the second-story window, amid her alarmed protests, where she then had to shimmy down a drain pipe in her socks in that pissing rain. When she had made it across the backyard without detection, the back gate wouldn't open. She pulled and pulled, silently cursing, the rain barreling down upon her, her feet wet bricks, and still the gate wouldn't budge. It was only after she placed one of her feet against the wall and used the full force of her body that the gate opened, sending its ruddy wood surface right at her face, and giving her a scar she would bear for the rest of her life.

Julia's face clenched as Clare spoke. Clare couldn't tell if it was horror or sympathy.

"The worst part is, I kept seeing him after that," Clare said, shaking her head in disgust. "Can you believe it?"

"I can," Julia said, sweeping her hand up and laying it flat on Clare's chest. "The heart is an asshole."

"You said you had news?" Julia sensed that Clare was headed somewhere far away and wanted to lure her back to the present moment. She sat straight up in the bed, hopeful, her small, mauve lips poised in anticipation.

"Yes," Clare said. "So, well, I have some ... hang-ups about dating people at work. And I don't want to jeopardize your job or mine, especially in light of your recent claim."

Julia nodded soberly. Clare continued, choosing her

words carefully. "I just ... I wanted to be sure before we ... I mean if we decided to pursue something, so I did some research into the company's divisions and hierarchies, and though I'm technically still senior to you, we don't operate in the same reporting structure!"

"That's fantastic!" Julia said, not understanding a word of any of it, but distracted nonetheless by Clare's enthusiasm and her eyes, which appeared green today. She noticed a pencil holding her dark hair in place, begging to be freed. "What does that mean? In non-HR-speak please."

"It means," Clare said, taking Julia's wine glass and setting it on the nightstand, and then removing Julia's glasses and placing them next to it, "that we can do this." Clare took Julia's face in her hands and kissed her softly. Julia relished Clare's lips, which tasted like vanilla, and welcomed the cold pads of Clare's fingers touching her neck, melting her into a heap of sighs.

Their mouths met again, harder this time, faster, and Julia's hands went to Clare's hair, removing the pencil from it, and feeling the soft, silky strands shake loose and fall to her slender shoulders. Trailing her fingers down Clare's arms, Julia noticed the fine dark hairs that came to attention under her teasing caress.

She guided Clare's arms up and over her head, then removed her blouse, admiring the lacy, teal bra she wore by outlining the straps with her fingers. Julia then kissed the supple mounds that peaked out from the bra, running her tongue down each slope and valley, before unclasping the bra, and letting it drop to the floor.

As Julia gently pushed Clare down onto the bed, nudging Clare's knees open with her own, the foot that was still touching the floor kicked something hard. The buzzing was powerful enough to be felt from the bed.

"Is that—?" Clare said.

"Fuck." Julia reached down to silence the Hitachi Magic Wand that she had accidentally switched on, and was about to shove it under the bed once more when Clare stopped her.

"Wait." She took the wand from Julia and placed it between her thighs, then beckoned Julia on top of her. Julia straddled her hips, feeling the gentle pressure of the vibrator between them. With one hand, Clare positioned the wand against their clits and turned it to the lowest setting, while the other hand massaged and pinched Julia's nipple through her tight shirt and bra. It hardened immediately and the ache of the vibration below sent her soaking right through her underwear and jeans.

Julia kissed her way along Clare's neck and jaw, down and down, until she reached Clare's breast, the pink murmur of her areola, and circled it with her tongue. Clare increased the speed of the vibrator, which sent a thousand surrenders coursing through Julia's entire body. Julia gently ran her teeth along Clare's nipple and, hearing her moan in response, increased the pressure there.

They moved their hips in unison, each matching the other's fervent rhythms until they were galloping wildly, legs straining, sweat pooling at the base of Julia's spine. She wanted suddenly to remove all the barriers between them —how had she not even undressed?—but her desire for Clare could not be stopped.

She leaned back, placing her hands on Clare's thighs as they rocked together, the vibration between them pitching to a fever, until they both came, and Julia collapsed on top of Clare, riding the last few waves of orgasm as they shocked through her.

Several moments later, as Julia lay on Clare's chest, her

mouth resting against Clare's collarbone, she whispered, "I'd love to take you on a date this Friday."

"Friday, as in tomorrow?"

"Yes."

Clare squeezed Julia tighter. "I'd love to."

She leaned forward to kiss Clare full and hard once more, her hair falling around them, and shook her head in disbelief. She couldn't believe this was really happening. It seemed like only yesterday that Clare had told her no, had run from her, and now here Clare was in her bed, legs butterflied open, eyes blanketing Julia's face with tenderness and heat.

Julia had to tell Clare about the rigged dates, she knew she did, but was now the time? When they were finally on the same page? When she could feel Clare's breath hot at her neck and her lips were so full and soft? And then, in perfect, perverse timing, Clare asked, "You said you had something to tell me?"

Julia's breath felt suddenly trapped in her throat. She didn't know a way to begin, especially a way that would make her come off not quite so badly as she knew she did.

"Well..." she started. Clare kissed her neck and her shoulder. It helped, in the sense that Julia didn't have to look Clare in the eye as she confessed everything, the crush that began months ago, the hesitation, the shock she felt when Clare told her she was going to be W;nkdIn's beta tester, and, finally, that she had been intentionally sending Clare on dates that she knew Clare would not enjoy. The kisses stopped gradually, though Clare's face still rested against Julia's shoulder as she broke this last piece of news. When Clare pulled away, Julia clung to her.

"I'm sorry, Clare."

"So let me get this straight. You had a crush on me. I

told you no. So you instead decided to sabotage my love life?"

"Well, when you put it like that—"

"Unbelievable."

"I know. It was wrong. I'm really sorry, Clare. I wanted more time to get to know you, and for you to know me."

Julia had never seen Clare look so betrayed before; it was unsettling. She looked hollowed out. Julia stretched an arm out to touch her but Clare rose from the bed and moved away from her. Julia felt herself sinking, a terrible dread rising from the depths. *I can't lose her*, she thought, scrambling to make it right. "But on the bright side, it seemed like you did enjoy some of the dates? You really Jenga'd with gusto! And ... and ... the mime class?"

Clare had to get away. Face hot with humiliation, she grabbed her clothes and purse and began to pace abruptly, looking for a way out. Her hands trembled and her legs were unsteady. She felt like she was walking on stilts instead of her own flesh and bones.

When she found a door, she made a beeline for it, only to realize too late that it was not the exit; it was the bathroom. She locked herself inside nonetheless and slid down the door until she was sitting on the floor. It smelled like fake-ocean, as if it had recently been cleaned, plus a dash of salt spray.

"Clare?" She heard Julia calling from beyond the door, her voice muffled with alarm and tenderness.

"I just need a minute!"

Her breath came out forced and labored. She tried to inhale deeply but couldn't. She felt like she might be having a panic attack and rummaged through her purse until she found the emergency number Luca had scribbled on the back of a sub club card. He didn't yet have business cards, he'd told her. "Plus," he said, "If you buy seven more subs, you'll get one free."

She dialed the number and pressed the phone to her ear. "Luca? Hi, it's Clare."

"Clare? Did I miss our appointment or..."

"No, you said to call this number if I had an emergency, and well, I have one."

"Are you okay? Do you need to call 911?"

"No, no. It's not that kind of emergency. I've locked myself in Julia's bathroom."

"And you can't get out? I've been there. Is there a window? You're probably slim enough to jimmy your way through—"

"No, I'm not trapped! I've locked myself in here *because* of Julia."

"The hot coworker?"

"Yes, wait, I never even described her appearance to you!" She was whispering now, attempting to keep whatever conversation she could muted from the rest of the house, lest Julia be on the other side of the door listening, which she probably was.

"Well, now's your chance," he said huskily. "I've got 20 minutes until this Peloton class."

"Luca! Focus!"

"Okay, okay." There was silence on the line for a few seconds, then, "So you're saying she's not hot?"

After Clare had finished rolling her eyes, she filled him in on what had just gone down with Julia. He sat quietly for a moment, then said, in a clinical way, "Sounds like you're running away again, Clare."

"I am not."

"You are, literally and emotionally. A twofer, Clare." He sounded winded as he said it, as if he was physically running to get the point across. As if she needed it to be *that* obvious, that spelled out.

"But she ... she tried to interfere with my love life!"

"So she set up some shitty dates, big whoop. Do you know how many shitty dates I've been on?"

An image flashed in Clare's mind of Luca sitting at a formal dining table with a white cloth, flashing his big white teeth at every woman who walked by, and none sitting down.

"53!" He said hoarsely. "And that's just this year."

Clare blinked, watching Julia's flamingo-patterned shower curtain dance softly in the breeze from the open window. She could easily imagine herself leaping out of that window in the next few minutes and the familiarity of the thought alarmed her.

"Also," he continued, "I mean, technically part of her job was to get you out of your comfort zone, right? Isn't that what you said?" Clare didn't want to admit he had a point, so she nodded silently, knowing he couldn't see her. "She likes you. Some might even call such a gesture *romantic*. And it's definitely way less offensive than most of the rom-com setups I've seen. Remember in *The Notebook* when Ryan Gosling threatened to publicly fling himself off a Ferris wheel if Rachel McAdams didn't go on a date with him? I mean, *that* ... that was offensive. And don't get me started on the late-aughts works of Kathryn Heigl!"

Luca's monologue was interrupted by Julia's soft knock on the door, which Clare felt against the back of her head. "I'll take myself off of your case, immediately," Julia said.

"I'll quit. Whatever you want. Just let me make it up to you!"

"She's chasing you, Clare," Luca said placidly, as if he just remembered he was supposed to be a therapist. "And you're running. It sounds like a toxic pattern you've been emulating for a while, possibly starting in early childhood. Say, were your parents alcoholics?"

"We'll discuss this at a later date," Clare whisper-screamed into the phone, and then hung up.

She opened the bathroom door to find Julia on the floor, her soft brown eyes looking up at Clare pitifully.

"Whatever you want," Julia said again. "Just tell me."

Clare's emotions ambushed her, running the full grief gamut: Denial, anger, bargaining, Taylor Swift, then back to denial again! Her shoulders sagged. Her spine slumped. She suddenly felt very tired. Emotions were exhausting. She didn't know how people did them regularly.

Still. Did Luca have a point? She did run. That was her habit. But she also knew that shitty behavior was worth running from. And Julia had betrayed her! And after she'd been so open with Julia. After they'd been ... *intimate*! Clare shuddered.

She thought of all the things she had wanted to say to Erik and hadn't been able to. She tried to conjure the feelings of rage once more, but all that came out was helplessness. Hot tears flash-flooded her face as she stepped over Julia on the floor and made her way to the door.

"I can't believe you did this to me," she said, her hand on the door knob, a chill gripping her voice. "I trusted you. I might have to talk to you eventually because of work, but don't ever think for a minute that what you did is okay."

twenty

OPERATION JULIA MAKES AMENDS

STARDATE **99434.24**

"Paula, what does *Star Trek* have to do with this?"

"Do you want her back or not?"

Julia sighed. "Okay, continue."

"As I was saying, Operation Julia Makes Amends, Phase 1. Acts of Service."

At the all-hands staff meeting, Julia enters the room with two cups of coffee. She holds one out to Clare, who has not looked up at her, but pretends to be engrossed in Yolanda's hair-care routine, which she appears to be explaining in exhaustive detail.

"...then I follow with a shine serum, and if it's particularly humid that day I..."

"Sorry to interrupt," Julia says. "But I got this for you. It has four sugars in it, just the way you like it."

At this, Clare looks up, her face a stone cliff, and says, "Thanks," before tossing it in the trash.

Stardate 99439.71 (3 days later)

Phase 2: Gift-giving

Clare arrives at her desk to find an original movie poster from *Labyrinth*, signed by David Bowie.

Julia, creeping from behind her cubicle wall, pitches with excitement as she sees Clare leave her office with the poster and walk right towards Julia. She imagines Clare thanking her profusely for the thoughtful (and expensive) gift.

Clare continues walking, however, past Julia's desk to Rodrigo's cubicle, where she finds him doing a series of prisoner squats. "Want this?" she says to him. Julia hears him squeal.

Clare does not look in Julia's direction when she makes her way back down the hall to her office.

Stardate 99458.97 (1 week later)

Phase 3: Words of Affirmation

It's after hours at W;nkdIn. Clare is on the phone, walking back and forth between her open office door. No one else is around. Julia walks cautiously down the hall toward her office and knocks softly on the door, her face a hopeful grimace. Julia holds a stack of oversized cue cards and a boombox.

Clare is puzzled. She stops pacing but does not stop talking to the person on the phone.

Julia holds up the first cue card. "Say it's carol singers."

Clare shakes her head, not understanding that Julia is attempting to recreate a touching scene from the movie *Love Actually*. Julia panics slightly, but sallies forth, turning on the boombox, which plays a riveting cover of *O Holy Night* by Justin Bieber.

The first cue card says, "Because it's Christmas ..."

Julia flips to the next card, her smile elvish with exaggerated glee: "Well, it's not exactly Christmas yet ..."

She flips to the next card: "but it's near-ish winter, and when it's near-ish winter, you tell the truth."

Clare closes the door.

Julia moves her face to the window next to the now-closed door, her eyes sparkling with pitifulness through the blinds. She holds up the next cue card, which reads: "I'm so sorry. I miss you. Forgive me."

Clare closes the blinds.

Stardate 99497.28 (2 week later)

Phase 4: The Big Guns

Clare hears a knock at her office door. She finds Paula on the other side of it. Paula deposits a three-ring binder in Clare's arms.

"What's this? The Affirmative Action planning binder?"

Paula shakes her head no. She then drops an origami envelope on top of the binder, and tells Clare to read it. Paula walks back toward her own desk.

Clare eyes the envelope warily, shuts the door, and returns to her desk. She opens the envelope to find Julia's tight, squirrelly handwriting staring back at her. It reads:

· · ·

Dear Clare,

In this binder, you'll find a series of dates tailored to your wants, preferences, and desires. There are more than 50 to choose from, and all the details have been arranged and paid for in advance. All you have to do is choose the days you want to attend. (If you want to attend at all, that is. There's no obligation for you to do so.)

If you do want to partake in any of these experiences, a plus-1 has also been accounted for, should you desire company. Whoever you choose to take is a lucky person.

On bended knee,

Julia

Clare flips through the binder. It's meticulously organized and color-coded with labels for Food, Art, Music, Cultural Events, and something called Surprise Me. Her eyes widen as she peruses the dates, marveling at how well put-together and on point they are. The most shocking is a reservation at La Fortuna, which is a restaurant her dad had wanted to take her to. After he died she couldn't bring herself to go. There's no way Julia could have known this, but it touches her all the same.

She turns the page to the Surprise Me tab, and finds maps of "beautiful, desolate places to scream into the void," a gift certificate to a cafe that sells Clare's favorite pastry (brioche donuts), which she hasn't been able to find in years, and a happy hour flyer for a plush hotel that offers free champagne to everyone in the lounge at exactly 4:32pm, called "the happy minute."

Clare notices that there are no experiences involving forced physical activity or getting-to-know-you endeavors, and smiles in spite of herself.

Paula, who is pretending to file client profiles but secretly watching Clare's reaction through the office blinds, smiles too.

twenty-one

CLARE CLOSED THE BINDER.

She felt a sinking yielding in her body, a dance both foreign and familiar beating its notes against her sternum. She hadn't felt seen like this in ages, and was both touched by Julia's gesture and confused by it. She heard her father's voice in her ear, telling her not to be "so stubborn," as he had done many times growing up.

Clare was still upset about what had happened, but maybe she'd been too hard on Julia. Maybe she deserved a second chance. Clare allowed a brief daydream to play out in her mind's theater—the two of them sharing a brioche donut, powdered sugar dusting Julia's lips, their hands intertwined under the metal cafe table.

Her smile faded when she heard a knock on the door and Nikki, her nemesis, stepped inside, a severe, almost cartoonish smirk on her face.

"You should really organize your desk once in a while," Nikki said. "Or are you secretly auditioning for a spot on *Hoarders*?"

Clare swallowed uneasily and placed the binder in the

bottom drawer of the desk. *Ha!* She thought. *Ha ha ha. Even my binder clips are organized (by size and color).* When Nikki didn't move or appear to be leaving anytime soon, Clare glanced at her aspirational calendar, which read, *The best revenge? No revenge. Move on, babe.*

"Good morning, Nikki," she said. "To what do I owe this unexpected pleasure?"

"Yolanda called a last-minute meeting. I was told to summon you."

"And you chose not to use your cauldron this time?" The best revenge was passive-aggressive comments, she decided. Nikki glared at Clare before striding to the desk and taking one of Clare's pens in her hand.

"You might want to think about having sex sometime this century," Nikki retorted. "It'd do wonders for that stick lodged in your ass."

Clare stifled a wince. She didn't want to give Nikki the satisfaction of getting a rise out of her. "Why are you like this? It doesn't have to be this way, you know."

"What way should I be, Clare? Tight-lipped and reserved like you?"

"I'm not that reserved."

Here Nikki laughed. "Please, you're so buttoned-up you literally won't undo the top button off your dress shirts. What are you afraid of? That someone will be unbearably aroused by your trachea?" She laughed again.

Technically, Nikki was right. She dressed modestly and happened to like the simple satisfaction of each button fastened. No button lonely and hanging out loosey-goosey without its hole mate. But she did not say this. Her dress habits were none of Nikki's business.

"Ten minutes," Nikki said. "Conference room C. Don't be late." She tossed the pen on Clare's desk.

Clare placed the pen back in its holder, next to the other blue .5mm pens. "What's this meeting about anyway?"

"Your guess is as good as mine, sunshine."

Julia barely had time to place the lid on her oat-milk latte before Paula had grabbed her by the elbow and steered her away from her desk toward a conference room.

"You're needed," Paula said, walking them briskly down the gray hall before Julia had time to protest or question her.

"Aw, I need you too, bae, but I also really need to pee, so gimme two minutes—"

"Not by me. You're needed in conference room C. I'm just the messenger."

"Oh! This isn't about Operation Julia Makes Amends?"

"No, I think that's going pretty well!"

"Is it about Callie ghosting you then?"

"No, but yes—later! I do need you to read this text message draft and tell me if it sounds too codependent. But first—"

Paula opened the door to the conference room and ushered Julia inside, where she was greeted by a sea of C's —the CEO, COO, CFO, and others she couldn't place, having seen their photos on the walls but never having met them in person.

Panic gripped her. This was it. She was going to be fired. For the harassment claim? For sabotaging Clare's dates? For having sex with her? She'd been so careful, and Clare said they weren't in the same reporting structure, but had they missed something? She gripped her latte hard, trying to calm the storm swirling around her stomach.

A few seconds later, Clare walked in, and Julia felt as if she might throw up. They'd both be fired! And this was all her fault! Clare had been right to blow her off. Why had she been so foolish? Why did she let her stampeding desire for Clare get in the way of her common sense? Her sister Candace was going to love telling their mother about how Julia couldn't hold down a job *again*.

But then something unexpected happened. Clare smiled at her.

"Hey," Clare said, sitting down next to her. Clare hadn't looked at her this kindly in weeks. "I got the binder. It was really sweet. Thank you." Clare squeezed Julia's hand under the table. Two quick pulses. Julia felt like she might have a seizure. "Let's talk after this, okay?"

"Okay." Julia's heart did a kind of cirque du soleil move in her ribs.

Then Clare stood up and took a seat at the far end of the table, next to a few people Julia didn't recognize. *She wants to talk! She loved the binder!* A thousand balloons sprung from her chest. And while she still did not want to get fired, who cared, *who cared?* Clare wanted to talk!

When everyone was seated, the COO, Gary Traynor, a bald man in a gray suit and cornflower blue tie, smiled cordially. "Thank you all for joining us, Rob and Jim, in particular, thank you for coming in from the corporate office."

Corporate? Did that mean lawyers? Julia blew on the too-hot latte, casting her eyes into its milky swirl, as if it could tell her the future and the future was bleak yet frothy.

The COO continued, "This is a very exciting day for us, and we hope for all of you."

Julia raised her head back up tentatively, fidgeting with the cardboard insulator on her coffee cup.

"As you know, we at W;nkdIn are dedicated to the welfare of our female employees. And we are excited to make good on that promise. Today we're announcing a new initiative at the company promoting visibility of female leadership in the field, and we want all of you involved."

Julia and Clare shared an uncertain glance. "Now," the COO said, "Before you ask the obvious question, yes, this project does mean longer hours on top of your normal workload. But we're going to make it worth your while. We want you to create and present a plan for the new initiative to the board at the annual meeting in Los Angeles."

Nikki interjected, "But that's only one month away!"

"We know it's fast, and that's why we've assembled the two teams you see in this room. You're going to work together to pull off the impossible. And the position doesn't come without benefits. Nikki and Clare—you'll be in charge of the two teams. Consider it a trial run."

"A trial run for what?" Clare asked.

Nikki cast a smug smile in Clare's direction and Julia had a sudden urge to toss her hot coffee across the table at Nikki.

"Ah yes, thank you for asking, Clare," the Chief HR Officer was speaking now, an elderly bespectacled man with two wild tufts of white hair seeming to spring straight from his ears. "I'm retiring at the end of this year, and I'd like one of you to succeed me."

"Me or Nikki will be Chief HR Officer?"

"You've got it," he said. "We want to see how each of you manage your teams and will be keeping a close eye on both of you. May the best man, er, woman win."

"Oh my god, sir, I'm so honored," Nikki said. "Of course I accept this challenge."

"Excellent." He reached across the table to shake Nikki's

hand as Clare tried and failed to suppress a pout. "As for the rest of you, Yolanda, Julia, Ben, Terese, you'll each be receiving new titles as well, along with salary increases."

Excitement coursed through Julia—a promotion! And here she thought she was about to be fired. She couldn't wait to see the look on her sister's face when she told her. And her mom. Plus, with the extra money she could finally make a dent in the debt Britt had left her with, instead of transferring the balance from credit card to credit card, like she'd been doing for months. But as the spark wiggled its way around Julia's stomach, a different fear stormed in.

"I have a question," Julia asked, a slight tremor in her voice. "Does this alter the reporting structure?"

"Yes," Gary said. "You'll be reporting to Clare now, who, I'm sure you'll agree, is the exact person you want to be under."

"I, well—" Julia stammered, as the weight of the news sunk in. Clare was her boss, effective today. There would be no date. No Clare. Not now. A pebble lodged itself in her throat, refusing to budge. But she refused to let herself cry, certainly not here, in front of all the higher ups, and definitely not in front of Nikki, whom she barely knew but already disliked intensely.

"Now, I know you have a lot of questions," Gary said, "so I'm turning this over to Rob and Jim, who'll be walking you through the roles and budget of the initiative."

Julia sat quietly through the rest of the meeting, wanting desperately to speak to Clare, but Clare wouldn't so much as look at her. Out of the corner of her eye, Julia could see that Clare's leg was shaking. Up and down, up and down the leg went, an ocean roiling and toiling beneath the surface of her skin while above, Clare's face showed nothing but placid, unflappable calm.

twenty-two

"GET OUT, NIKKI."

"I came to congratulate you," Nikki said, sitting once again in Clare's chair, after the meeting had ended. "And to scope out my new office. What do you think about a faux-alpaca-fur rug right here?"

Clare seethed. A chorus of no's reverberated through her body and she reared up like a wild horse. She had been preparing for just this moment. A propulsive force slammed through her, only startling her a little. She grabbed Nikki's briefcase and escorted it just beyond the open door, where she set it down gingerly on an end table next to some promotional brochures. Nikki followed, to Clare's surprise, to retrieve it. As Nikki bent to recover her briefcase, Clare whispered in Nikki's ear, "I hope your day is as pleasant as you are," and shut the door.

Her first order of business as CHRO would be to put Nikki in charge of the Forced Fun committee, which is what Clare called the office social events W;nkdIn put together. Maybe the best revenge was revenge after all, it turned out.

Once her anger subsided, Clare sat back down at her

desk and lay her face in her hands, feeling her features about to crumble like a cake taken out of the oven too soon. Happiness and devastation eddied about inside of her like a revolting soup. A trial run as Chief HR Officer. A C-suite position! The job she had been coveting ever since she started here two years ago, and which she thought was still years beyond her grasp, now set directly in her lap. And she couldn't even celebrate, and she most definitely could not be with Julia now. Her donut fantasy image from earlier that day vanished in a powdery poof.

Clare couldn't even bring herself to look at Julia during the meeting, for fear that she would never be able to stop, that she would dissolve into a puddle of whipped cream right there on the office floor. And how on earth were they supposed to work together now with all the *possibility* that lay between them? She imagined the long, late hours side by side, Julia's sleeves rolled to her elbows, sharing furtive glances as the tips of their fingers met over poignant Excel spreadsheets. *I'd love to expand your row,* one of them would say. *Only if I can insert a column,* the other would reply. Thinking about even the small torches of their fingers meeting across a table sent a wave of desire through Clare, who fanned herself with a stack of post-its like a corseted southern belle in need of smelling salts.

Maybe this could still work! she told herself, desperation dotting her cheeks with red. Maybe if they only—no, that wouldn't help. Or what about—no, she had just checked that yesterday. She rapped her fingers against the desk, thinking, *thinking*.

But it was hopeless. She'd heard what the COO had said. Julia would be reporting directly to Clare. There was no loophole, no workaround. She could either pursue her dream job—or the girl of her dreams. There was no in-between, no third choice, no obscure bylaw that would save them. Defeated, she reached for the bottle of Cognac hidden in her desk drawer and took a long swig. The fire it sent down her throat soothed, if only for a moment, the fire that Julia had ignited in Clare's heart.

———

A soft knock.

It was after work hours and Clare was still in her office. Julia had waited as long as she could for Clare to come talk to her, but at this rate, she'd be waiting all night. And so, she knocked. A mouse knock. A whisper-mouse knock. When Clare didn't answer, Julia opened the door, walked in, and shut it quickly behind her.

"Hi," Julia said, sitting down across from Clare, whose head lay in her arms on her desk. The lights were off, but it seemed wrong to turn them on, so Julia didn't.

"Hi," Clare said, not lifting her head. Julia noticed the bottle of amber liquid by her head and joined her, taking a swig straight from the bottle. The burn felt harsh and good. "You can't be in here."

"I know."

Julia took another swig of Cognac and wiped her mouth. She felt a little like a sheriff in a western, except it was herself who was about to be carted off to jail. Emotional jail! The valves in her heart opened and shut wildly like swinging saloon doors. "Did you still want ... to talk?"

Clare sighed as she placed her fists into her cheeks. "I loved the binder dates. They were perfect. I was going to ask you to come with me to La Fortuna tonight, but ... well."

"Does that mean you," Julia gulped, "forgive me?"

"Mostly."

Julia's heart pounded. "I'm not going to stop making it up to you."

"I'm happy for you, by the way. Associate VP of Experiences. That's big. You should be proud."

"I'm happy for you, too," Julia said.

Clare clasped her hands in front of her on the table and Julia longed more than anything to hold them. "I suppose now we shouldn't go to La Fortuna. Right?"

"No," Clare said. "We shouldn't."

Julia didn't realize until she said it out loud that she was hoping Clare would argue with her. But that was too big an ask, Julia knew.

"Don't look at me like that," Clare slurred. "I didn't want this. ... I mean, I did want this. But I also want to go to dinner with you. That magazine was wrong! You can't have it all."

"What magazine?"

"All of them!" Clare hiccoughed. "Especially that one with the souffle recipe. Beat the egg whites until dry, it said! They're liquid! They don't dry."

Julia chuckled. She had never seen Clare tipsy before and was rather enjoying it.

"What if," Julia offered tentatively, "we dated ... on the sly? No one would have to know."

"No, I can't do that again—I won't." Clare wiped her eyes and straightened her shoulders, as if attempting to posture herself back to sobriety. "And I don't want to do that to you. I don't want you to know what that feels like, to be someone's secret, to lie to people you care about. I did it with Erik. It's awful."

"Could it really be worse than this?" Julia asked. "Having you inches away from me when I can't kiss you? To

159

work alongside you almost every day, pretending that the mere sight of you doesn't unravel me? Is it really more awful than that? Maybe it'd be better if I quit."

"You can't do that," Clare sighed. Clare remembered the stack of bills she'd glimpsed in Julia's apartment, and while she didn't ask questions, it seemed obvious to Clare that Julia needed the money. She didn't know how to say this, however, so instead replied, "You said all you wanted was to be taken seriously. This is your chance. You can't quit."

———

They sat in silence for several minutes. Clare considered things. Perhaps this was a sign. The universe's way of telling her that love was not in the cards for her. Perhaps the universe was saying, *You know what? You have a great 401K. Let's leave it at that.* And she had tried, hadn't she? No one could say she hadn't tried—not even her mother, who would surely have lots to say on the matter. Not that she planned on telling Carole anything.

Because Clare's office was so full of beige, it gave the room a sad sepia tone that matched her mood. She realized that was why she chose the color—to reflect her sadness, not because she loved taupe. No one loved taupe. Except maybe camels.

She wished suddenly that she *had* become a lawyer. Maybe then she could effectively argue this. She could point a finger in the air and say, "I object!" And a jury of her peers would nod in sympathy and understanding.

But she wasn't a lawyer. She was Interim Chief HR Officer, a reality she loved, loathed, and finally, accepted. The job was as good as hers. If only she could resist Julia. Her skin was already starting to redden and swell again. Of course. The eczema. It was back. It would always be back. Nothing ever changed, not really.

"It's going to be okay," Julia said, breaking the muted, maudlin, old-timey photo that the room had become. "And by okay, I mean it's going to be terrible."

"That's maybe the first pessimistic thing I've ever heard you say."

"Yeah, well ..." she trailed off into nothing.

The room was entirely dark now, only the faint glow of the street lights shone through. Julia reached across the desk and gripped Clare's fingers and together they sat this way, in the dark, saying nothing, their lives an ellipses, a dot dot dot, a breath that would never complete, the lungs filling and filling and filling.

twenty-three

"MAYBE YOU NEED A NEW HOBBY," Paula said, pausing just long enough for Julia not to be able to interject. "Aside from the K Stew Haiku Review."

Julia sulked. "I'm not good at anything else."

They were at a Chili's in a suburban mall, sitting on the same side of a booth, sharing a deep-fried onion flower and drinking some kind of blue cocktail that tasted like a grape Jolly Rancher. Paula, who had recently dyed her hair purple because she "needed a change," aimlessly swiped left and right on a dating app as if, well, nothing had changed.

"Oh please," Paula scoffed. "You're good at everything I've seen you try. Don't act like it's such a burden to be preternaturally talented."

"That's not true. Remember when I tried making macarons? They turned out lumpy."

"Who cares? They were delicious! Lumpy, pfft."

"And the hip hop class? The only popping that occurred was when my shoulder dislocated."

Paula nudged her phone in Julia's direction, ignoring Julia's pouting. "What about her? Yay or nay?"

Julia scrolled through the woman's photos. "You hate camping."

"So?"

"She's camping in six of her photos. In the seventh, she's fishing, which you also hate."

Paula smiled and swiped right. "Like I'd take love advice from someone with blue teeth."

"*Your* teeth are blue!"

A group of raucous elderly women walked in and sat in several booths nearby. One whooped and slung her arm around like she was lassoing an invisible cowboy. Others were less mobile, leaning against canes and walkers, but no less enthusiastic. Julia noticed they were all wearing matching lavender t-shirts of a tortilla chip wearing sunglasses that read, "Nacho Bitch."

"Can we get shirts like that?" Julia asked, nudging Paula in the arm.

Paula's mouth hung open, then she started typing, "Adding to cart right ... now."

Julia slumped over in the booth. "It's just so unfair. I finally earned Clare's trust back. And then someone comes along and builds this giant wall between us. Now I don't know what to do. Do we just work together and that's it? Do I move on? I mean, don't get me wrong, I'm happy I got promoted. It's sure as hell gonna help with all my debt. But what if Clare's my person, and we're losing out on something momentous because of a dumb technicality?"

Paula's eyebrows fluttered. Julia could tell she was trying hard not to roll her eyes. "Hey, at least you got a glimpse of her. At least she likes you back. At least your desire is reciprocated. I can barely get a woman to return my texts or say yes to a second date. And while you're drowning in your pity party, some of us are still stuck in our dead-end jobs here with no hope for advancement."

Julia's shoulders tensed. She felt guilty for wallowing but also irritated by her friend for consistently trying to date people who were so emphatically wrong for her. "You're right. I'm sorry. I know I'm not the first person to be twat-blocked by capitalism."

Julia tapped Paula's arm. She wanted her full attention. "But also, stop wasting your time on people who don't make time for you. Stop pining for the people who ghost you. Stop swiping right on people who have nothing in common with you. Say no to the unavailable women—I don't care how hot they are." Julia knew she was lecturing but she couldn't help herself. She'd witnessed Paula spiral downward for the last year and wanted so badly to shake her out of it. "If you want things to change, you have to actually change. And I'm not talking about your hair. Demand more. You're worth it. Once you believe it, others will too."

"Damn," Paula said. "There's an order muppet in you, after all."

Paula put her phone down and looked at Julia. "Okay, but also. Since we're truth-bombing: Don't let your whole life revolve around Clare. She's great, but so are you. You deserve someone who'll tear down any walls standing between you."

In the next booth, the elder ladies began pounding on the table, chanting, "Chug chug chug chug," and then bursting into applause. Someone named Ethel was slapped on the back in congratulations. Julia saw herself in 40 years, slapping Paula on the back. It made her smile.

Julia looked at Paula again, at the ordinariness of their lives. The sexagenarians were nobody's bitch, yet clearly

Julia and Paula were. They were stuck in their habits, their individual hamster wheels. The world revolved around them while they stayed in still-motion. Going nowhere. Julia felt this acutely, like a question nobody had to ask. And then she blinked and the feeling was gone. She dipped a piece of fried onion in ranch dressing and felt sorry for herself once more.

"Plus, let's be real," Paula said, apropos of nothing. "Could you really be with someone who's never seen a Kristen Stewart movie?"

twenty-four

"THE ANCIENT JAPANESE art of kintsugi is part of a long and storied tradition of beautifying imperfections," said a white man in his fifties with graying temples and a full, unkempt beard. His name was Dave. He was broomstick-shaped and wore a black shirt with the name of a band Clare didn't remotely recognize. Vicarious Death Machine. It took Clare a while to figure out the words, as the font was reminiscent of blood splatters.

Dave and the vicarious death machine were slowly walking between two rows of long white tables, where a handful of students sat with broken bowls in front of them. She couldn't quite believe she'd taken advice from her mother's "lover" Simon. But the macrame hobby clearly wasn't going anywhere good and Clare needed something to distract herself from thoughts of Julia—anything.

Outside the small classroom, which smelled of spilled milk and bleach, the rain came down in sheets, the sky grim and monotone, which matched Clare's mood a little too precisely.

"My roots to Japan go far and deep," Dave said. He told

the class that he was a self-taught kintsugi artisan. "I minored in bonsai pruning and tea ceremony at the University of Phoenix online. I was also a dishwasher at Benihana for a number of years."

Clare doubted very much that these things made a person qualified to say they had "Japanese roots," but she had already given Dave her money and broken one of her bowls for the purpose of repairing it, so she decided to just let it go. She glanced around at the other well-meaning white people in attendance, all of whom watched Dave with rapt attention. Most were middle-aged or older, with a distinct mommy blogger vibe. Clare looked down at her own clothing, the chunky beige cable-knit sweater and capri pants, and realized she fit in a little too perfectly. The thought depressed her, but she couldn't articulate why.

"Kintsugi translates to *golden joinery* and this is what you'll be doing throughout this class. We'll be taking broken dishes and repairing them with beautiful gold seams, returning them, and some say, returning *ourselves*, to a state of wholeness."

Dave continued to monologue. "When we not only embrace but glorify our flaws, we give the pieces a new identity, a new lease on life. We say to the Universe, 'I may be anxious, have child-sized hands, and call my mother every day, even on my honeymoon, but I am still worthy of love, Sharon!' Now, ready your epoxy."

Clare examined the pieces of her white bowl from Target. It was made to hold fruit, but since Clare rarely bought any, she figured it was ripe for the chopping block.

She got to work, examining the broken pieces, the brushes, the epoxy, and trying to figure out a plan to put them back together. No matter how much she dusted and glued and corrected, however, the bowl remained hideous to her. Sweat trickled down her spine. Rather than take on a new, resurrected life, her bowl had instead become a zombie. While she worked, she looked over at the other women in the class. They seemed placid, content, as if this was a meditative experience for them. A few chatted jovially with one another. None appeared to be struggling like she was, not even the woman to Clare's immediate left, who was clearly not following the directions at all. Her bowl was no longer a bowl, but some kind of glitzy, broken tower of Babylon, teetering. Or perhaps it was supposed to be a plate of nachos, the gold glue serving as cheese. The woman noticed Clare staring and gave her a Gollum grin. Clare looked away.

"Nice work, Amanda. Very creative," Dave said.

As Clare puzzled over the woman's creation, Dave floated by and picked up Clare's bowl, displaying it before the class. "Now this is a perfect example of what *not* to do."

Really? Clare thought. *Golden Nachos over there is fine, but mine is wrong?* She said nothing however, and listened to Dave mutely.

"You're trying to attain perfection, which is not the aim. Do you see how the cracks here almost look as if they're trying to be covered up and diminished? This is the opposite goal of kintsugi."

He looked Clare in the eye as he dropped the bowl on the floor, where it broke into even more pieces. Clare wished at that moment that there was some private place she could retreat to and cry. Just for five minutes. A power cry. Not a full-on sob session, but a brief rejoinder. She refused to give Dave the satisfaction of knowing she was so easily broken. How she *was* the Target bowl. Dave moved on, picking up other students' bowls and either praising or condemning them.

Clare bent down, crawling under the table to sweep the pieces of her bowl up. One jagged piece pricked her finger, a bright red spot of blood forming. She dabbed at it with a piece of tissue she had in her purse.

"In life, we hide our brokenness," Dave said, continuing his slow stroll around the room. "Because we don't want to seem weak or incompetent or admit that we don't know how to program the smart TV. We don't, okay, Sharon? Get your know-it-all nephew to do it if he's so smart!"

Clare sighed deeply, surveying her pieces of broken bowl and daunted by the task of starting over. They only had a few minutes left before class ended and she had nothing to show for it. Unless you counted the literal blood, sweat, and soon-to-be tears. Perhaps she should count it. It wasn't nothing.

"But kintsugi teaches us to *honor* these broken bits, as they are testaments to our *surviving* in the face of the poo-poo pile that is life. You know what else rises from the shit? Flowers! And hallucinogenic mushrooms. " He picked up another student's bowl and held it over his head triumphantly. "These cracks, you see them? That's you growing and healing. Own them! Say yes—to crack."

Clare considered her life. How had it gone so far off track? The whole weekend stretched out before her depressingly. It was too early for the pie-sized chocolate chip cookie in her fridge that she didn't finish the night before. It was too early for anything. She glanced at her phone and saw a text from her mother. **Darling. Have you made a plan for scattering the ashes yet?—Mom** [plus the emojis: fried shrimp, gray square, and prayer hands].

She ignored it. She didn't need any more pressure right now, certainly not from her mother. It wasn't Clare's fault her mother didn't know how to grieve properly, that she had moved on so seamlessly from her father to another man. The more she thought about it, the more she wished she had another bowl to break.

When the class finished, the students shuffled out of their seats, smiling with their bowls or bits of bowl, and headed down the long dark hallway to their Priuses and their beautifully flawed lives. Clare was the last to leave on purpose and, glancing swiftly each way to make sure she was alone, dropped the pieces of her bowl into the trash, and walked on.

twenty-five

"LET'S cut to the chase, Clare. Let's get down to brass tacks. Let's stop beating around the bush and start tweeting around the tush."

"What?" Clare asked. Luca was making even less sense than usual.

"Let's stop wasting time with trivialities and get to the meat of things."

"Okay." Clare held her breath. Luca's gaze was fleeting and apocryphal. She wondered if he might start reciting Proust or burst into song.

"Who's your favorite Spice Girl?"

Clare unheld her breath. "Ginger Spice."

"Really?" Luca said. "I thought it would be Posh."

"Everyone thinks that," Clare smiled in a self-satisfied way, as if she'd gamed the system somehow. As if she'd won some kind of cultural lottery.

"What do you think of the question as a first message on dating apps? Too dated?"

"Are you trying to date women your age?" Clare asked, realizing that she had no idea how old Luca actually was.

He could have been 22 or 42, or existed on an age-plane that defied numbers.

"My range is set from 21 to 99."

"Really?"

"Age is just a number, Clare. But do you think it's good? As an opener?"

"It's definitely better than the usual heys, hi's, and what's ups."

"I'm sayin'." Luca picked up his phone and started pressing buttons, as if he had lined up five such Spice Girls messages and was merely waiting for Clare to give the okay before sending. Then, he smiled and put the phone away.

Clare glanced at the corner of the room, where the upturned womb chair jutted out awkwardly. It was buried in even more manila file folders now, plus a Costco-sized box of Skittles, and a small velour box tied with a purple ribbon.

"Can I ask you something unrelated to girl bands from the '90s?"

He shrugged, "It's a Spice World. I just live in it."

Clare took this as a yes. She realized she'd be breaking the therapy script with her next question, but well, her sessions with Luca were anything but conventional. "What happened, with your parents?" She gestured to the womb chair. "Why did they say those horrible things to you?"

"Oh. That. Well—" He fidgeted, then rose from his chair and began pacing. "They're cafeteria Catholics but also middle-class white liberals. So, you know, constantly at war with themselves and their ideals." He paused, poking one of the legs of the womb chair with his pen. "They were fine when I came out as queer in high school, but when I started transitioning and taking testosterone, they really lost it. Refused to call me Luca or use my preferred pronouns. My dad told me I was a blight on mankind and many other terrible things that don't bear repeating in the presence of a lady—"

Clare blushed a little at being called a lady. It seemed too gallant a word to describe her. She looked at Luca, at his adult acne and valiant attempt at a beard, and certain things began to crystallize in her mind and snap into place. His unabashed love of rom-coms. His preternatural ability to suss out Clare's feelings. A tenderness washed over her.

"—I haven't spoken to them since. The chair was their first attempt at contact in four years. If you can call that contact, anyway. And I don't know what to do with it. Hence—" He prodded the chair once more, as if making sure it was still not alive. "We're in a stalemate, presently."

"A stalemate?"

"They got me the chair. So I got them his-and-hers weighted slankets. Then they bought me an enormous box of Skittles. Then *I* bought them a cigar wrapped in blue that said 'Congrats! It's a boy!' Then *they* countered with something entirely unexpected."

Clare sat breathlessly. Her mother was skilled at subterfuge and subtle manipulation but it was nothing like this silent game of gift-chicken. She was riveted. And depressed. And riveted some more! Who were these people? Who had wounded them so?

Luca walked over to the chair and picked up the velour box with the purple ribbon. He opened it the way one might a tiny coffin that had once held a very tiny someone dear. "My grandfather's cufflinks." He held them out to Clare to admire, and admire them she did. They were beautiful, ornate, but not showy, with gold toggles and posts, and a dull, onyx front face relief of what looked to Clare like the winged horse from Greek mythology. Pegasus? She couldn't bring herself to interrupt. "I always coveted these cufflinks, and was never allowed to wear them as a kid. When my grandfather died he left them to me, but at that point my parents and I weren't speaking, so I never saw them. And this is—" His face appeared pinched and pained, as if holding back a tremendous amount of fury or a side cramp. "—a kind of apology, for them."

The worlds lolled around on his tongue, as if he'd just encountered a Skittles flavor he wasn't sure he enjoyed. Then he grinned, a flash of teeth like lightning, that disappeared as quickly as it struck.

Clare settled back onto the couch. She relaxed her shoulders, which had rolled up toward her neck. She hadn't realized she'd been tensed and leaning forward as Luca spoke. "What will you do now? Will you reach out?"

"You don't understand—talking to my parents, it's like dismantling a piano ... while it's on fire ... and surrounded by crocodiles ... and the crocodiles have swords!"

"Okay okay, I get it."

"Do you?"

"Actually no, I'm distracted by the image of crocodiles with swords. How do they hold them?"

"Look, the point is ... talking to them ... it's a logistical and emotional and physical undertaking. It requires all of my faculties. And I'm not sure I'm ... ready."

Clare shook her head sadly. She was all too familiar with the unwinnable war of parental disappointment.

"Let's just say you're not the only one who's avoiding their problems," he said, closing the cuff links box and setting it delicately on top of the upended womb chair, manila folders, and candy. Then he sat back down abruptly across from Clare. "Speaking of" he said, "let's talk about your mom. You've been avoiding it."

Clare feigned surprise. "*Oh*. Okay. What's there to talk about?"

"How about that you're jealous of your mother's sex life?"

Clare's face twitched and contorted into something resembling lumpy gravy. She had been one of those lucky kids who never walked in on her parents having sex, and she'd certainly never visualized her mother and Simon in bed together, as she'd assumed, with an ageist or daughterly plea, that a woman in her sixties would be done with "all that." But now that Luca had uttered it, irrefutably, there the image was. And it would not dislodge itself.

She shook her head violently, as if taking a magnet to a cassette tape in hopes of erasing it. She was even more abhorred to realize that she *was* jealous, good gods, and not only that, she was enraged on her father's behalf. How dare her mother move on, leaving Clare to hold the torch! It was as if she needed her mother to keep pining for Yuri, as if to not do so was to dishonor his memory somehow, even though, as her mother was want to point out, this was something she and he had discussed before his passing, and he was not only fine with the idea of Carole dating once he was gone—but he had even jokingly written an online dating profile for her in the last months of his life. Clare was too distraught to read it, especially because she knew her father had a foul mouth and was not above sending his mother dirty limericks that rhymed with words like *runt*. So what was Clare so upset about? Why did her mother seem to move on so quickly while Clare limped along, inert and estranged from happiness?

She gulped. "It's not the ... sex—" she could barely bring herself to say the word without activating her gag reflex.

"Oh no, it's more than that," Luca said. "You only get

one life, Clare. Your mother devoted most of hers to being with your father and raising you. Now that he's gone and you're grown, she's taking charge of her life. She's looking after herself for a change and having the time of her life! You seem threatened by this. Either that, or maybe it's easier for you to judge your mom than to face yourself in the mirror."

Clare's heart swelled up into her throat.

When had Luca become such a know-it-all? Weren't therapists supposed to ask you gentle, leading questions until you figured out your damage on your own? Luca's method seemed to be the opposite of that—to bludgeon Clare with her damage until she was no longer conscious, and then to wave some smelling salts under her nose to revive her. Not to help her up, no. But as a courtesy to others walking by who might step on her.

"I am not ... threatened." Clare felt her eczema flaring on her thighs. She scratched through the fabric of her pants, which only seemed to make the itchiness worse. Her fingernails turned white. "All my life she's told me no. Don't do that. Don't *be* that. And then one day she wakes up and decides she's going to do all the things she claimed to despise! It's deceitful. It's wrong. And I mean, come on, a woman her age! Galavanting around the world with a man she just met! It's *obscene*. It's improper. It's not ... ladylike. Oh god."

It was then that Clare remembered how her mother had hurled such words at her. How such words had been weaponized, meant to stop Clare from doing anything too unusual or off-the-cuff or *queer*. And how Clare had listened! All her life. She laid low. She stayed the course. She followed the rules. And where had it gotten her? Here Clare was, repeating her mother's admonishments like the burning garbage that they were. Clare was judging her mother for doing the very things Clare wished she could do. Wished she *had* done.

Not only had Carole forsaken Clare's father, she left the actual country, and Clare, in her mourning. To figure it all out on her own. While Carole traveled with her "lover" and saw the world, Clare had been left holding the bag. Or box, rather.

Luca's phone chimed in his pocket. He looked to Clare as if to say, *I understand you're having a dark epiphany right now, but can I just check this one thing? I think it might be Chrystal, the tai chi practitioner with the amazing rack!* And Clare looked back at him, as if to say, *You might as well. It's not like my life is going to magically get better in the next few seconds. One of us should have a shot at happiness and why not you.*

He subtly glanced at his phone, and unable to contain his excitement, said, "Chrystal wrote back! Scary Spice! She's such a Scary."

twenty-six

A FEW WEEKS went by without incident.

Fall had turned to winter, which, in the Bay Area, did not make a noticeable difference. The fog rolled in off the Oakland hills in the dewy mornings, and then rolled right back out in the evenings.

There was something comforting to Clare about this, the consistency of the fog soothed her, like reliable commuter trains or friends who didn't need to ask first before stopping by. In and out. Down and back. Their ghostly gloom a thick wool pulled over the eyes, especially useful when one did not want to gaze too keenly at the scope of one's days. As Clare did not.

Clare and Julia worked together with their new team at W;nkdIn, brainstorming and building a plan on female leadership that they could bring to the board. Because time was not on their side—this worked in Clare's favor, as she barely had a moment to blink or breathe, let alone fantasize about the relationship that could have been or about anything else.

The distraction was especially welcome after Clare's realization that she had accidentally become her mother. She often threw herself into her work whenever she found her emotional life too taxing. Had she not done this very thing when Erik chose his wife over her? And had she not worked her ass off then? And was she not now the Interim Chief HR Officer? She was! Sure, she was just as alone, but her avoidance had paid off then, so why couldn't it work again? Thankfully, she found the demands of her new role especially challenging. She wasn't used to being responsible for so many people, and welcomed the relief of having something to fixate on other than Julia and her family baggage.

No, Clare would be good. She would be aloof and leaderly. She would not succumb to her baser wants or instincts and she would also not allow Julia to slip up either. They both needed this to work out. It was the responsible course to take.

So, when Julia walked into the breakroom as Clare was pouring herself a cup of coffee, Clare froze, mug in both hands. It burned her skin but she couldn't put it down. She couldn't move. Julia paused when she saw Clare, then scurried quickly to the fridge where she stuck her head in for what seemed to Clare like an unusually long time.

"Can you hand me the creamer?" Clare said, still unable to move from her perch but was grateful that at least her voice worked.

"No." Julia's voice echoed, her head still firmly in the fridge.

"No?"

"No."

"Okay."

Julia shut the refrigerator door and walked out with nothing. Clare sighed, the tension lifting from her shoulders. She hadn't realized she'd been holding her breath.

In another instance, Clare had walked into the bathroom and saw Julia waiting in line for the one stall. She thought about turning around and leaving, but was overcome by the urge to stand next to Julia silently, to perhaps feel the brush of her shoulder against hers, for a moment. Clare leaned back against the wall, her heart thudding against her ribs. Julia kept her eyes forward, toward the mirror that reflected their bodies back to each other.

The antiseptic smell of the bathroom was sharp in Clare's nose. She was hunting for Julia's scent but the cleaning products overwhelmed everything else. Glancing back to the mirror, Clare allowed herself to sneak glimpses at Julia. The pleated purple pants she wore were billowy and hung from her hip bones. Clare thought about how easy it would be to tug them down, how satisfying it would be, then chased the thought from her mind. It was followed by a more tender one: Had Julia been eating? She looked wan, her eyes blank and glassy.

A flushing sound and then a faucet running interrupted the silence that stretched before Clare, and before she knew it the person had gone and it was just the two of them standing there. Clare's ears rang with tension; she felt uncomfortable in her clothes and in her skin and in the room and the entire world.

As Julia pushed herself away from the wall and toward the now empty bathroom stall, Clare gently maneuvered her body into Julia's way, allowing their shoulders and elbows to brush briefly and filling Clare with more exhilaration than she'd felt in weeks.

"Clare."

Hearing her name on Julia's lips made her heady and her throat lumpy. She swallowed loudly. Then she realized Julia's voice had been stern, almost a reprimand.

"Hm?"

"No."

"No?"

"No."

Unlike Clare, Julia was good at saying no. Too good. Perhaps this would be the only conversation they would ever have again. Rooms filled with agonizing tension and the swift deflating of it.

Clare looked into Julia's eyes, expectant, waiting. Something twitched in Julia's jaw, the muscle pulsing and tensed. Clare reached for it unthinkingly, but Julia backed away. So much for Clare's willpower.

"Rules. We need rules." Julia's shoulders slumped. She pulled the waist of her pants up higher, but they fell right back to her hips, the sharp creases hanging on for dear life.

"Okay. Like?"

"Like, we can't be alone together."

"Right, yes, of course."

"And no 'accidental' touching." Clare's face burned, but not with shame or embarrassment exactly, more with the thrill of being caught. "And no 'on purpose' touching either." Here Julia looked away, her own face bright with crimson. She was blushing. Clare had made her blush. She reveled in this, and her hand itched to touch her again. She resisted the impulse, instead making two tight fists with her hands. They hung by her sides.

But even as her hands and arms obeyed, Clare felt herself drawing nearer to Julia, leaning ever so slightly in the direction of her lips. She didn't realize she was doing it and the movement was so slow and so pronounced it was almost comical; it felt to her as if her lips were operating under a spell or potent curse.

Blood pulsed in Clare's hands, tingling and strange, when she looked into Julia's face and saw that she was moving, too. Her twitching jaw tilted, leaning toward Clare's, her eyelids heavy and closing as she did so. Sweat slick on her lower back, heart pumping full of adrenaline, Clare closed her eyes as well. If they didn't see it coming it wouldn't count, right? The heat in the small room reached Clare's consciousness, along with the antiseptic smell again, which had only grown stronger. Clare felt faint with want, her eyes shut tight against it. Any second their lips would meet. Any second—

The door whooshed open, waking Clare from her trance. Her eyes widened just in time to see Julia enter the stall and close the door with a clang behind her.

"Hey," Yolanda sang. "What's shaking?"

"Nothing!" Clare shouted

"Nothing!" Julia shouted from behind the stall's door.

Yolanda looked at Clare quizzically but only for an instant, then her face returned to its usual chipper demeanor. "That you, Julia? You need anything? Toilet paper? Magazine?" Yolanda winked at Clare.

"No! Be out in sec."

Clare's fists remained at her sides throughout this exchange, as if she was being restrained. She smiled tightly at Yolanda and forced a small laugh. It took several minutes before her heart started to slow to a normal rate. But it appeared Yolanda hadn't seen anything, and if she had, she didn't let on.

After this incident, however, Clare decided not to take

any more chances. She would use the cafe's restroom next door to W;nkdIn, just to be extra precautious. It wasn't that she didn't trust herself or Julia. She just wanted to be on the safe side. She'd worked too hard and too long for this promotion to let it slip away.

twenty-seven

JULIA HAD BEEN HAVING DREAMS. About Clare. Dreams that caused Julia to wake with a start in a sweat, itchy, enthralled, a warm glow pulsating in her center. She could only remember bits and fragments of them, these dreams. What was more clear was how she *felt* when she woke up, which was almost worse. She rolled over and reached for her Hitachi, trying to soothe the ache of absence that filled her on these mornings.

It was the run-in with Clare in line at the bathroom that had done it. Agitated Julia, filled her blood with madness and longing. She'd have to be more careful. She'd have to ensure that she didn't end up too near Clare or be alone with her. It sounded easy enough. But then, it always did, until you failed.

The money was helping a little. With the salary increase she'd been able to pay down one credit card and pay off another one entirely. She even paid her rent on time for once. If she kept this up, within a year she might be mostly debt free. It was an enticing premise. To be free. Free from the shackles that bound her, kept her up worrying at night, cauterized her joys when she made frivolous purchases, like a sweater that was decorated with dozens of pink nipples. She shouldn't have bought it, she knew. But it was so perfect! She couldn't help it. Plus, she was celebrating paying off the one credit card. And she needed it, this tiny victory. Anything to help distract her from the tidal force that was Clare, working with her, sitting next to her in meetings, avoiding her in common spaces. She never knew it could be so exhausting to resist a person. But then, when did she ever have to?

She thought about wearing the nipple sweater to work that morning, but decided it would be a stretch, a little too risque even for a casual-attired startup. So she chose instead a bright orange sweater, purple tights, and a long brown, faux fur-lined trench coat. She still wanted to look good for Clare, for Clare to notice her, to *know* that Clare noticed her, even when Clare kept her face rigid and unreadable.

Julia was starting to learn Clare's little quirks and ticks. She was becoming better at reading her. For instance, when Clare was stressed, her temple pulsed. When she was flustered, she hid her hands from view—probably to avoid people seeing them shake. It was a tell-tale sign that Julia began to look for. While she didn't want Clare to be flustered, she did want Clare to be flustered, at least as much as Julia was. Fair's fair, right?

By the end of the work day, Julia's energy was waning. The days were shorter now, which meant she was leaving the office in utter blackness, something that always depressed her. Where had the day gone?

She congratulated herself, at least, for making it through another day resisting the woman she wanted, and then felt sad for it. What a terrible goal! She reminded herself that she wanted Clare to succeed, to get the promotion she wanted. Julia inhaled deeply, to strengthen her resolve. She was headed for the doors to leave when Paula grabbed her by the coat sleeve.

"Psst, come here."

"Are you whispering? Why are you whispering?" Paula leaned halfway out of the door to a small conference room. The lights inside the room were off.

"Come here," Paula beckoned again.

Confused but resigned, Julia followed her friend into the dark conference room, wondering what kind of crisis she was going to be helping Paula with and why it had to be pitch black to do so.

But the room was not empty. Ten to 15 W;nkdIn staffers sat and crouched and huddled in the small space, whispering among themselves. Julia could hardly see who they were and hoped (and did not hope) that Clare was among them.

"It's Ben's birthday," Paula said. "We've all been working so much that we almost missed it. But we figured a small surprise party was in order. There's cake!" She pointed her thumb at a desk, which ostensibly had a cake on it, though Julia could only see shadowy blobs. "Shit, I see him at the end of the corridor! Get ready, everyone!"

Paula closed the conference room door as Julia pushed her way further into the darkness. Feeling her way around the edge of the table, she maneuvered among the bodies, trying not to bump into or disturb anyone.

"Excuse you," said a woman, probably Nikki, whose shoulder Julia had touched as she passed.

"Sorry."

In the dim light, Julia found an open space and wedged herself into it, crouching down so that she'd be mostly out of view when Ben opened the door. Her hand rested on the table's cool, round edge, the other was on the industrial carpet.

She smelled Clare before she saw her. That clean, honeyed scent, something sweet, milky, and soothing, like a lavender tea macaron. Julia turned to the left, where she could just make out the long outline of Clare's neck. As her eyes adjusted to the dark, Clare's other features began to sharpen into focus—that dark hair and pale skin, the long bow of her, the graceful lines of her. She was so close that Julia sucked in her breath and momentarily lost her balance.

Clare's hand reached out to steady Julia as she shuffled back into a crouch, her hand further out on the carpet to steady her. Their shoulders touched and her heart beat its tiny wings against her ribs. The outside of her pinky was now touching Clare's, which flooded her synapses, sending a rushing whir to her ears and back down.

What was taking Ben so long?

Julia didn't move away from the soft sigh of Clare's pinky touching hers. Each agonizing second that passed sent a jolt to Julia's center. Her lips parted. Her fingers began to crawl over Clare's until her entire hand rested on top. Clare's hand was clammy and cold, which felt nice against the furnace of her own. She leaned closer, her brain at war with her body. When had her body become such a traitor?

The wings of her heart beat faster. Her stomach tightened. She could see more of Clare now, those changeful green eyes were looking right at her. They searched Julia's face, hunger and immensity and desperation burning in her eyes, until she closed them, tilted her chin toward Julia's. Their mouths a whisper away, Julia closed her eyes, too. She had no defenses left. Clare was a black hole, her vast gravity pulling every bit of Julia's matter into her, consuming her.

And just as Julia felt Clare's breath hot on her lips, the lights flipped on.

"Surprise!" the group yelled, each popping up from their crouched position on the floor. Julia was one of the last people to rise. Her hands tingled and tremored as Clare offered her hand, then dragged Julia up with her.

The room was full—far fuller than Julia had expected—and Julia looked out into the sea of familiar faces, her heart galloping as Ben walked in. He clutched his chest, a grateful smile spreading across his face. "You guys! You shouldn't have."

The group began to sing happy birthday to Ben as the outside edges of Julia's and Clare's hands touched by their sides. To remove them would be painful. To not remove them would be painful.

The group's tinny, off-key voices rang in Julia's ears until the obligatory applause forced their hands apart. Julia pressed her hands together forcefully, hoping the sound might stifle the blood that bloomed in her ears at being so close, *so close* to Clare's lips again.

twenty-eight

THEN, late on a Sunday evening, the inevitable happened.

It was a day before the conference. After the team had worked through two rounds of drafts and several helpings of Thai food, Clare and Julia found themselves alone for the first time since the bathroom incident. Even the meandering, disruptive Nikki had gone home, but not first before complaining that Clare was setting an unhealthy work-life example for her team.

Sifting through the remnants of a plastic container of pad see ew, Clare plopped herself down on the modular gray couch. Julia joined her, grabbing her Pad Thai and sitting as far away from Clare on the couch as she could.

The moments seemed to slow and grow heavier. An invisible force seemed to draw them together. Clare searched Julia's face, her eyes following a route that ended at Julia's mouth. Clare was tired of resisting. She kissed her then, pushing Julia down onto the couch and reaching, unthinkingly, for Julia's shirt, to pull it over her head. Julia moaned in response, taking Clare's lower lip in hers, but also placing her hands over Clare's, to stop Clare from removing her shirt.

"We can't. You said—" Julia groaned.

"Forget what I said. I want you. I need you—"

Clare reached once more for Julia's shirt, placed her fingers on the side where her bra strap had fallen and—

"Clare! Are you still in there?"

Clare awoke with a start, hair matted with sweat. She had only meant to rest her eyes, not fall into a full-on lucid dream fantasy.

"Yes?" she called out, not recognizing the voice beyond her office door. She straightened herself, sat upright, and wiped at her mouth with the back of her hand.

"Go home!" Yolanda poked her head inside Clare's office. "The flight's at 9am tomorrow and we want you in ship shape to present at the conference."

"I was just finishing up some things." She looked around the desk, patting the air, as if the 'things' in question were invisible, unruly dust mites needing herding. She found a solitary post-it that had fallen from its place and stuck it back to the board, pleased with herself.

"Okay, but don't stay too late! You keep startling the janitor."

"Well, if he'd turn down that Skrillex I wouldn't have to yell to get his attention." Yolanda ignored her, but in her usual attentive, affirming way. As she was about to shut the door, Clare called out to her.

"Wait! How was your weekend? Did you and Brian do anything fun?"

Yolanda raked her acrylic nails against the door frame,

thinking. "It was good! We went for a long hike. He wore me out! But it was worth it."

Damn, Clare thought again. She'd never learn if Brian was a human or mutt at this rate. She resigned herself to not knowing. "That sounds wonderful."

"The door code's set," Yolanda chirped. "Be out in 30 or the cops will come! See you tomorrow, Clare Bear. Bright and early!"

Once Yolanda had left, Clare began gathering her things. She was still flustered from her earlier dream-fantasy, her fingers tingling with sensation and when she locked her office door behind her, she noticed too late that her briefcase was still inside, which housed all the information, handouts, and notes she needed for tomorrow's presentation.

"Shit!" she said loudly, knowing no one was around to hear her. She searched for the keys, but they too were in her briefcase, locked inside. "Shit. Shit. Shit."

Panic slid through her. Yolanda was gone. Even the janitor had left. Clare didn't realize how late it had gotten. She pressed her clammy hands to her forehead and closed her eyes, trying to think.

When she opened them, Julia was walking toward her and she thought briefly that she was hallucinating. But then Julia smiled with her perfect slightly gap-toothed smile and Clare realized she was searingly awake.

"I thought I heard someone cursing."

"Julia, oh my god. What are you doing here?"

She held up her Walkman and large padded headphones. "Forgot this. I need it to drown out all the crying children on the plane tomorrow. What are you still doing here?"

Bright patches of red colored her cheeks as Clare said, "I locked myself out."

"Ah, no problem."

Julia took a step closer to Clare, who in turn stepped back more forcefully than she meant to, and found her back against the door. "Rules!"

Julia laughed, reaching into her back pocket and pulling out a small hook and rake. "No funny business, I promise. I'm only going to pop your lock."

The suggestiveness of this comment did not escape Clare, but what could she do? She needed Julia's help. "You'll need to hurry. Yolanda set the alarm."

As Julia shimmied the tools into the lock and rocked them back and forth, Clare's pulse rose. She felt giddy and nervous, as if they were doing something illegal.

Within a minute, Julia had picked the lock. It was the hottest thing Clare had ever witnessed and she needed a minute to take it in. Julia held the door open for Clare, that smile melting her and melting her and melting her.

"Oh my god, thank you!" Clare retrieved her briefcase and keys. "I would have been so screwed."

"Just doing my job," Julia said, repeating the words Clare had said to her after she'd taken care of Julia's harassment claim.

Elation pummeled Clare in the ribs and she briefly forgot herself as she leaned forward to kiss Julia on the cheek at the same moment Julia turned to say something. Their lips met, two sets of struck matches igniting quietly in the empty office. Only this time, Clare didn't fight it. She let herself tumble down the hill of Julia's soft lips, her fingers dancing on the edge of Julia's nape and in her hair. She let the quiet fire brighten and burn through her until she felt her flesh and bones turning into the most exquisite rubble.

They might have kept on this way, tangled in the soft fury of their roaming hands and mouths, had it not been for the security alarm beeping its 5-minute warning, alerting them to exit the building immediately.

Clare broke away reluctantly, a dreamy wildness blanketing her features. "Okay, I'll, um, I'll see you tomorrow then."

"Tomorrow, yes," Julia said, gathering her tools and bag, disappointment registering on her face as large as a billboard. "Tomorrow."

twenty-nine

EVEN THOUGH IT was technically winter, Los Angeles was balmy with summer, cloudless skies from here to the Pacific. But Julia barely felt the warmth inside the air-conditioned hotel that was hosting the conference and board meeting. Her fingers were purple with cold and she blew into them as she paced. Her team was slated to present their initiative on female leadership in less than an hour and she was the opening speaker.

Nerves made Julia the early bird for once, and she was already outside the conference room. She had never been keen on public speaking and was so nervous that she hadn't been able to eat or drink anything, her stomach a tilt-o-whirl. So she instead fixed her attention on the hotel's curious carpet, whose geometric pattern and green-yellow-orange color combination was clearly a holdover from groovier times.

Clare wasn't here yet, which comforted Julia. Last night they had messed up. She had been so surprised and swept up in "rescuing" Clare that she hadn't thought clearly. She kissed Clare. And Clare had kissed her back. On the early plane ride, Clare had avoided her. Which rules were they following now? Julia had begun to feel strange. Hopeful. Fearful. A knot in the gut tightening and loosening. She recognized this bubbling and tipping and flurrying sensation as the beginnings of love, but Julia hadn't expected them to come so quickly or so assuredly.

Besides, she had no idea how Clare really felt about her. Was she still mad about the date sabotaging? Julia spent so much time lately trying *not* to feel, it seemed, that things had muddied in Julia's mind. Perhaps Julia was making things bigger than they actually were. In the real estate of Julia's heart, Clare had gone and built an amusement park. Britt had always said that Julia had an overactive imagination and that she believed too much in fairy tales. Perhaps Clare merely viewed Julia as an enticement, a new shiny, and that was all. Plus, so much was riding on this initiative, perhaps Clare hadn't even had time to consider Julia as anything other than a colleague. A colleague she had intense sexual chemistry with, yes, but a colleague nonetheless.

"Nice blazer, Julia, " Ben said, chucking her shoulder as he walked by. "Break a leg in there."

"Thank you."

She at least looked the part of a woman who was put together, taking a cue from Clare, who suggested she "tone it down" for this meeting. Not trusting Clare's fashion sense— the woman was beautiful but she dressed like a Williams Sonoma showroom—she asked Rodrigo to weigh in. He told her she could also stand to dress a little less "flamboyantly for the capitalists," so she tapped into her inner-dandy, a side she hadn't paid heed to since her college days as an amateur drag king. Her stage name had been Dick Dodger, and nothing delighted him more than performing show tunes and jazzy covers of "Baby Got Back" to a small but enthusiastic crowd of women's studies minors, Students Against Sweatshops activists, and a scrum of intramural rugby players.

Today she wasn't quite so over the top in her attire, choosing gray tweed pants and a matching vest, her hair styled in a high, severe ponytail that she hoped made her appear older than she was. A red pocket square provided the only pop of color on her person. That is, until Clare walked up, sending a splash of crimson to each pale cheek.

"You look sharp," Clare said. "Ready to K some A?"

"What? Oh, yes. I mean, I think—I hope," Julia demurred. Sometimes the way Clare spoke reminded her of a well-meaning kindergarten teacher.

"You're nervous," Clare said, smiling. "Want to do it with me?"

Julia's heart pounded and her vision blurred. "What?"

"Do you want to practice your part of the presentation with me again?"

"Oh," Julia stifled a smile. Of course Clare had not been suggesting *that*. "Yeah, actually, that'll help me calm down some, I think. Let's walk while we do it so I can burn off some of this nervous energy."

They set off down the hall, making a wide circle around the hotel's perimeter. "First," Julia said, "I'll do my part of the presentation, and then I'll introduce you. You'll start on slide 14."

"Right," Clare said.

She rehearsed once again the lines she'd practiced over and over again the last week as they slowly walked past the coffee stand, row after row of monotonous conference rooms, and the sleepy, unopened restaurant. After they'd made four rotations around the hotel perimeter, Julia's breath began to soften and her confidence rose. She had this presentation down, she was certain.

And just when she was about to suggest to Clare that they head back, Julia overheard someone say Clare's name. She glanced to her left, about 15 feet away, where Nikki sat, her back to them, on a plump orange chair, talking to someone Julia didn't recognize.

Clare placed a hand on Julia's shoulder to slow her and steered them toward where Nikki sat. She didn't know why Clare did this exactly, curiosity perhaps, or masochism, or an uncanny ability to discern when others were talking about her behind her back.

As they got closer, Julia began to pick up what Nikki was saying.

"It's in the bag, I'm telling you," Nikki told her companion. "Gary told me this morning. Did you know her nickname is Elsa?"

"Like the Ice Queen?"

"Yep."

The man laughed. "Did you start that rumor?"

Nikki pressed her lips together and flicked her hand, as if throwing away a key. "Anyway, there's no way they'd let someone so frosty be Chief HR Officer."

"Here's hoping she can '*let it go*,'" the man sang-laughed. Nikki laughed along with him.

Julia's stomach sank and her fists clenched at their sides. She hated the idea that Nikki was talking shit about Clare, and starting rumors she sincerely hoped weren't true. Then she remembered that Paula had called Clare an 'Ice Queen,' too. Before she had time to follow this train of thought further, however, they were close enough that Nikki's companion saw them and gave Nikki a little kick under the table. "We should be getting back, yeah?" he said too loudly.

Nikki glanced behind her to see Julia and Clare a few feet away and stammered, "Ye-yeah we should. Let's go."

When they were out of earshot, Julia squeezed Clare's hand and let it go. "She's jealous. Don't let her get to you. That's exactly what she wants."

Clare's mouth twisted. Julia reached for her, but Clare's arm jutted out to stop her.

"If you hug me, I'll fall apart, and I can't fall apart," she said, her eyes shining wetly. "Not here. Not now."

"Okay," Julia said. She rubbed the back of her own neck, feeling helpless.

She wanted more than anything to comfort Clare, to say something that might take the sting out of Nikki's ignorant words, and to reassure Clare that they were utterly false, but when she opened her mouth to try, nothing came out.

Feeling useless and strange, Julia was struck dumb. How do you begin to comfort someone so selfless and giving? Someone so smart and funny and tender and together? Julia couldn't begin to tell Clare how much she meant to her, how even knowing Clare for a few short months had changed her. Faced with the surging and inappropriate need to confess these things, Julia stopped herself. "We should get back," she said. "It's time."

———

Julia's stomach was in knots when she walked up to the podium to present her piece of the initiative. She looked out at the sea of faces, some stern, some familiar. A few shifted in their seats as the silence between them grew. At the end of the first row of navy blue chairs, Julia saw Clare sitting on her hands, legs crossed, her top knee bouncing restlessly. When Julia's eyes fell upon Clare, the bouncing paused, and even though it was obvious to Julia that Clare was distressed, she still gave Julia a thumbs up. That was Clare. Relentlessly rooting for you. Kind. Hopeful, even in the face of the most absurd or unlikely circumstances. Julia's heart swelled. She glanced at her index cards, and then set them aside on the podium. She knew what she wanted to say.

"Thank you, Jerry, for that lovely introduction, and thanks to all of you for attending," Julia started, her voice rising and falling before settling into her usual calm, clipped tone. "Before I get started, I'd like to thank all my colleagues who contributed to this presentation, and whose hard work, long hours, and dedication made all of this possible."

She paused, her hands shaking. She was glad the podium hid them from view. And she was even more surprised that her voice did not falter as she continued, "I'd like to give special thanks to one colleague in particular, Clare Kolikov, who embodies the commitment, keen insight, and fierce determination that we are striving to model in this initiative on female leadership."

Julia scanned the crowd as she spoke, but her eyes lingered on Clare's, attempting to tamp down every fear and doubt that loomed inside of her as she continued off the cuff, "I'm used to people ignoring me. Not taking me seriously. I'm used to people telling me I'm pretty, but they don't particularly care to listen to what I have to say."

Julia looked up to see hundreds of eyes gaping back at her in stunned silence. She cleared her throat and kept going. "That was never the case with Clare. When I first met her, I was in a state of crisis. She didn't know me. I was just an employee—number 328, according to my file. And I came to her with a problem that many others have swept under the rug in the past. They pretended to care, but what they really cared about was preserving the status quo. But Clare didn't do that. She *listened*. She listened to my concerns with empathy and compassion, and then she took action.

"She didn't even have to help me that day. She could've just filled out a form and sent me on my merry way, never thinking twice about it. But that's not who Clare is. And not only was she able to help me in spite of the hurdles I've faced as a woman—the glass ceiling, the constant push back, the comments on my appearance—she makes you believe that you can do great things. That you deserve a seat at the table. If you have something to contribute, she'll find a way to make sure you're heard. She taught me to trust my inner voice and not be afraid to own my success. This is leadership. And I've seen her do this countless other times—not just for me—in the few months that I've known her.

"We have this janitor in the Oakland office, Raj. He loves Skrillex and Dolly Parton and makes a surprisingly good Shepherd's Pie. He and Clare both work late a lot, and got to talking one night. He told Clare that he wanted to be a software engineer, to go to college, something he hadn't been able to do, raising three young children on his own. And what did Clare do? She petitioned W;nkdIn to start a company tuition reimbursement program, knowing that Raj's new engineering skills would not only help him but help the company, too. That's just one small example of the kind of magic Clare makes happen. She helps people. She wants you to grow, to be your best possible self, to harness your super powers, whatever those may be. And she doesn't stop until it happens. Sometimes to the detriment of her own life. I mean, Christ, has this woman ever taken a vacation?"

Laughter erupted from the rows of chairs.

"I'll be the first to admit that she's not the easiest person to get to know. She's not bubbly and she hates small talk and has strong feelings about jazz for some reason, but in spite of these things, she always has your back. She's *always* looking out for the people she works with. And I can't imagine having a more thoughtful leader, or a better partner, than her. So thank you, Clare. For making this all possible."

Picking up the index cards in front of her, a lightness overtook Julia. She smoothed down her shirt and noticed that her hands had stopped shaking. She marveled at this, that something so simple—so cliche—could have this effect on her. She shook her head, a half smile tilting upward. The truth, it *did* set you free. What she didn't know was what the hell she planned to do about it, now that she knew for certain that she was falling for Clare. She steeled herself as this truth wound its way through her.

"Next slide please."

thirty

THE REST of the day blurred for Clare. As soon as Julia had said her name, had said those lovely, inspiring words about her in front of the board and all her colleagues, Clare felt as if she had gone into a low-grade black out. Still reeling from Nikki's insults, but bolstered now by an audacity to prove Nikki wrong, and by a surging affection for Julia, time passed for Clare in fits and starts.

Here was another person shaking her hand, congratulating her on the presentation, and thrusting a business card in her direction. And here was Ben, telling Clare that she had killed it, and that they were all meeting in the hotel bar for drinks. And here was the board chair, regaling her with a story about his own stint in HR. He must have mentioned this history before, but she had no recollection of it. Still, he was smiling, and enthusiastic in the board's unanimous approval of the initiative. And here was Yolanda, telling Clare that she and Julia made a terrific team, and that they could look forward to working closely together over the next year to put the initiative in action.

She smiled through all of this, at the rotating cast of faces offering their hands, their praise, their stories, all the while searching for Julia in the crowd. Where had she gone? Clare had lost her in the aftermath of bodies and grins and handshakes, and each time she set about trying to look for her, another person swarmed in.

"Come on, Clare," someone tugged at her elbow. "First drink's on me!"

"I'll meet you there," she smiled, pulling away. "I just need to—" she jerked her thumb in the air behind her, and took off down the hall in search of Julia, leaving the rest of her sentence to dangle in the air unfinished.

She wasn't in her hotel room, at the cafe, or the coffee cart, or by the hotel pool. She wasn't outside with the smokers or sitting in the lounge area. From a distance, Clare even peeked into the bar, where everyone had gathered, drinks sweating in their glasses, but Julia wasn't there either.

Riding the elevator up, Clare wondered if perhaps Julia didn't want to be found. Maybe she regretted what she had said about Clare earlier. Or maybe it was spoken in haste in order to make Clare feel better and now she was embarrassed. She decided to try Julia's room one last time before giving up. But when she knocked, it yielded to her. She realized the door was ajar and stepped inside. She found Julia sitting on the edge of the bed, chin in hand.

When Clare walked in, Julia rose and stood before her. Clare felt suddenly flayed and exposed, even though she wore all of her clothes. Time slowed. Clare felt herself draw closer and closer to Julia until their faces were inches from each other. She half-expected herself to turn away, to be the ever responsible one, to flee, but she did no such thing.

She looked at Julia wolfishly, as if it was taking every ounce of her willpower not to devour Julia on the spot. For a moment, neither of them moved. Clare felt locked in place and time. Then Julia placed her fingers on Clare's waist, the softness of her hands a kind of anchor, which had the effect of both soothing and agitating her in excitement.

She turned her face up toward Julia's, expecting a kiss, but instead Julia found her neck and began to softly rake her way down and down with her teeth. Clare felt this in her shoulders, her spine, and the soft valley of her lower back. Clare's heart fluttered with each tiny flurry of movement. She kept her eyes closed, to feel every sensation more fully.

Clare teased the skin on Julia's arms, running her fingers up the downy length of them. The hairs there stood at attention each time Clare made her ascents and descents. When Clare undid the buttons on Julia's vest, she felt herself evaporating. What a curious sensation, she thought, to feel as weighted as a mountain, and also as wispy as dryer fluff. She feared that if Julia removed her hands from her body that she might float off into space.

But that didn't happen. Clare removed Julia's vest and then her bra, sending them to the floor with a soundless flourish. Her hands were like beautiful thieves, moving and discovering and capsizing every ounce of Julia's flesh as she moved. She didn't falter or fumble—her hands knew precisely where to exact the most pleasure, the most teasing, expansive pressure.

With that same deliberateness and dexterity, Clare undid the top button of Julia's dress pants. The stretchy fabric yielded easily, and within moments Clare was pulling down the zipper, and then tugging further still as the fabric slid down Julia's thighs and around her ankles.

Clare removed her own dress shirt, feeling the cold rush of air on her bare arms mingling with the fever of her ardor. But she wanted to take her time, to *relish* Julia, delicately trailing her fingers down the backs of Julia's thighs, stopping just below the wet, swollen folds that begged for attention.

And then suddenly Clare blushed and looked down, away from Julia. Julia reached for her, pulling her back to standing and placing her palm on the back of Clare's neck.

Drawing her closer, Clare said, "Did you mean it? What you said?"

"Every word."

At this simple, monumental admission, Clare gently pushed Julia back onto the bed, straddling her hips and kissing her as she sat on Julia's lap. Julia closed her eyes and Clare noticed her eyelashes for the first time, which were long and black, with tips that lightened at the end. She kissed each eyelid, inhaling the salt of Julia's skin. Julia's hands gripped Clare's waist tighter as she performed this ritual, reverence mixing with desire and tenderness. The room's A/C whirred awake, which sent an army of goosebumps to Clare's skin. She trembled when Julia's hands ran the lengths of her arms, warming and igniting her, amazed that they could read each other so well without saying a word.

Mind spinning, Clare lay on top of her, and slipped her tongue into Julia's mouth, relishing the taste that was at once foreign and familiar to her. How strange to feel so strong and weak in Julia's hands, the pleasure of it so intense it bordered on pain, each sensation exponential, as if a hundred hands extended from her body and a hundred hands reached back toward her own.

Clare paused in her wonder, removing the rest of her

clothes as swiftly as she could, and kicking the last tangle of fabric onto the floor before climbing back on top of Julia.

Julia's head thrust back into the white bedspread when Clare placed her mouth upon the hollow of her throat. When Julia moaned, she pressed a little harder, teeth dragging a jagged line across the pure, unmarred canvas of Julia's skin. Clare had the sudden urge to mark Julia, to possess her, even if it would fade in a few days, but held back, as she didn't know if such a gesture would be well received.

Clare worked her way down, lavishing Julia's breasts with attention and softness. Julia gripped the back of Clare's head, pressing her closer, and then surprised her by urging Clare's body upward, pulling her until Clare's thighs straddled Julia's face, her cunt poised directly above Julia's eager mouth.

The suddenness and intimacy of this position unhinged Clare. A surge of wetness coursed through her. Her cunt brushed against the tip of Julia's nose, but Julia did not greet it with her tongue. Instead, she slowly drew her tongue along the ridge between thigh and lip, nibbling softly at the flesh all around it. Julia's mouth was so firm and so soft that Clare felt every insecurity and doubt melting away, leaving a tremulous trail of desire and longing in its wake.

Julia's hands massaged Clare's thighs, which were tense from holding herself up, and relaxed when she leaned back a little, letting her ass rest on Julia's chest. Her hands continued to explore Clare's body, tentatively, and then more assuredly cupping Clare's cheeks with both hands as she pressed her tongue to the most sensitive part of Clare. Clare groaned as Julia's tongue teased and tasted her, and she moved her hips slowly back and forth in rhythm with Julia's movements. When Julia glided her hands upward, along Clare's back and then around to her breasts, Clare clenched her thighs around Julia's face, pleading for more.

Pinching and rolling Clare's nipples in her fingers, Julia's tongue began to move faster, and Clare didn't know how much more of this she could bear before losing herself entirely. She felt the sensations everywhere, each pinch of her nipples sending trails of fire from the base of her skull down to her toes. Her skin prickled with cold from the A/C, mingling from the sweat on her torso and lower back as she pitched herself harder against Julia's mouth.

And then, wanting Julia to experience the same ferocity she was, Clare reached her hand back hand between Julia's thighs, and began to stroke Julia's clit.

Julia's hips rocked against Clare's hand, slowly at first, and then faster. When Clare dipped a finger inside Julia's wet center, her hips began to plead with the same ferocity as Clare's and together they rode the wave of each other's pleasure, a fury and agony overtaking them, until Clare felt that she might shatter into a million pieces.

There was an unbearable urgency to their movements, each thrusting of their hips became an offering, a seamless, wordless unity, as tender as it was frantic, as reverent as it was animal. When Clare came moments later, Julia held onto her, to keep as much of them touching as possible as she rocked and moaned and coiled into a fuse of luminous electricity, and holding on further still as the convulsions radiated through her skin and out into the air, in an ecstatic procession of tumbling, tenuous, neverending light.

Right before she felt her body disassembling, Clare called out Julia's name, her voice almost unrecognizable to herself, her voice a wild bird caught in the throat, her thighs singing, trilling to a song her mind had forgotten but which her body knew by memory.

Spent, sweaty, hand clenched in a fist of Julia's hair, which Clare did not let go of, until finally she did, softly, slowly, releasing Julia from her grip as the final riptides of pleasure carried her out to sea, until the only part of her capable of movement was her own mad heart.

After the strength in her limbs had returned, after Clare had clung to Julia like a salve for hours and hours in the large, unfamiliar hotel bed, their legs twisted in the sheets, Clare somehow mustered the resolve to rise. She had no idea what time it was; the light from outside had long since extinguished.

Kissing a sleeping Julia on the forehead, she dressed quickly. Even though it was dark, she knew her clothes were hopelessly wrinkled, her hair disheveled, and her neck throbbed in the place where Julia had raked her teeth against it. Clare both wanted and did not want a bruise to appear there, but she wouldn't know for sure until she returned to her own room and surveyed the damage under the unforgiving light of the hotel bathroom.

With the lights off, she couldn't help but sneak a glance at herself, the dark hair falling around her face, curled and snarled from sex and sleep, her lips swollen. The mauve lipstick she was wearing earlier was no longer there, though she could see traces of color on her shirt collar. She examined her neck, the mark that might or might not appear later, which bore traces of red.

Clare almost didn't recognize herself. And she liked it. Glimpses of former lives flitted before her. The Clare who once took risks, who collected traces of wildness, who stayed up late to map the contours of a person's skin with her tongue. She thought she'd locked these selves away, threw the keys in the ocean. But Julia found them, found *her,* these parts that Clare had assumed were wrong, unworthy, unflattering.

Shoes and jacket in her hand, Clare couldn't keep from smiling as she opened the door and slipped as quietly outside into the hallway as she could, hearing the lock click in place just as a glimpse of motion entered her periphery. Without thinking, she glanced in the direction of the woman walking toward her, fear freezing her in place when she recognized who it was.

Clare's eyes widened, clutching her shoes and jacket to her chest before her gaze dropped to the floor, but not before she saw, to her horror, Nikki's face transform into a wicked grin. Keeping her eyes to the floor, Clare braced herself for what Nikki might say when she hurried past, and was not prepared for the even worse option—that Nikki said nothing, leaving Clare's mind to loop into a panic.

How much did she see? Did she know this was Julia's room? And if she did, would she say something? Would people believe Nikki over Clare? Would Clare be able to lie about this, about her feelings for Julia, when she now felt so strongly? Could their reputations recover from a scandal like this? This lapse in judgment dooming the careers they had worked so hard to build?

Thoughts short-circuited and whirled around as she shuffled along the carpet to her room, collapsing onto the bed as all the joy of the night seeped out of her body like a balloon. An image of Nikki's twisted grin appeared once more in Clare's mind, causing her to grimace.

But then, a surprise. There was Julia's scent, which lingered on her breath, her face, lips, and fingers. She placed a hand up against her nostrils, breathing in the delicious salt and musk of Julia, letting it fill her lungs. The smell of Julia was a balm that eased her weary mind. She let it coat her breath as fear and uncertainty began to wind up the base of her spine.

What am I going to do? What am I going to do?

thirty-one

THE K STEW HAIKU REVIEW

Clouds of Sils Maria
This movie was so
French. How ironic that it
had zero frenching!

Frenching was on Julia's mind that morning. Clare had managed to slip out of the hotel room without waking her up, which wasn't a surprise, as Julia slept like the dead. She also snored like a lawnmower, which she hoped wasn't the real reason Clare had left early. Britt had needed both ear plugs and a white noise machine when they slept together, so Julia knew it wasn't exactly her most endearing quirk.

But Clare left a note, a sweet one, scrawled in her scrupulous cursive script. "My body hums for you.—C"

Julia couldn't keep herself from smiling all through the shower, while getting dressed, and heading out the door to grab a coffee in the cafe on the ground floor. She stopped smiling when, as she shut the door to her room behind her, she ran right into Nikki, who was so close, it was almost as if she had been waiting for Julia to open the door.

"Jesus Christ," Julia said.

Nikki, not in the least embarrassed, responded by laughing. "Oh, this is too perfect," she said, tossing her brown, mongoosey hair over her shoulder. It looked as if Nikki had been out all night—her eyes sagged, her blazer bore a yellow-ish stain on the forearm, and she blinked in rapid, almost violent succession.

"Excuse me?"

"Nothing, nothing," Nikki continued to laugh as she brushed by Julia and continued down the hall toward the elevators. "Enjoy your morning!"

Julia shook her head. Her eyes were beginning to strain from all the rolling. But then she remembered Clare, the sweet sigh of Clare's straddling hips, their skin hot and alive, and the smile returned to her face. *This is called taking the high road*, she thought to herself, then flipped Nikki's back the bird.

"Darling, you wouldn't believe it!"

Sitting on an aggressively art deco chair near the hotel's lobby, Clare forgot her self-imposed rule of not answering her mother's phone calls before coffee. She wiped the sleep from her eyes and took a too-hot sip that burned her tongue.

"Have you been drinking more tap water?" Clare asked.

"No! Well yes, but no. We're in Bulgaria and I've just had the most delicious Dunkin' Donut of my life."

"You went all the way to Bulgaria to eat at Dunkin' Donuts? You know they have one in Walnut Creek, right?"

Clare's mother ignored her. "Its flavor was called The Mozart and darn if they weren't right because there's a symphony being performed right here on my tongue!"

"I'm happy for you, mom." Clare took another sip and singed her own tongue again. Violin Concerto in Third-Degree Burns.

"Are you all right, darling?" she said. "You sound pale."

"I *sound* pale?"

When had her mother started speaking to her this way? Infancy? How was she so sure of herself? Had Clare ever been this sure of herself in her life?

"I'm sorry, I'm—I'm a bit out of sorts this morning," Clare said. "I am though, I'm happy for you, I promise."

"Is this about your father again? Because you know, we talked about this when he was first diagnosed."

"No, mom—it's not that—"

"He said, 'Carole. When I die, I want you to be happy—"

"Please stop."

"'Take a lover,' he said. 'Take several! And don't you dare let that bunion situation stop you from getting back on that horse because you are cute as a zipper and any man worth his salt will see that—"

"I said please—"

"And you know what? I *am* happy, Clare! Simon makes me happy. And the bunion was temporary, remember?"

Clare closed her eyes, clasping a palm to her forehead. "Yeah, yes, we gave the big blue shoe to Goodwill, I remember. It's not Dad. I'm glad you've ... moved on. I just—"

"I'm worried about you, darling. You seem ... closed off."

"To what?"

"To everything—joy. I don't know. Since your father—

you've been different. This is why I think you should scatter the ashes. It's like you're a faucet someone's pinched shut."

Eyes still closed, Clare felt around the low table in front of her for the coffee. When she couldn't find it, she opened one eye in time to see Nikki galloping toward her with a stride as crooked as her smile.

"Mom, don't be worried," she said, heart lurching into her stomach. "I'm fine, really. Everything's fine."

thirty-two

WHEN CLARE HUNG up the phone, there was Nikki, towering over her. Though she really didn't want to get up, she stood anyway, as she was at least half a foot taller than Nikki and didn't want Nikki to feel like she had anything over her.

Nikki pointed to the phone Clare clutched in her hand. "Who was that? Julia?"

"I don't see how that's any of your business."

"You've made it my business though, haven't you?"

"What?" Whatever Nikki thought she knew, Clare figured it was best to play dumb, to not let herself get caught in any trap Nikki might be trying to set for her.

"Oh, now she plays coy. Like I didn't catch you in your little early morning walk of shame."

"I don't know what you're talking about, Nikki, and frankly, I don't care. Are we done here? Because I'd like to enjoy my coffee in peace." She burned her tongue again. Still too hot. At least now it was numb and she couldn't really feel the pain. She took an even longer, more masochistic sip.

"I haven't finished, actually."

Then, out of the corner of her eye, Clare saw the worst possible thing. The best-worst. It was Julia, looking refreshed and radiant, as if she hadn't lost a wink of sleep over their late-night rendezvous, which Clare supposed she hadn't. She was coming right toward them. Clare begged silently with her eyes for Julia to trip or to realize she'd forgotten her wallet, her hotel key, her sanity, anything, and turn in the opposite direction she was walking.

Instead, Julia smiled at Clare. She must not have noticed or recognized Nikki with her back to her.

"...fucking your subordinates *is* absolutely my business," Nikki was saying. "And it's certainly information that the CEO would be interested in hearing about, especially in light of this trial run..."

Clare kept an eye on Nikki, half-listening to her diatribe, and another on Julia who would be here in four seconds if something or someone didn't stop her.

Clare had never believed in *manifesting* before. Sure, she had read *The Secret* just as everybody had, and sure, she dabbled in the occasional, vaguely uplifting, socially acceptable forms of woo, but for all her wishing and hoping and willing things to be, nothing had even remotely come close to fruition for Clare. Until that very moment.

A man, portly and balding, appeared before Julia, stepping in front of her. He began trying to engage her in conversation. *Yes*, Clare thought. *I manifest you to talk for a good, long while, sir! Take your time. Tell her about how the NFL works or about how you once took apart the TV remote and were almost able to put it back together.*

Whatever he said must have worked, as Julia stopped walking toward Clare and Nikki.

"...and you had better believe I'll be watching you, Clare

Kolikov, because if I so much as catch even a whiff of illicit or wrongful behavior from you *or* Julia, I'm reporting both of your asses to the CEO myself!"

Nikki huffed off then, just as Clare wondered if it was possible to feel both panic and relief at the same time. Surely the Germans must have a word for it, she thought, as Julia reached her, sitting on the arm of the aggressively art deco chair and then, thinking better of it, standing.

Clare suddenly felt exhausted by everything. The presentation, the travel, the job, Nikki, Julia. Julia, Julia. They'd had an amazing night together, yes, but now this— the stress, the hiding, the threats. How easily her world could collapse. Secrecy loomed. Sleepless nights. Weren't relationships supposed to be the *easy* part?

She found herself thinking back to her boring life from just a few months ago, the life that was so tepid and unremarkable her own mother had chastised her for it. But wasn't there something to be said for a life where not much happened? Weren't the Buddhists always going on about such things? Hell, all they did was live in caves and eat plain rice and no one was telling *them* to live a little!

What was so wrong with routine and security and domestic complicity? Clare prided herself on these things. So what if she hadn't taken a vacation in ages. Or been out of the country in years. And then she remembered Erik. The last great rend in her life. How much had that relationship cost her? How much had she sacrificed to be with him, and for what? She swore she wouldn't put herself through that again. Yet here she was. Fretting. Fearful. Secretive.

Maybe her mother was right. Maybe she was like a faucet that had been pinched shut. Maybe she had to be, or else she risked her whole damn house flooding.

"Hey you." Julia wasn't sure how to greet Clare. They had just spent a wild and intimate night together, yes, but they were also in a hotel lobby where any number of colleagues could walk by at any moment. She extended an arm, then reeled it back in. Clare made no motion to touch her. Also was it just her, Julia wondered, or did Clare not look particularly happy to see her?

When Clare didn't say anything, Julia forged ahead anyway, telling herself that Clare was probably tired and ready to go home. "You wouldn't believe what just happened to me," Julia said, barely able to contain her irritation.

"What?"

"Did you see that guy? He just came up and started explaining the NFL to me. Like, hello! I went to football camp when I was nine. Please."

thirty-three

THE K STEW HAIKU REVIEW

Charlie's Angels
Stew wears a leopard
print lounge suit. ... ... I'm sorry, does
something else happen?

Julia shut her laptop. She couldn't shake this sour mood. Not even the sweet comments from her blog fans could cheer her up. It made sense, of course. These people weren't real. She wasn't even real herself. She was an avatar. And her readers were responding to Julia's profile and words, which were carefully calibrated to display her exceptional cleverness about a movie star who would very likely never know Julia existed.

She missed Clare, who did know Julia existed, but she wouldn't know it from the way Clare had ignored all of Julia's texts since they got back from L.A.

Outside, fat, noisy raindrops seemed to throw themselves at her windowpane. *You and me both, rain*, she said morosely to no one.

She texted Paula, but Paula was on a date. **I have a good feeling about this one!**

Oh? Julia texted back.

Yeah! She loves *Dr. Pimple Popper* **and Coke Slurpees.**

Julia waited for Paula to say something else, something *more*, or at least more substantial, but nothing came. **When's the wedding?** Julia texted.

Paula: **Is that sarcasm?**

Julia: **No! Show me a relationship that** *hasn't* **been founded on reality TV and carbs.**

Paula: **Ours certainly was.**

Julia: **See? Kismet.**

Paula: **I've gotta go. She's coming back from the bathroom now. Wish me luck!**

Julia texted several peach emojis, water droplets, cats-with-heart-eyes, and lastly, fireworks.

She wore a thin gold chain that Britt had given her for one of their anniversaries. Six years? Seven? They had been together so long that Julia had started to lose track of the time. They'd become complacent, both of them, Julia had realized, after Britt left, as fuzzy and worn around the edges as a tattered pair of childhood slippers.

Julia reasoned that she should probably take the necklace off, that it was in some way keeping her tethered to the past, but at this point the necklace felt like a part of her. She touched it whenever she felt nervous, not unlike the way her grandfather would worry his rosary beads during Mass. Back and forth, she ran her index finger under the chain, the hairs on her neck softly sighing at attention.

It was only when it broke, the limp halves of it falling

partly into her sweater and partly onto the floor, that Julia was agitated into action. She was tired of being complacent. She was tired of waiting. She was not a person who stood idly by while the world around her spun. She was a *spinner*! She was so spinny she could teach a goddamn spin class! And with that, she squeezed into her worn leather boots, threw a jacket on, and headed for the door.

Julia knew that they were breaking so many rules already. She didn't know how she and Clare could possibly sustain this—she only knew that she *must*.

If Clare had known she was going to have company, she would have put the coffee cups away, or at least come up with some plausible deniability. As it was, the sight of Julia —drenched, hair sticking to her forehead, a too-small jacket covering a too-large sweater—didn't leave Clare much time to think, let alone hide anything.

"You're shivering, come in, come in." Clare ushered Julia inside and began removing her clothes, the too-small jacket, the combat boots, the socks with a hole in each big toe. Only when she had gotten Julia down to her bra and underwear did she realize the intimacy and brazenness of her gestures. But she didn't let that stop her for once. Instead she threw Julia's clothes in the dryer and wrapped her in a large flannel robe.

"Are you busy?" Julia asked.

"Um. Well..."

Julia looked suddenly embarrassed. When she'd arrived, she'd had a "storm the castle" look as it were, but now that she was dried and covered in tartan, Clare noticed she looked morose and more than a little lost.

Clare decided to go the honesty route. "I was just having a chat with my dad."

"Oh god, your dad is here! You could have told me before you stripped me to my bloomers." She gripped the robe tighter about herself, even though she was already covered.

Clare smiled sympathetically. The coffee had just finished brewing. She could smell its earthy, deep aroma from where they sat in her bedroom. "It's not like that. Come." Clare held out her hand and Julia took it.

The round, dark brown kitchen table was set with two beige placemats, two coffee mugs, and a tray of chocolate chip cookies in between them. On the chair farthest from them, against the back wall, sat a black plastic box with a pair of thick, wire-frame glasses on top.

"Julia, meet my dad, Yuri." Julia shifted from one foot to the other, her gaze between the box and Clare's calm demeanor. "He died a little more than a year ago. Lung cancer."

"I'm so sorry—" Julia interjected, but Clare went on, determined.

"My therapist suggested that I try 'talking' to him, that it might be a way to release some of the grief that felt like a human-sized brick covering me after he died. That when it felt like I was in a dark hole I would never crawl out of, to wonder, what would my dad say about it? At first I dismissed it as stupid. Who talks to dead people? But then, after nothing else seemed to be working, I gave it a go one night, and you know what? I felt a little bit lighter after. Still silly, yes, but it was like I could hear his voice so clearly— and it was nice. I felt ... less alone. So I kept it up."

"And the cookies?"

"His favorite. He'd wake up every night around

midnight and eat Chips Ahoy. I think he needed something, after he quit drinking, to, I don't know, be addicted to."

"There are worse vices," Julia laughed.

"Want some coffee? I just made it."

Julia sat down in the open seat next to the ashes. "Did you steal these mugs?"

Clare reddened, a lump forming in her throat. "Define 'steal.'"

"You totally did, didn't you? It's not like IHOP hands out commemorative mugs."

Clare poured them coffee, avoiding Julia's eyes. "Fine, yes, I stole them. And I feel really bad about it. The only other thing I've ever stolen was a skull-and-crossbones pog and that was in first grade."

"What's a pog?"

"Oh, never mind."

"Well, I am shocked. Dismayed. To think I'm attracted to a *criminal*. I should haul your ass down to the pokey right now."

"Keep it up, Dawes, and you're not getting any cookies." Julia made a reach for the tray, but Clare snatched it, sliding it to the far side of the table.

"I take it back! I've always believed in your innocence. Free Clare!" She pounded her fists on the table.

"That's better." Clare slid the tray back.

"Pushover," Julia said triumphantly, crumbs falling down around her chin as she smiled.

"*Blogger*."

And then, laughter poured out of them, first Julia, then Clare, so much so that by the time they had finished, each had to gasp a little for breath.

As their laughter quieted, so did the rain, which had

ceased its onslaught. Only a faint, cursory tapping filtered in through the windows.

Julia titled the IHOP mug to her face and sipped. "What does your dad think of your lawless ways anyway?"

Clare smiled. "He stole the one I'm holding." It had a small chip on the handle and Clare rubbed at it with her thumb. "When I went off to college in New York, he wanted me to have a little piece of home."

"They don't have IHOPs in New York?"

"You're missing the point, Julia."

"Right, sorry. Continue."

"I thought, well, when he died, I thought a ritual would help me to feel close to him, to keep him with me in some way." Julia reached across the table and took hold of Clare's fingertips. "You think I'm nuts, don't you? This is a 'aw, poor nutter' sympathy hand hold?"

Julia shook her head, "No, no, it's sweet. Unorthodox, perhaps. But harmless." Clare wiped away the tears threatening to fall down her cheeks. "Do you need the ritual to feel close to him?"

"I thought so, but I'm not so sure. Anyway, my mom's been on me to scatter the ashes."

"Is she?"

"Yeah."

Julia looked around, suddenly skeptical. "She's not here too, is she? In that flower vase?"

Clare laughed again. She couldn't remember the last time she'd laughed this much. "She's alive and well, thank you. Somewhere in Eastern Europe currently. Budapest, I think. She's traveling the world." Clare hadn't meant for the last sentence to come off quite so disdainfully.

"Good for her," Julia said. "It's a struggle to get my mom to travel beyond the couch."

"It was a struggle for mine for ages, too. And now she's a damn globetrotter. It's a little embarrassing."

"Why embarrassing?"

Clare was caught off guard by the question. She was used to her mother embarrassing her, as all mothers embarrass their children, but the truth of this particular situation was, she realized, different from the usual parental blights.

"Well, I suppose I'm jealous. With work being what it is, and you know, who can take a vacation anymore, and ..." She trailed off, exhausted by her own excuses before they even left her mouth. "I haven't been anywhere in a decade. Oh god. *I'm* the embarrassing one, aren't I?"

Julia's face softened. Her words rose barely above a whisper as she said, "Clare, you're not embarrassing. You're too hard on yourself."

There it was again. Julia's seemingly inexhaustible optimism. How did she do it? How did she retain her enthusiasm in the face of the world's daily, crushing blows? Her whole oeuvre was one, long, tireless yes. *You want a thing? Get the thing!* And when Julia said it, Clare almost believed it. She wanted to. Julia made the present seem so effortless. So full of promise.

Clare shook her head. "No, I *am* embarrassing, I mean, look." She swept her arm across the table. "I was just hoping maybe you wouldn't mind so much." Her heart hammered. She felt as if it had dislodged itself and was making its way out through her esophagus. "And I'm sorry, too. I know I've been a little distant. Things have been ... weird."

"It's okay." Julia squeezed Clare's hand tighter. Clare relished the warmth and comfort of so simple a pleasure.

At this, Clare grabbed Julia by the flannel belt loop and

playfully pulled her onto her lap. Clare's hand found Julia's waist, the other resting against Julia's outer thigh. Clare felt the warmth of Julia's breath on her face, the scent of cinnamon that seemed to follow her everywhere. Clare also smelled the sweet, creamy coffee on Julia's lips, and saw the rise and fall of her chest as she breathed unevenly.

Julia closed her eyes and kissed Clare, who felt herself brightening and slipping. Her mouth blurred with possibility, with longing.

She pulled back reluctantly, and gently guided Julia back to the chair she had been sitting on, facing the window. "I have to tell you something," Clare said.

"Okay." Someone who didn't know her might not have noticed the barely perceptible knot that formed on Julia's brow when Clare spoke. But Clare noticed. And it worried her.

"It's Nikki. She saw me leaving your hotel room."

"So that's why she was hovering outside my door like a vulture. Ugh."

"She doesn't have proof of any wrongdoing, but she did say she'd be watching us."

"Fucking hell. Why didn't you tell me?"

"I didn't want you to worry unnecessarily. Instead I made the obvious, rational choice to ignore you for a while!" She smiled a little maniacally. "But now, well, I figured it's best ... you know ... I thought maybe we should cool it ... for a while."

Julia seemed to shrink into the chair. Clare felt like the worst kind of coward. She *was* the worst kind of coward.

"How long is 'a while'?"

"I don't know," Clare answered truthfully. "Until the trial run is over? Until the initiative is on the ground and running? Then I can ... I can talk to the CEO about .. I can tell him—I mean, I *will* tell him ..."

"Christ, Clare, you can't even say it."

Behind Julia's head, lightning splayed its hand across the sky in the kitchen window, setting every word on fire. A terrific crash of thunder followed. It was as if the hand of a deity had reached down, took hold of Clare's lapels, and scolded her. Her eyes flashed.

"I want to be with you," Julia said. "I want to shout it from the rooftops. Hell, I'll hire a plane or a marching band."

"I want that, too. I just ... I just need a little time to work out the details," Claire said. "Can you be a little patient with me?"

Julia smiled. The knot at her forehead softened as she scooched her chair over to Clare, then rested her head against Clare's shoulder.

"Also, I don't need a marching band," Clare said. "I'm more of a string quartet kind of gal."

Clare closed her eyes, allowing the warmth and nearness of Julia to spread through her, while outside, the sky cracked once more, illuminating the still houses, the peopleless cars, the distant, bald hills, before banishing them all once more to darkness.

thirty-four

IT HAPPENED ON A THURSDAY MORNING. The best news of Clare's life. Or at least what she thought would be the best news of her life.

The CEO sat Clare and Nikki down, told them they'd each done a phenomenal job with the initiative and with their teams, and that, because Clare had more years of experience, both in HR, and at the company, she'd be given the role of Chief HR Officer. Nikki, too, would be given a promotion, Senior VP of People.

"The official announcement will be on Monday," he said, lightly karate-chopping them each on the shoulder, as if he was knighting them but forgot a sword. "Until then, keep this information between us, okay?"

Nikki's mouth hung open, but for once, it seemed she had nothing to say. Clare couldn't believe it. The job was hers. She won. Her face felt like a twisty set of funhouse mirrors. Was she smiling or grimacing? She couldn't tell. Was it both? Was she Julia's permanent boss now? She was. She was! No, no, no, yes, no.

"Bang up job, both of you, I mean it," he said. "We're

gonna do great things around here." He stood, shaking each of their hands with finality. "Hey, stick around a few minutes, won't you, Clare? I've got an invoice from a mime school and the expenses are all written in emojis. I can't figure it out."

And with that, Nikki left the office without so much as a glance at Clare. It was unlike her not to grimace or sulk, and Clare didn't trust it. She would've paid more heed to it, except her schedule that day was already jam-packed, including a virtual therapy appointment with Luca, which she had rescheduled several times this month already.

Because she had been so busy with implementing the new initiative on female leadership, she hadn't seen him for several weeks. After interpreting the mime emoji invoice, she dashed to her office and shut the door.

Luca was late for their appointment, so Clare clicked over to Pizzazz.com, a self-help magazine disguised to sell beauty products, while she waited. She remembered seeing a *Pizzazz* magazine on the coffee table in the waiting room during one of her earlier sessions. The homepage showed a wan, pale woman in her underwear with more abs than could feasibly fit on a torso. Clare counted them, 13. A baker's dozen of abs. She knew it was photoshopped, but still felt depressed about her own, perfectly fine, healthy body.

She lifted her shirt slightly to count her own abs. There were none, but in the right lighting, she occasionally could make out the faint, ghostly outline of 1 or 2. A two-pack. A ghost of Tupac. Underneath the woman on the magazine cover was this headline: "Are You Mysterious or Just Avoidant? A Quiz."

Thankfully, before Clare could get too deep into the quiz, Luca's face appeared on screen. The crookedness of

Luca's grin told Clare that he likely wasn't wearing pants, though she of course chose not to confirm this.

Clare fished around in her desk for her stack of therapy coupons. There was only one left. This was her eighth session with Luca. Where had the time gone? "Hey," she said, "It looks like this is my last coupon. Assuming I'm still broken in the next hour, you'll have to start charging me full price."

Luca tilted his head at her. "Right. Okay."

"What?"

He scratched his head, hesitating just a beat. "Well, actually, that coupon was only good for one session."

Clare shook her head, confused. "But you've been charging me half price all this time."

"Yeah." He smiled at her boyishly, as if he was getting away with something, and not Clare.

"But why? Why would you do that?"

"I figured you needed someone to talk to and that you might bolt if you found out the coupons were bunk."

Clare considered this. She certainly might have. Her tendency to bolt was strong, as was her distaste for therapy. At least, it was when they'd just started. "Luca! You didn't have to do that."

"You took a chance on me," he said. "The least I could do was return the favor."

Clare clutched at the fabric near her heart, subtly, as she stared into the screen. Her throat became full and tight and she wondered if she might cry.

"But I have some good news actually," Luca said.

"Yeah?"

"I passed my board requirements. I'm officially a licensed psychotherapist."

Clare beamed. "Luca! I'm so proud of you. Congratulations!"

"Thank you, thank you. I'm def gonna start charging you more now that I'll have a fancy framed certificate on the wall."

"As you should."

"But anyway. Down to business. The talks with your dad, they're helping?"

"I think so, yeah."

He looked down at his crotch. Was he not wearing underwear either? Clare wished she hadn't wondered.

"Sorry," he said, "I'm a little out of it."

"What happened? Did you talk to your parents?"

"Kind of. We're supposed to have coffee. It's a tentative cease-fire."

"Good! That's good, right?"

"It's weird, but yeah, maybe good. But that's not why I'm out of it."

"Oh. Then what?"

"I was just text-fighting with one of my slosh ball teammates."

"Slosh ball?"

"It's kickball, but with drinking. So, like, to determine who goes first, both teams drink a beer. Whoever finishes first, kicks first. And instead of second base, there's a keg. And you have to round the bases holding a beer—"

"I get the idea."

"Right, well, Trevor thinks it was my fault we lost last Saturday's game, but I got a *cramp*. I could barely walk! Let him try running with 800 ounces of light beer sloshing inside of him."

He paused, looking imploringly at Clare, as if their roles

were reversed and *she* was supposed to be helping him. Then he seemed to remember himself, and a placidity overtook him. His voice lowered in pitch to a Bob Ross level of soothing.

"Anyway, tell me about you. How's Julia? Are you two getting it on yet or what?"

"So, actually, I have news, too. I got a promotion. I'm Chief HR Officer now." Luca's eyes widened so dramatically it was almost as if his eyebrows had shot arrows at Clare. "I'm Julia's boss. And we slept together anyway."

Clare cupped her hands up around her mouth. She hadn't said this out loud before, and the effect was dizzying. She forced herself to acknowledge the short, staggered breaths pushing against her hand, reminding her that she was alive.

"Craaaaap-ola," Luca gasped.

"The promotion I'd been wanting forever, mind you," Clare said. "The promotion I thought would make my life feel worthwhile, instead of this waiting, waiting, waiting. And you know what? I felt the joy of it for about 15 seconds. A pin prick of joy, before the whole thing deflated, leaving me sad and shriveled on the sidewalk. Why does it feel this way? Why can't I be happy about this thing I've wanted forever and finally got?"

"Because it's not actually the thing you want?"

"Yes it is! Have you been listening? Are you Tindering right now?"

"I'm not Tindering, you're Tindering!"

Clare said it again, softer this time. "This is what I want."

"Okay," he said thoughtfully. "Then, why don't you celebrate? Take yourself out on the town. You achieved a goal! That deserves a nice dinner at least. Or something. Don't wallow thinking about the pussy you could be eating this weekend. Wallow in the lobster you *are* eating."

Clare considered this. Maybe celebrating her accomplishment would make her feel better, or at least make her feel *something*. They were quiet for a while, though Luca's brow flexed and released occasionally, perhaps from compassion, the shared and strange intimacy of their unlikely union. Clare felt more at ease already, simply sitting across from Luca on a screen. Perhaps because she had such low expectations of him, she didn't worry too much about whether he was judging her or thinking that her meager problems were meager.

But then he spoke. "I can't believe we lost that game."

Clare looked into Luca's wild eyes, his eyebrows threaded with worry and regret, and said, "You have to let it go."

The silence filled their individual spaces and then radiated outward, into the wide, gray, chaotic world. She told him to let go of the slosh ball game, of the awful things his parents said to him, of the 53 dates he went on that year that went nowhere, as well as all the women who didn't write him back. She told him to let go of not having the greatest therapy boundaries and his grandfather's cufflinks and of everything else that was plaguing him.

And then, something strange happened. She took what she had given to Luca and she turned it right back on herself. She let go of not having 13-pack abs and of every time she disappointed her mother. She let go of all the mistakes she had made with Erik. She let go of the eczema and of not knowing how to grieve the loss of her father, the only person who had loved her unconditionally. She forgave herself for not moving the way everyone thought she should have by now. She let go of the fear of loving Julia. She let go and let go until they were both leaning forward on their desks, heads in hands, sobbing, and then she whispered it again, "It's okay to let go," realizing that it was the thing she had most needed to hear in her life, that it was perhaps the only thing she had ever needed to hear. And how easy, she thought, and how true, that she could have given such permission to herself at any time.

thirty-five

THE NEXT DAY, on Friday, at 4:30 p.m., Nikki walked into Clare's office and shut the door.

Without saying a word, Nikki held her phone in the air and pressed play. Clare heard her own voice played back for her in crystal clarity. "I'm Julia's boss. And we slept together anyway."

Nikki played the recording again, watching as Clare's face fell a few octaves each time she pressed the button. "I'm Julia's boss. And we slept together anyway."

Nikki sat down in the chair across from Clare's desk, the same chair that Julia had first sat in when they met, in what felt like another lifetime. But instead of a beautiful beginning, as with Julia, Clare saw her life for what it was in this moment, a series of rapidly closing doors.

"Here's what's going to happen," Nikki began. "At the all-hands meeting on Monday morning, instead of accepting the CHRO position, you're going to resign. And you're going to recommend me as your replacement. Or I'm going to anonymously play this recording over the loudspeaker in front of everyone."

"You're blackmailing me?" Clare knew that something dark simmered inside Nikki but she hadn't thought Nikki was capable of this kind of malice.

"We're just talking," Nikki said casually. "Just having a little conversation."

"You recorded a private conversation between me and my therapist. Do you know how many ethical and legal lines you've crossed? Do you really think you'll get away with this?"

Nikki leaned back in the chair, her fingertips creating steeples against each other. "I highly doubt my name's the one that's going to be dragged through the mud when people find out you've been sleeping with your subordinate."

Clare shrank inside herself. She felt like someone had lobbed six inches off her person. All she could do was shake her head. "I can't believe you'd do this."

Nikki smirked. "You have the weekend to decide. And if you decide to resign on Monday morning, then your precious Julia can at least keep her job."

Nikki rose from the chair, tossing a pad of blank post-its in Clare's direction.

———

Julia had been so ecstatic when Clare said she needed to see her that she prepared a special outfit. It involved an asymmetrical military-style jacket with brass buttons and a collar that would not go down. Julia was as excited as that collar. *This is it*, Julia thought. *Clare's figured out a plan and we're going to be together for real now.*

She decided to try her hand at macarons again. *Clare*

would like that, she thought. *She's never seen my domestic side.* Julia half toyed with the idea of putting on a hip hop dance workout while she beat the meringue, but she thought it might be overkill. Plus, what if she dislocated her shoulder again? She'd need her joints in working order for all the sex they were surely on the verge of having.

The doorbell rang and Julia twerked her way over to it, but instead of being greeted with a wet, passionate kiss, Clare breezed by her and sat down on the bed.

"I got it. And she knows," Clare said.

"What? Longer sentences, please."

"I got the promotion. And Nikki knows about us. She recorded my conversation with Luca. Either I resign on Monday or we both lose our jobs." Julia joined Clare on the bed as Clare explained the whole sordid situation. This was not how she saw the evening going for them.

Julia's throat felt rock solid. She tried to swallow but couldn't, her whole body suddenly filled with rage toward Nikki. "Don't let her win," she said. "Let me take the fall."

A litany of *fucks* fell from Clare's mouth. It sounded so strange, this small, obscene word, coming from Clare, so out of place. Clare shook her head, her voice shrill and jittery. "It wouldn't matter. The damage is done. I fucked up. I'm your boss and I should have known better. I should have known *better*."

Julia tried to comfort Clare by placing an arm around her, but Clare stood up suddenly and began to pace. Julia had never seen her like this before, so panicked yet robotic. It was as if Clare had become a wind-up car ramming into the wall again and again.

"Maybe this is a sign," Julia said.

"A sign?"

"That it's time for a change? Let's run away together and start that savory cheesecake business."

"Julia, this isn't funny!"

"Okay, okay, sorry. You're the one who always knows what to do! I'm flailing here."

"I'm fucked." Clare paced the small studio, six steps up, six steps back. "What have I done?"

Julia's forehead knotted. She had to think. The edges of her vision blurred and a bile rose in her throat. She tried once more to touch Clare, who breezed by her again. "We'll figure it out, okay? Together."

"I can't believe I let you talk me into this."

"Me? I talked you into this?" Julia's throat locked again. "So I'm what? Just some obstacle standing in the way of your precious job, is that it? Is that what I am to you?"

"No, sorry, that's not what I meant. I just, I—it's all wrong. This isn't me. This isn't me." She continued to pace and stare at the floor, her words stuttery, her head shaking, as if she was in a trance. Julia opened her mouth to speak just as a smoke alarm startled and shrieked through the house. "Fuck! The macarons!" Julia shouted.

Smoke billowed through the studio apartment, permeating the air with a cloying sweetness, as Julia ran around opening windows and waving a towel at the ceiling. When the horrible noise stopped, she removed the charred bits of macaron shells from the oven and threw the tray on the counter. Several landed on the floor with an airy plonk.

Clare came into the kitchen and began doing the only thing it seemed she knew how, trying to fix it. Julia looked at Clare on her knees and Clare paused in her tidying and gave Julia a pleading look. A look as if to say, here I am on my knees for you, is that not enough? Julia decided that it wasn't. It was not enough. Screw the job! She wanted to be chosen. She wanted to be first for once in the grand scheme of things. And in the microscopic scheme of things. In all the things!

The noise had stopped but the alarm inside of Julia continued to sound.

She felt like she had been moving through life in a driverless car, as if her days were something that were happening *to* her, she was just along for the ride, and would only need to nudge the car occasionally to get back on the right track. But she realized now how wrong that was.

"You're not even thinking about me are you?" Julia's voice was quieter now, with riptides of anguish nipping at her syllables.

"She's blackmailing me, Julia! Have you ever been blackmailed? Because I sure haven't and I could use a little support here."

"You know what your problem is? You're a coward. This isn't about blackmail—it's about you being afraid to stand up and say, Fuck your stupid rules! They don't matter. I want to be with her. But you can't. You can't say that. You're too afraid the world will implode if you break the rules. You're too afraid of being judged for it."

"So what if I am? We can't all be like you, Julia, with your whimsy and your roller skates and change-jobs-when-ever-you-feel-like-it ways. I've worked my ass off for years at the expense of everything else in my life, so don't tell me it was all for nothing!"

Julia swiped at her eyes. This was the problem with loving people. Once someone *knew* you, they also knew precisely where to dig a thumb into your rawest, softest parts. "You know, I admired you," Julia said. "I saw you as this incredibly put-together person. Who always had the answers. I've seen you stand up for so many others, myself included, against the bullshit bureaucracy and toxicity and whatever was standing in the way of their dreams. But you don't do the same for you! You won't stand up for yourself, or for us." Julia shook her head sadly. Her voice felt heavy and slow, like a clogged artery. "You've been chasing this dream that you think you should be chasing, while your life —and all the things that really matter—pass you by. What do you really want, Clare? I'm asking you. No, I'm begging you. Choose me. Choose us. We can get through this —together."

Clare stopped pacing and looked at Julia, as if for the first time. "Julia—it's not that simple."

She looked into Clare's eyes, waiting for her to say more, to reveal more, to fight for them, but when Clare didn't, Julia understood that she had her answer. She felt like the ground beneath her had swallowed her, and that she might never rise again. "Well, you know what?" Her voice cracked. Sadness throttled her senses. If she didn't say this now, she would lose all conviction. "Let me make it simple for you."

Julia marched to the door and flung it open.

"Julia please—let's talk about this." Clare did not rise from her knees. She was crying now, crawling from the kitchen to the front door, clutching at the charred bits of cookies in her hands.

"We have talked about it, Clare. Over and over again. I'm done talking now. I'd like you to leave."

The tears that fell silently from Clare's face were almost enough to crack Julia's resolve but she somehow held firm long enough for Clare to rise and shuffle through the door-way. When she turned back to plead with Julia once more,

Julia closed the door. Not swiftly or even hard. Just with enough force for the lock to click into place. And then Julia collapsed against it, sliding on her back down its blue wooden frame. By the time she reached the floor, she was sobbing.

thirty-six

THE TROUBLE with thinking that alcohol will solve all your problems, Clare decided, after polishing off half a bottle of malbec, was that it *did* solve all your problems ... for a little while. She swayed unsteadily, glancing at her neatly made bed. She wanted to lay down on it, but then she'd have to remake it, and she wasn't sure she had the motor skills to do so to her specifications just then. So instead Clare laid down on the floor next to her bed, sweeping her arms and legs into a wide snowless angel.

She felt warm and loose in a way she hadn't in ages. The sadness that swarmed like a dense cloud of gnats after her fight with Julia moved away from her heart temporarily and instead filled her stomach. She recognized the feeling, somewhere in the region of her awareness, as nausea. But she didn't get up. Not yet.

Instead she picked up her phone and bought a full set of mime makeup, a pair of rainbow-colored roller blades with light-up wheels, and a tie-dye T-shirt that looked similar to one she wanted when she was eight that her mother refused to buy for her. *Ha!* She thought. *I do what I want!*

She did not have Julia and soon she would not have a job, but that was okay, because soon she would have this T-shirt. With the T-shirt and the mime makeup and the roller blades, and the rest didn't matter, she decided.

As she looked at the T-shirt, an anger welled up inside of her and out her fingertips. She put on Celine Dion's "My Heart Will Go On," lip-syncing along earnestly. Emboldened by Celine's crescendo-ing conviction, Clare texted her mother. **This is all your fault. I was never good enough in your eyes. I was always a disappointment. And guess what? Now I'm a disappointment to Julia, too. Congratulations! [Beaver emoji]**

The beaver emoji was a mistake, but Clare enjoyed its subtle lesbian symbolism. She threw her phone down on the hardwood floor where it clattered. Then she crawled her way to the bathroom to throw up.

Afterwards, she felt strong enough to stand. She wiped her mouth, lit a vanilla candle in the bathroom to disguise the smell, and hobbled over to the kitchen, where she pulled a box of cookies from the pantry and the IHOP mug her father had stolen for her. She filled the mug with tap water and set it down on the counter. She hobbled over to her closet to find her father's ashes, which she also set down on the counter, next to the mug.

As she retrieved the ashes, Clare passed her phone, which was pinging like crazy on the floor where she had flung it. Her mother, probably. Clare left it, allowing it to continue its futile song, sure her mother would give up in a few minutes and leave her alone.

Clumsily, Clare began arranging the cookies, the coffee mug, and the ashes in her usual ritual on the dining table. She drank the water swiftly and unceremoniously, suddenly aware of how thirsty she was. She refilled the mug and sat back down, trying to muster up an unclouded-ness needed to perform her grief ritual. The room swayed. Clare shut her eyes, which only made the swaying worse.

Ping, her phone sang. *Ping ping ping*.

She opened her eyes, glaring in the direction of the phone. She shoved a cookie into her mouth, its buttery crunch sounding impossibly loud in her ears.

And then her phone rang. *Ring ring ring, ping ping ping*. A furious ballet of mechanical raindrops filled the air, infringing upon her drunken pseudo-peace. Annoyed, Clare waited, her fists tight at her sides, ready to strike at some-thing—anything. She swayed in her chair, bolstered by a few seconds of blissful quiet.

When the phone pinged again, Clare was furious. She leapt up from the table, the force of her thighs striking its rounded ledge as she rose, sending the whole thing careening up and over, and spilling its contents onto the floor.

It seemed to happen in slow motion. Clare watched in disbelief as everything she held dear crashed to the floor, the mug shattering into a dozen pieces, the lid of her father's ashes cracking open and sending up a plume of gray and white dust that coated the floor, the counter, Clare's skin, everything. Everything.

The wail that escaped from Clare's throat at that moment sounded inhuman to her. It was bestial and low and unlike any noise she had ever made thus far in her life. With ineloquent motion, Clare clumsily rose and reached for the dustpan, sweeping artlessly at the floor. Whether because of her drunken state or some perverse karma, the charred bones of her father refused to be contained. The more Clare swept, the more they seemed to fly around out of the pan, reaching new, previously clean surfaces. After a few futile minutes of this—if that's indeed how long it was, Clare no longer had a sense of time—she collapsed onto the kitchen floor, clutching the dustpan and its ashes to her chest and sobbing. Each heave of her lungs sent a flurry of ashes skittering in the air, where they came to rest on Clare's starched shirt.

She held onto the pan, clutching it as desperately as she clutched for air, and cried. The tears flowed torrentially out of her as she looked at the mess she had made. Not just in her kitchen, but the mess she had made of her life. Her breath stuttered and fell from her lungs. Stuttered and fell and stuttered and fell until every inhalation brought her lower than she ever felt before. She descended to a watery and vivid hell. For a brief moment, she looked at the jagged fragments of the broken mug and thought the ugliest thoughts. She had always known such thoughts were there, lurking in her, but each time she had been able to push them away.

Reaching for a fragment of the mug's handle, she ran the sharp edge of it against her thumb. Her breath pulsed loudly in her ears. Her hands moved as if through molasses. She dug the shard into her thumb, and a bright red drop bloomed on her skin. She stared at the cut and then she lost focus of it and stared widely out into her house. This house that her father had helped her buy. This house that she had meant to fill with his love and instead filled with minimalist, utilitarian bullshit.

The beige was everywhere, her furniture, her floors, her skin. And then she looked at the bright red spot on her thumb, this small, irrefutable proof of her aliveness, a beacon shining into the storm, and she felt an eerie calm. A certainty rose from the depths of her, seeming so absurd in this moment that she actually started laughing. Her laughter rang out, reverberating against every hard surface and wall of the dining room, so that it seemed to Clare as if a hundred people were laughing. A manic chorus of glee. A stadium full of mirth. She laughed again, rolling onto her side and reaching for a kitchen towel to wipe her face and her hand.

Despite her anxiety and fear and worries for the future, the certainty stayed with her. She knew what she would do.

thirty-seven

IT TOOK a few more hours before Clare had sobered up enough to get behind the wheel of her car. Mount Diablo was not very far, but it felt far as Clare wound her way up to the summit. She'd gathered up her father's ashes, a warm coat, and all the resolve she could muster.

It was dark out, the kind of late that soon begins to be early. And cold, even in the car. Clare wrapped her coat tighter around herself. When she arrived at the summit's parking lot, dawn had just begun to filter through the horizon, a pinkish orange breaking against the jagged edge of the treeline.

Cradling the box of ashes gingerly as if it were a baby, Clare got out of the car and stepped as close to the edge of the railing as she could, staring into the vastness below.

Her mother sounded confused when she answered the video call. "Clare? Do you have any idea what time it is?"

"No," she answered truthfully. "Were you sleeping?"

"No," Carole lied, wiping the sleep from her eyes and sitting up in bed. The soft wheeze of Simon snoring littered the background. "Where are you?"

"Mount Diablo. I wanted you to be here when——" She held the ashes up so her mother could see.

"Oh." A sharp wind blew in from the range. Clare clutched the ashes to her chest once more. "Clare, are you all right? Are you ... are you angry with me?"

Another gust of wind came and stung her cheeks with cold. "I was," she said, "but now I'm not."

"Oh," Carole said again. "I know that I'm ... that I can be ... hard on you." Her mother seemed to be struggling to find the words. "I just ... you and your father were my whole world. I married young, I never got an education. I worked and cleaned and changed diapers and fed you. And well, I ... I wanted more ... for you. More for your life."

"I'm sorry I disappointed you."

"Darling, you haven't disappointed me."

"That's not true. You say I haven't and then you make all these little comments that show how you really feel."

"I'm sorry, Clare. I'm trying. It's not always easy for me to see why you do ... certain things."

"Like date women?"

"Well, yes, frankly. That's one of them."

"Because I want to. My sexuality isn't some rebellion or getting back at you. I don't know why that's so hard for you to understand."

"Clare." Her mother had never used her first name this much. When she was a child she had thought her name was darling until she was five and someone finally clued her in. "I only want your life to be easy. And if you end up with a woman your life will be harder."

"Everyone's life is hard, mom. And it's way harder if someone goes against who they are. ... And I do love a woman. Her name is Julia. I might have lost her because I was afraid to be myself. I don't want to lie or hide or be careful with my heart anymore. Not with her or with you or anyone."

They were quiet for a few moments. The wind continued to whip itself into a frenzy, twisting Clare's hair this way and that. Clare wrapped her coat still tighter around herself, as if it could protect her from her own heart. "You sound like your father," Carole said sweetly. "I see so much of him in you."

"You do?"

"Yes, all the time." Clare held the box to her chest. It was surprisingly heavy. "You're both stoic on the outside but actually big softies. Remember how your father would cry during any movie where a dog died?"

Clare did remember. "It was the only time I saw him cry." Her father, like most of the men in her life, had been hard to read. Clare conjured up an image of him, not from when he was dying, but long before, to a time when Clare didn't even know the word cancer. She thought of his broad features, his wispy hair, his masculinity neither brutish nor overwhelming. The way he had 15 pairs of the same jeans and flannel shirts. The way he shuffled everywhere, feet whispering on the linoleum floor, on every surface. That draggy walk earned him the nickname Shackles, which Clare both abhorred and begrudgingly respected. (Clare only ever had cutesy nicknames that she hated. Clare Bear. Clare-inet.) The way he was always adjusting his thick bifocals, especially when he was reading, usually some cheap thriller. Something unknown and unknowable in his eyes that Clare had been desperate to understand. She knew a vulnerability was there, but it had not been offered to her. That she would never know that part of him filled her with an immense sadness, as if she had failed an impossible test.

When he died, she felt like someone turned the volume

of her life all the way down. She hadn't meant to mute herself—she only wanted to feel closer to him. Perhaps if she became unreadable she could tap into some hidden vibration, some cosmic jostling of the particles that she shared with him. But instead it only hardened her, gave her a glossy, candy-coated shell that kept everyone at a safe distance. Everyone except Julia.

"I think he's ready for his last adventure," Carole said.

Wiping the tears from her face, Clare set the phone down on a rock nearby, tilting it so her mother could watch. Then she removed the lid, heaved the box high up above her head, and sent the ashes flying. The wind picked up, sending a cloud of white down the side of the mountain, billowing up and over and nibbling on the trees and branches as it sailed past.

Together they watched in silence as the ashes performed their beautiful and strange choreography. Clare knew she and her mother had a long way to go toward understanding each other, and maybe they'd never get there, but for now, Clare looked out into the pink-gray dawn, at the promise and possibility and vastness of the future below, and she let it be enough. She let it go.

thirty-eight

THE K STEW HAIKU REVIEW

Lizzie
Lezzie Borden! See
What I did ther? I'm funk. FUNK!
I'm SRUNK. Dammit.

#FreeLezzzzzie

When Julia woke up, a team of horses stampeded through her head and she was wearing all of her clothes. It was night still. How could the day not be over? The whiskey had done a shitty job. Julia rubbed her eyes, which were itchy and dry from falling asleep in her contacts. She sat up, then decided to brush her teeth and get some water. To have something to do. She changed into her glasses and got back into bed, pulling the red duvet cover up to her chin.

She thought about calling Paula, who was better in a crisis than she was. But then, Julia had been calling Paula a lot that weekend. Maybe she deserved a respite from Julia's imprecise yet all-consuming pain.

She then thought about calling her mother. It had been a while, though, since Julia had called. Her mother might be mad at her for not calling her as often as Candace did. How often *did* Candace call their mother? Daily? Every few days? Julia couldn't remember but it felt like too much when Candace had mentioned it.

Maybe Julia should hit up the thrift or vintage stores. That might make her feel better. She'd have to wear sunglasses to disguise her ugly-crying, but that would be fine. Maybe it'd make her feel glamorous and European. Maybe she'd don a frilly scarf and toss her head frenchfully. But then she remembered it was nighttime and no stores would be open. She hunkered deeper into bed, wishing somebody would bring her a Totino's Party Pizza. Or a hug. Or both.

The phone rang and excitement leapt into Julia's face. Clare! But then she recognized "It's a Small World," and realized it was her sister, the precise last person she wanted to talk to. Maybe she'd locked herself out of her car again, which would give Julia about three seconds of schadenfreude-induced joy. She pressed accept.

As soon as Candace said hello, however, Julia began to weep.

"Oh," Candace said, startled, unsure of where to begin. "Are you okay? What is it? What happened?"

Julia didn't know if it was her rawness or the hangover or loneliness or sheer dumb timing, but she found herself telling Candace everything—what had happened between her and Clare, about the failed business Britt had dragged her into, and the resulting debt she was shackled with. And about how she might lose her job on Monday.

"How much did Britt leave you holding the bag for?"

Julia told Candace the amount and thought she heard her sister gasp, ever so softly. And then she said, "Okay. I'll Venmo you. What's your handle?"

"What?" Julia must've misheard.

"What's your handle? I'll send it to you."

"No no no. I couldn't do that to you. It's not your problem, it's mine. I'll handle it."

Candace sighed. "I know it's not my problem, dummy, but let me help you."

"I can't."

"Christ on a stick, Julia! You've been doing this for years. You think you're such a cowboy and you don't let anyone help you."

"That's not true."

"Yes, it is. So stop being a dodo and let me do this for you. We all need help. How the hell do you think I got through medical school? It wasn't a magical fairy!"

Julia stammered, clutching the blanket tighter around her like the child she suddenly felt like she was. "Are ... are you sure? You don't see me as ... a loser?"

"Asking for help doesn't make you a loser, *loser*—it makes you human."

Julia paused. Her heart began to pound. "Are you gonna tell mom?"

"Not if you don't want me to."

"Thank you." Julia felt the whiskey leaking out of her face. She felt both relief and embarrassed and wished she could take back her earlier unkind thought about Candace locking herself out of her car.

"I don't know why you're so secretive, though. Mom

cares about you. She just wants to know what's going on with you. And so do I."

"You and mom have your little party of two. I'm just a third wheel—always have been." Julia felt pouty and tragic. She wished she hadn't finished off the whiskey and that her head wasn't pounding.

"Is that what you think? Really? You left us. You left the actual country, remember? For years! You disconnected yourself from us. You didn't even come home for the holidays!"

"I sent a postcard," Julia muttered weakly. Her phone chimed. Candace's payment had gone through.

"You did," Candace admitted. "And mom still has it up on her fridge all these years later. I have to see that stupid cartoon elf mooning me every time I get a La Croix." Candace's voice still seethed at Julia, but she was laughing now. A stocky laugh. A soupy, swimmy laugh. Big and coarse and undelicate, the same way Julia laughed.

"You've always been the 'cool' one, you know? The free spirit. The adventurer. For chrissake, you should never be able to get away with half the weird shit you wear, but somehow you make it work. I've always felt boring and predictable by comparison."

Julia could not believe what she was hearing. *Candace, the doctor! The successful one! The golden child! She compared herself to me?* How had their lines gotten so crossed? How did they not think to reach for each other amid such a glorious and wrong tangle? She felt a thrilling lightness at this novel image of her sister. She seemed to Julia like a wholly new thing, a Magic Eye painting she had been staring obliquely at for years, only to finally glimpse the unicorn inside it while not even trying. She was so moved she thought she might cry again.

"I wish I could hug you right now," Julia said.

"Hug me tomorrow morning. Mom wants to do breakfast at IHOP. You should come."

"Okay," Julia said, elation mixed with sadness at the thought of Clare and her father, all the coffee they would no longer enjoy together. Someday her mother would be gone and Candace, too. But tomorrow, they would eat pancakes and Julia would tell her mom about her life. No more lying. No more hiding. "Oh, Candace?"

"Yeah?"

"What were you calling about?"

"Oh, right. Mom wants her Tupperware back. Bring it tomorrow or else you're banned from breakfast from here on out."

———

Clare arrived early at work on Monday. She didn't bother with makeup. She threw her hair in a bun sloppily, then fished out the only pair of jeans she owned from the back of her closet. They were from college but with a little squirming, she was able to get them on. *HaHA! Take that, time.*

She felt free already. She briefly considered rollerblading to work, as her drunk impulse purchases had arrived that morning. The look on everyone's faces as she rolled off into the sunset, not even bothering to look back at their stunned mouths and crinkled eyebrows, would really be something.

But Clare did not know how to rollerblade, not even as a child, and she wanted her last day to be as triumphant as possible, considering the circumstances. Perhaps she'd go rollerblading later, however. She would have plenty of free time, after all.

In her office, she packed up her few possessions, including a W;nkdIn hoodie, which she unfolded and placed over her head, feeling its cocoon of softness overtake her like a hug. She glanced at the inspirational quotes calendar, which read, "Nothing is impossible, unless you can't do it." She didn't like that one, however, so flipped forward a few days until she found one that she did. "Today is the first day of the rest of your life."

Better.

With her chin high, she walked slowly down the hall toward the rest of her life, which was in conference room C, where the all-hands meeting was about to take place.

The people at W;nkdIn glanced briefly at Clare, then returned to their chittering. Rodrigo adjusted his pompadour while looking at his phone. Yolanda was discussing the latest TikTok meme with Sofie or Saffron, the intern. Clare was embarrassed to realize she never did learn her name. The Sara/hs were unwrapping a loaf of seitan, which Paula obligingly sliced and placed small servings on paper plates to pass down. Julia stood up to help her, refusing to meet Clare's gaze when she looked in her direction.

Clare expected this reaction but it still stung. She resisted the urge to run to Julia and beg on her knees for another chance. But no. She would stick to the plan. The plan was the thing! The thing that would convince Julia that Clare was worthy of her forgiveness.

Nikki sat with her hands clasped together on the table. Her face was placid, almost pharmaceutical. The recording she had made of Clare's therapy session sat just to the left of her, as if she couldn't wait to press the trigger. Clare took a deep breath and stood at the back of the room. Her hands were shaking so she shoved them into her hoodie pocket.

Feeling the safety of this warm and fuzzy pouch, she suddenly saw the allure of hoodies.

"Hey, hi, everyone," Clare started. "I have something to say."

People shifted in their swivel chairs and bounced on their yoga balls. Sarah blew a little too hard on her oolong tea, sending its nutty aroma toward the front of the room.

Yolanda scrolled through the virtual agenda. "I don't see you on here," she said.

"Right, no, it's not ... official."

"Is this about how the snack tray is empty by 9:03 a.m.?" Rodrigo said. "Because I have feelings about that. Also, could we get some new bubbly water flavors? Lime is so last Hot Girl Summer."

"And there's, like, not enough dairy-free coffee creamer alternatives, which I find oppressive," said Sofie or Saffron, the intern.

Paula muttered but not softly enough, "We have soy, almond, and oat milks! What more do you want?"

"Cashew, walnut, macadamia, hemp," Sofie or Saffron said. "I could go on."

Clare cleared her throat and steadied herself. If she didn't speak now, she might never do it. Not simply due to nerves but also because the alternative milk wars were not likely to cease within the next hour. "Today will be my last day at W;nkdIn."

It's not that Clare expected fanfare, or a chorus of gasps and shocked faces when she announced that she was quitting. But she expected more than the *nothing* that had followed. She cleared her throat awkwardly.

"Is this because of the beta dates?" Rodrigo asked, still texting.

"No," Clare said, correcting herself, hands shaking in

her hoodie pocket. "Well, kind of, actually. I'm quitting W;nkdIn because I'm in love with Julia."

That did it.

Rodrigo stopped checking his phone. Yolanda's eyes widened. Sofie or Saffron began live-tweeting Clare's confession. Nikki sniffed at the air, confused. Sara's mouth fell open and Sarah clasped her hand against Sara's mouth, embarrassed. Julia twined bits of hair in her fingers, a habit she engaged in when nervous, Clare knew.

"I have been in love with Julia for a long time, since before I was her manager." She glanced at the Sara/hs and the CEO, who sat motionless and unreadable. Everyone was looking at Julia, who in turn would not shift her eyes up from the table. "I ... I should have said something sooner, and I didn't mean for this to happen, but well."

Come on, Julia, Clare found herself silently pleading. *Look up. Look up!*

She looked at the Sara/hs and the CEO. "I know I let you down. My behavior is inexcusable, and that's why I'm stepping down. You deserve someone better. Someone who can uphold the appearance and reputation of the company." She paused briefly. "But not Nikki, who secretly recorded a session between me and my therapist and was prepared to use it to blackmail me for my position."

A communal gasp rose from the table. "Nikki!" the CEO shouted.

"Don't believe her! She lies, she's lying! I would never ... I ... how could you trust someone so—" Nikki clasped her hand over her phone and placed it in her pocket.

Clare forged ahead, her neck as straight and tall as an archer's bow. "In keeping my feelings for Julia a secret, I let myself hurt her ... hurt us ... and all because I was so scared of losing this job ... and of you finding out I wasn't ... who you thought I was."

She wiped a tear from her cheek brusquely, annoyed at its presence at such a time, and walked slowly toward Julia, who was tearing a napkin into a thousand pieces. "But I'm not going to lie or hide anymore. I won't do that to Julia or to myself. No more secrets."

When she got to Julia she kneeled on the industrial carpet in front of her and said, "I love you."

"I quit, too!" Paula shouted, knocking a small tray of artificial sweeteners off the table accidentally. She knocked over a few more intentionally, for good measure. "I've had it with this dead-end job with you entitled snobs always whining about snacks and macadamia milks while I wait on you like a servant. Fuck that, I'm out!" She stormed out the door of Conference Room C.

"Sara and I are getting divorced," Sarah shouted.

"Sarah! I thought we were waiting until after the holidays."

"I got swept up!"

An eruption of conversations, quacking, honking, and disarray burst forth into the fluorescent room. Nostrils flared angrily. White boards were aggressively erased. In the tumult, Julia ran out of the room, leaving Clare in her position of penitence by the table.

"Wait," Clare shouted, chasing and catching her at the far end of the hallway. "Where are you going? You don't have anything to say to me?"

Julia looked longingly at Clare's face. She lay her hand gently against Clare's cheek, where the heat of it coiled down the length of Clare's spine. "I love you, too," Julia whispered. "And I can't. It's too late. I'm sorry."

Julia took off down the hall and toward the double doors that led to the outside world, the sound of her combat boots ricocheting on the hardwood floors sounding to Clare like the cruelest applause.

thirty-nine

AT THE 7-ELEVEN around the corner from W;nkdIn's office, Julia met up with Paula.

"I did it!" Paula squealed. "I left! Ha! *I* was the one to leave, for once. This demands a celebration. Wherefore art thou, carbs?"

Julia's stomach churned. Her insides, once neatly and delicately arranged inside of her now felt like a 10-car pileup.

Paula picked up a candy bar. "Soy lecithin, PGPR ... what on earth is—oh fuck it, we're celebrating." She grabbed five of them, a bottle of sparkling champagne, and a large bag of Funyuns and headed for the register, tugging Julia by the arm. "Are you okay? That was ... a lot to take in."

"Yeah," Julia could barely muster a response. "I did the right thing though, didn't I? I ... I stood up for myself?"

"You don't sound so sure."

Julia searched Paula's face for backup, or at least some certainty, but instead found something akin to confusion, pity, and gastrointestinal upsetness. "Okay, what? Say it, whatever it is."

"Real talk?"

Julia winced. "Real talk."

"I don't get it. She loves you. She quit her job for you! Clare! And you're gonna walk away? Now?"

"I tried, Paula. I really did."

"Oh, you mean like how you *tried* to run an essential oils business or how you *tried* to be a wedding planner."

"I'm not sure what you're getting at—"

"Even when your shitheel boss in the Peace Corps fired you. You loved that job. You loved those kids. And you just walked away. You didn't even try to fight."

"What the fuck are you talking about, Paula?"

"You are my favorite person, Julia, and I love you, but you can be a quitter. Especially when things get tough."

"That is not fair—" Julia felt a defensiveness well in her chest, prickly with spines.

"And some things are worth quitting—I'm not saying that's never the case. Like when Britt ran off with that Auntie Em girl, I was like, 'Bye, Felicia' because good fucking riddance! But I can't sit here in silence after having listened to you tell me how much you love this girl and then watch you walk away without even so much as a shrug."

"But you ... you told me I deserved someone who'd go to bat for me."

"Look, I'm not saying Clare doesn't have her issues. We all do. But she went out on a limb for you today. She's *trying*. And she didn't have to, especially after all the shit you've pulled."

Julia trembled. She felt her throat tighten and a sour, vinegar taste coat her tongue. How had it come to this? She wondered. How had she become such an asshole? And not only that, but an asshole crying in a 7-Eleven?

Paula placed a gentle arm on Julia's shoulder. "You

know I'm here for you and will be no matter what you decide. Just, you know, think on it."

"Okay," Julia said.

"Okay, boo. Take a candy bar." Paula deposited the chocolate bar into Julia's coat pocket and wrapped her in a hug. "You don't get enough PGPR in your diet."

———

A week passed and Julia still didn't know what to do with herself. She got in her car and drove East until she found herself at Middle Harbor Shoreline Park overlooking the San Francisco Bay. The smell of goose poop was over-whelming and Julia tried to step around the many brown and white piles, as if they were land mines, while she walked to the water's edge. Enormous lifts and colorful shipping containers flanked her on all sides, which made her feel somewhat protected, as if being guarded by ancient sentinels.

The cold wind whipped her face as she walked, her engineer boots crunching against the small strip of sand that masqueraded as a beach. She imagined herself here with Clare, walking hand in hand as the wind reddened their cheeks and knocked their hair all around. The image filled her with such immediate sadness that tears threatened to erupt out of her like a volcano. She stifled them by trying a trick she'd read on Reddit about how to stop unwanted erections—by flexing her bicep with all her intensity until the blood drained from elsewhere and surged into her arm. But it didn't work. The tears came anyway and then the mucus and then her arm felt sore from the straining, so she flexed the other one to even them out.

A fisherman in a hooded coat on the pier smirked at her as she performed these movements, so she pretended she was doing a workout, lifting her arms over her head, bending at the hip. She didn't know why she cared what the fisherman thought of her. Maybe it was simply posturing or wanting to be as alone as she felt. His presence disrupted her sadness, rendered it performative and strange somehow, so she then behaved performatively and strangely.

She kept walking, her mind a plastic bag caught on the antenna of a junked-out car. Clare *loved* her. She'd said it; she'd meant it. She'd done what Julia asked, what she'd wanted—so why was Julia so conflicted?

Maybe Paula was right. Maybe she was a quitter.

Clare came into her life like a tornado, uprooting houses and breaking levees and filling everything with water and trees and the detritus of the universe. How could she ever rebuild after such a reckoning? Wasn't it better to just start over?

And then it hit her. They needed to start over. Sometimes only a fire can show you the way out.

Julia had always been the bold one, the reckless one. The one who took chances and faced down demons and became ill with dysentery trying to teach elementary school students how to read. Her life was too much like a struck match, quick to ignite and just as quick to extinguish.

Clare tempered her, she realized now. Clare was the wet wick upon which her light could carry on. Clare was the quiet, simmering, radiant moon, its steady, subdued light bursting in the lining of Julia's skin. She had to find Clare! She had to tell her she was wrong. She had to apologize and make it right. But more than that, she needed a plan.

She called her sister. "Hey Candace, it's me. Does Johnny still play the cello?"

After hours and multiple phone calls, her legs ached, she smelled faintly of algae, and she had multiple blisters on her toes and heels. But she was almost done. Or at least she thought she was.

Paula was the last on her list. Her voice jumped as she told Paula her plan.

Paula was strangely quiet, before saying, "Uh, when do you plan on doing this?"

"I booked them for 8 p.m."

"You might want to do it sooner."

"What? Why?"

"Rodrigo told me that Clare is flying to Europe tonight to see her mom. Her flight leaves in 2 hours. She asked him to watch her sad plant while she's away."

"What!"

"I know! That thing is not even alive, I'm pretty sure."

"Not the plant, Paula!"

"Oh right. Shit, yeah. You better get going!"

"I'm trying!"

"Do or do not do—there is no try!"

forty

THE DAY WAS WANING by the time Clare had finished packing her suitcase. Clouds crept over the setting sun, plunging the world into darkness and light, darkness and light. It felt right somehow, this changefulness. Like a toddler playing a cosmic joke on the grand light switch of the world.

She only had a few more minutes before she had to leave for the airport. Her mother would be thrilled to see her after so long, at least. And she hoped the last-minute trip would distract her from stampeding thoughts of Julia, even though she knew it wouldn't.

A sharp, fiery knot found its way to her center, something rude and obvious and gutting. Clare could feel the sadness rub up against her like a cat. An ocean of heaviness washed over her.

But then, something unexpected.

Music. Soft and serenading. Quiet and surging. Where was it coming from? Clare looked down the hallway, half expecting to find a celestial cloud chorus in her living room, brandishing brass trumpets and smiling through chubby cheeks.

But that was absurd. Clare grabbed her coat and suitcase, and the music continued to come. Louder now. It sounded as if it was right outside her house.

She flung the door open, goosebumps lighting up her arms like prayer votives when she saw Julia standing at the bottom of the steps. She wore no coat, smelled strongly of algae, and was clearly out of breath. When Julia looked back at her, the sun broke through the clouds once more, flooding the sky with lightness.

"I know I messed up," Julia said, rising up the stone steps and closing the distance between them. "Many times, it turns out. I was hurt and I was angry ... but I ... I love you. Don't go. Stay with me. I want to spend my life loving you. I want to have adventures with you and be silly with you and receive your imaginary mime flowers and laugh with you when you lock yourself out of your office—"

"That was one time—"

The clouds pushed their way forward again, sending the sun backstage. Julia stepped closer, worrying the hem of her shirt. "Will you give us another chance? Please? Will you give me another chance to make things right?"

"What about W;nkdIn?"

"I resigned. A few days after you did. I realized it didn't matter." Julia clasped Clare's hands in hers. "Nothing matters if I don't have you."

The bushes on the edge of Clare's yard began to rustle, and a stranger appeared, along with the soft, sweeping sighs of a violin concerto. *No, it couldn't be,* Clare thought. Then three others emerged, a cellist, a violist, and another violinist. The source of the music she'd heard coming into view.

The string quartet emerged from the bushes they'd been hiding in, dusted off the leaves and bits of trees from their black ensembles, and started up again. They played a song that sounded to Clare like everything in her dismantled life had been put back together.

It might not have been exactly the way it had been before, but that was, perhaps, the point.

The bows glided along their strings and Clare was reborn. She clasped Julia's face in her hands and she was reborn. And then they were kissing, Clare's synapses hot and alive in Julia's arms and she was reborn.

The sun made its last bow before sinking beneath the horizon, streams of red and pink tendrils reaching, interlacing with the shadows as the music played. Clare saw Julia's searching eyes and felt her breath, which came out in short, staggered bursts, on Clare's cheeks. And then they were laughing, big, coarse laughs with ruddy cheeks and tear-glistened faces.

"I guess this means you read my comments?" Clare laughed.

"What comments?"

"Oh my god, you didn't check your blog?"

"Um no. I was busy trying to convince a string quartet to serenade your bush."

"Well? What are you waiting for?"

Julia fired up her phone and was startled to find dozens of notifications on the K Stew Haiku Review blog.

She clicked on the latest comment, under Julia's review of *Happiest Season*.

It read:

Hold your chestnuts. This
is a great Christmas rom-com.
So merry and gay.

Julia clicked through several others. There were dozens of haiku comments. Almost one for every movie she'd reviewed. Julia clicked through and scanned as many as she could, transfixed. She felt the words were dancing with her own. She felt amorphous and strange, alternately heavy and buoyant, excited and a little nauseous.

It was Clare. Clare wrote these. All of them. She must've spent the whole week watching these movies for her, writing these little love letters to her. And Julia hadn't even seen them.

"You didn't," Julia said, kissing Clare up and down the geography of her face, across her jawline, on her nose, and each corner of her lips.

"I did."

"You watched a hundred Kristen Stewart movies?"

"Just about. And I gotta say, I'm starting to see the appeal. Who knew she had such range? And that Princess Diana portrayal—" Clare chef-kissed the tips of her fingers.

" I am so completely in love with you."

"I'm so completely in love with you, too."

"Is that a yes, then? You'll stay? We'll be together?"

"Yes, yes, yesyesyes."

The violins swooped and swarmed, the music pitching into a frenzy as they kissed once more, Julia's happiness kaleidoscopic, shifting with each brush of the light and Clare's fingers and the ruthless and strange and beautiful world shifting beneath their feet.

She tried to hold onto the moment, even as she felt it slipping through her fingers, even as she knew she would forget and then remember and then forget again the unbearable romance of a beautiful woman hiring a string quartet to play you a song, reminding you how sweet and tender and perfect life can be.

epilogue

CLARE SAT down at an outdoor table at the tiny cafe in Le Marais district of Paris. She brushed a few croissant crumbs off her mustard yellow blazer and the blue-and-white striped sailor shirt underneath it that showed a tasteful hint of cleavage. She still wasn't used to wearing such bright colors or of wearing clothing that showed so much skin, but allowed herself to be not-so-subtly influenced by Julia's fashion-forwardness. Plus, she hadn't had an eczema flareup in months, and Clare found it freeing to not have to cover up, the way she used to with her blemishes and red patches. She noticed more than a few heads turn as she sat at the cafe's small table, its maroon awning offering protection against the slight drizzle.

A small part of her still couldn't believe she was here. The last time she was in Paris she was 18, a moon-eyed teenager ogling the bare-chested dancers at Moulin Rouge and trying to pretend not to in front of her high school boyfriend, whose parents had paid for their trip.

Julia came out of the cafe holding a cappuccino with a heart-shape swirled into the foam. "Your coffee's coming out in a minute," Julia said, a coy grin on her face, which Clare briefly wondered about but didn't question.

Julia squeezed Clare's hand when she sat down next to her. It had been raining when they walked to the cafe, but neither woman cared. Julia described the slight, chilly spray as "the most beautiful angels spitting on me," and Clare fell in love with her even more.

They were celebrating so much on this trip. The first was the one year anniversary of their new business, an all-female led organization that trained, prepared, and mentored women who were looking to get back into the workforce or to switch careers entirely. Clare and Julia co-founded the organization at the suggestion of one of W;nkdIn's board members, who was impressed with the work they had done with the female-leadership initiative and offered to be an angel investor.

Though still in the early stages, their reputation was spreading, and they were already making headway, helping women with their resumes, interview skills, researching, and scouting out potential new career tracks—one of whom was Paula.

With Clare's expertise and Julia's innovativeness, they were able to help Paula land her dream job, a spot as a costume designer (and dancing Stormtrooper) in Disney-land Paris's *Star Wars on Ice*. This was the second reason they were celebrating, to see Paula's show and to meet her new girlfriend, who played both an ice-skating Twi'lek and a cuddly Ewok in the show, respectively.

"I can't believe Paula finally found a steady girlfriend," Julia said, stroking Clare's thigh under the table.

"Me neither, but did she answer the important question?"

"Which is?"

"Is she an order muppet or a chaos muppet?"

Julia laughed. "Chaos, for sure."

"So there's hope for us yet—two star-crossed muppets."

Clare leaned forward and kissed Julia softly on the mouth, surprised at how her insides melted under Julia's touch as if it was the first time.

Clare snuck a sip of Julia's coffee contentedly, relishing the warmth of it against her cold lips. "I can't believe you're finally going to meet my mom," Clare said. "Though I feel like you have already, given how much she video calls you."

And then Clare's cell phone rang, as if she had summoned her mother telepathically. Bemused, Clare picked up the phone and held it horizontally so both of their faces fit in the frame.

"Hello, darlings!" Carole said. "My, Julia, you just keep getting more beautiful. And Clare! I can ... barely see your pores." Carole whispered to Julia, as if Clare couldn't hear her, "The snail cream I sent must be working."

Clare laughed and rolled her eyes. Some things might never change, but maybe this was okay.

"Simon and I are in an Uber. What's the name of the cafe again? Oh, two hands on the wheel, Pierre, *si vou plait!*"

"Trois cerises—it means three cherries," Julia said. Clare smiled at Julia again, remembering their first drink at 1221 and the three cherries Julia requested in her manhattan. She couldn't believe how long ago it felt. And also how short. With Julia, it seemed like Clare was making up for several lost lifetimes. She blinked and 50 years passed. She blinked again and it had only been 5 seconds. She hadn't known such happiness could exist and how perfectly it fit in her arms.

"Trois cerises," Carole repeated to the driver. "Pierre

was just telling us that he broke up with his boyfriend of seven years because he wouldn't commit. Let that be a lesson to us all, hmm? Carole winked at Clare. "It's time to get that D on lock. Tick-tock."

Julia pulled her face out of the frame so that she could laugh-cough into her napkin. Clare's insides clenched, her face began to redden. "I don't know what you think the D stands for, mom, but—"

"Why, for Dawes, of course," Carole interjected. "Anyway, Simon and I got you a housewarming gift. It's a Monstera Deliciosa—a Swiss cheese plant! Very rare, but hard to kill, darling. Perfect for your lack of nurturing experience." Carole shoved the plant in the phone's tiny frame, filling the screen with a blurry green.

Clare couldn't help but be touched. She'd finally have a new plant for her macrame plant hanging. "That's really thoughtful of you, mom. Thank you," Clare said.

"Oh, don't thank me, thank Simon. It was his idea."

Simon's nostrils appeared in the frame. "You're welcome, loves. About time Clare had some color in her home, eh?"

"Oh, slow down, darling," Carole said to Pierre the driver. "It's not a race." To Clare she said, "We'll see you soon, darlings. Ciao ciao!"

"See you soon!" Julia said.

As Clare hung up the phone, a man passed by the cafe with a Shar-Pei. Julia pointed excitedly, "Oh, that looks just like Brian, doesn't it?"

"Brian?"

"Yolanda's dog, remember? He came to the office every Friday!"

A thousand volts of recognition hit Clare, as she remembered this previously unsolved mystery. "Oh my god! Brian, yes. Her *dog*, of course." Clare chuckled to herself. "Not her husband then, but her dog."

"What? Oh, her husband's name is Brian, too."

"They're both Brian?"

"Both Brian." Julia nodded.

Clare laughed even harder, just as a waiter dressed in all black appeared with a silver tray from the cafe.

"Votre café, m'dame," he said and set down a mug that Clare recognized immediately. It was the IHOP mug that Clare's father had given her—the mug that Clare had broken into a dozen pieces during her drunken night of reckoning. It was no longer broken now, Clare could see, but was instead threaded through with the most beautiful seams of gold.

Clare's legs felt liquid. She was glad to be already sitting down lest she faint right here in this Parisian cafe.

"Surprise!" Julia said. "I found your kintsugi supplies in the closet. Happy anniversary, beautiful."

Clare couldn't speak. Words eddied and swelled in her tidally but when she opened her mouth, the waves did not break against her shores. Instead they dove back inside of her and erupted as tears instead.

She pulled Julia's face to hers, inhaled her cinnamon lips and earth-smelling musk, kissed her again and again. Clare closed her eyes against the soft of Julia's hands, moving her face into the comforting curve of it. When Julia's fingers lightly brushed her lip, she opened her mouth, and kissed the tips of Julia's fingers, tasting the skin and wanting more salt and more heat and more *more*.

For the millionth time this year, she'd found herself marveling. The button of Julia's nose, which turned ever so slightly upward at the tip. The rose petal maze of her lips. The four gray hairs that Julia was self-conscious about and which Clare found irresistible. The toned sweep of her broad back, her always warm hands, her garish, unstoppable laugh. Clare loved all of it, loved all of *her*, and could not believe her incredibly good fortune at having found Julia in spite of everything life had thrown at them.

She picked up the mug and watched the steam rise in the cold afternoon. The air tasted better here, she decided, unsure whether it was Paris or her new life or happiness— or some combination of everything. The air was denser, fuller. Each breath she inhaled felt like her nostrils were wrapped in an embrace.

"To us," Clare said.

Julia picked up her cup in kind. "To us!"

Clare raised the coffee to her lips, the bright-bursting earthiness filling her mouth. She let it coat her tongue.

pivot

Read on for a teaser of Pivot, *the next romantic comedy in the* Love Where You Work *series by Anna Pulley. Coming August 2022.*

Paula Suarez could never get her tentacles to stay.

She adjusted one—a long, thin latex tube dyed blue that bobbed just to the side of her face. It was one of the many tubes that made up the elaborate and heavy headpiece she was wearing. Some fell almost to her knees, where they dangled like puppy-less leashes in the refrigerated air of the massive convention center hall.

It wasn't like her to be so fidgety, but then, it wasn't like her to do something as grand and potentially humiliating as she was planning to do today. She smoothed a hand over the skin-tight metallic baby blue bodysuit that hugged her every contour. It was her best costume yet. She knew it. And this knowing filled her with an admiration and confidence that didn't exist outside the world of cosplay, as much as she wished such confidence would eke into her ordinary, day-to-day life.

She pressed her fingertips into the intricate black neck, waist, and wrists adornments and grinned. In spite of the limited mobility of the dress, it made her feel celestial and powerful. Like a goddess. A shiny, blue, alien goddess, a queen, a mother of dragons, going warp speed ahead! Not to, you know, mix fandoms.

And then, she tripped.

Her lithe regal form twisted into a grotesque flail as she stumbled forward into a group of My Little Ponies, clutching one by their rainbow tail in order to keep herself from falling face first to the ground.

After apologizing profusely, she realized her confidence was no longer so godly.

She texted Julia for backup.

Paula: **Tell me I'm great. Please.**

Julia: **You're a national treasure! Why? What's up?**

Paula: **I'm about to hit on the most popular cosplayer in the continental US at one of the most popular Cons in the US.**

Julia: **Nerdi Gras???**

Paula: **Ahem, Just Cos Con. We've been DMing about costume design and I think … she might be into me. But you don't just waltz up to Mistress Riina and ask her out. She's too famous. It needs to be big. Bold! A grand romantic gesture.**

Julia: **You know I love a grand gesture. So you're gonna do it after all?**

Paula: **I am! Soon. But right now, I need validation.**

Julia: **Your eyes are like deep pools of awesome sauce. Your style is so en pointe it makes ballerinas give you unintentional bitch-face, which everyone knows is a sign of respect amongst ballerinas. (I know because I was one for seven minutes in second grade.)**

You make great totchos. You know how to fold a fitted sheet!

Julia's odd compliments were working. She had started to feel a little bit better, but then Julia continued.

Julia: **But, wait! Are you sure about this? A public declaration of love is no small thing. I don't want to see you get hurt.**

Paula: **I have a plan! Plus, the situation is perfect. I'm dressed as The Diva and she's dressed as Leeloo.**

Julia: **?**

Paula: **For the love of Joss, from *The Fifth Element*! Bruce Willis and Mila Jovovich. Only one of the greatest sci-fi action movies ever?**

Julia: **Oh, right! Yes, so you're the blue alien super star singer and she's the orange-haired hottie and clearly Bruce Willis was just a diversion until her true lesbian love came along?**

Paula: **Exactly!**

Julia: **Well, that is romantic. I'll give you that. Best of luck, bestie! Give me all the details later.**

Paula: **I will, but it might be a while, considering all the hot gay sex I'm about to have.**

Julia: **You are so cocky when you cosplay. I love it. I guess I won't bore you with the hot gay sex I've been having with Clare.**

Paula: **Gross.com/barf**

JK love you, boo, and I'm so happy for you and Clare!

Paula put her phone in the strap of her boot and jumped up and down a few times, both to ensure her head piece was secure and to work off some of this nervous energy.

Outside in San Jose, the sky was so blue it burned. She'd been too busy inside the hotel convention to pay much thought to the outside world, but had to admit it was beautiful out. Perhaps Paula and her soon-to-be lover would make sweet love on their hotel room's private balcony later and enjoy this fresh, spring air.

Mistress Riina was conducting an interview about 15 feet from where Paula stood. She looked fantastic as Leeloo. The tight, gold leggings with black trim hugged her muscular thighs perfectly. The short, tousled orange hair and micro-fringe bangs looked so real they might not have been a wig. The short, ribbed crop top showed Riina's taut midriff, and the orange rubber suspenders that led down and down to the V of her perfect—

Focus, Paula! She chastised herself. *Don't screw this up.*

When Riina finished her interview, an adoring entourage of fans, handlers, stylists, vloggers, and TikTokers followed shortly behind her. This was it. Paula's chance. She cleared her throat, the lump of her nervousness a hard Werther's candy in her esophagus, and stepped in front of Mistress Riina's path.

Time slowed and blurred as Paula opened her mouth, fearful suddenly that nothing would come out. But then–miracle–it did, and she began to sing The Diva's song, "Il doce suono," changing the name to that of the object of her affection. Not that anyone would know what she was singing. Unless they spoke Italian.

At first, Paula's voice could barely be made out among the clatter and clang of the convention space, but when Riina looked at her–Paula was 6-feet tall in heels–and smiled, a surge stormed through her and she sang louder, with more conviction.

A crowd began to gather, wanting to witness the spectacle, or perhaps were merely confused by the tall, blue, celestial alien singing off-key (yet enthusiastic) soprano at the most famous cosplayer in the United States.

Paula glimpsed in her eye's corners the blue screens of the phones all around her, recording her. She hoped her singing wasn't *too* off. Though Paula had taken singing lessons when she was younger and apprenticed with a musical theater company in college—an apprenticeship that birthed her love of theatrical costumes and also annihilated her spirit—that all felt like another lifetime ago. Even though it was, in reality, four years ago. She hoped any missed notes would come off as endearing to Riina, rather than embarrassing.

As Paula's aria swooped into its dramatic crescendo, the notes swelling and burning as they crossed the threshold of her lips, she dropped to her knees, which was difficult to do in the blue leather mermaid dress. She held out her hand, her lungs galloping, her heart stampeding in her chest, as the song reached its peak.

Riina reached a hand out toward Paula and Paula felt as if she might faint. Out and out the hand went. Where would she touch her? Was it possible to die by fingertip brushing? Paula would soon find out.

But then, as the song eddied and swirled inside of her, releasing all the longing and pent-up agony in Paula's weary soul, Riina's hand found its way to Paula's head piece. She patted her on the head, tenderly, gingerly, as if Paula were a kindergartener or a golden retriever, and continued on past her, into the convention hall.

Nita Funmaker sat with a recorder and a notebook in the hotel's cafe, scribbling to herself. The white lab coat she wore had been accidentally helpful in carrying around all the things she needed to cover the Con. If she'd known being a fake scientist came with this many pockets, she might have considered an earlier career switch.

Her phone pinged in her pocket. Another email from her editor. Nita glimpsed at the text preview.

"Just checking in. How's the story coming along?"

She put the phone away and sighed. If she didn't come up with a story idea soon, Marcus, publisher of the East Bay Weekly (and also her father) would be, to use his words, "majorly bummed."

If she came all this way and failed to sniff out a good story, she'd be too hard on herself about it, then her dad would lecture her on how she was "too serious," and sign her up for an appointment to get her chakras aligned with someone named River or Nyx. She still didn't know what exactly that meant.

In any case, Nita had never been to a cosplay convention before and wasn't sure why he'd chosen her for this assignment.

That was a lie. She knew why he'd chosen her. It was the same reason he'd chosen her to cover DomCon: Strapped for Cash, and the Sacred Sex Goddess Tour, and Fur Real.

You're all business, he'd said to her, on more than one occasion. *There's a wide, wonderful world out there just waiting to be explored.* Her hippie father was possibly one of only a handful on earth who hoped his daughter might discover a newfound purpose in life at the annual furry convention.

She hadn't, but from that assignment, she had developed an appreciation for soft things.

Still, her pieces were popular. She knew this was likely due to the subject matter more than her sparkling prose, but still, she loved the praise. Readers had devoured her piece on the sex goddesses from the Pagan conference. They also loved the piece from the BDSM conference on DIY sex toys, where she'd learned how to fashion a flogger out of rubber bands and a No. 2 pencil. Not that she'd ever flogged anyone. Or had anything approaching intimacy in months. Even her brother's ferrets scurried away when she came near them. Too needy. They could smell it.

Nita sipped at the last dregs of her coffee and looked around her. Everyone else seemed to be having so much fun. Why couldn't she? Maybe her dad was right. Maybe she was too "business." Maybe it was the bad wig.

Just as Nita was about to give up for the day and go back to her hotel room for a nap, a tall woman dressed entirely in blue leather began to sing opera about 15 feet away from where she was sitting. *Well, this may be something*, she told herself, and joined the throng that began to gather around the scene.

Nita finally managed to push her way through to the front of the crowd of sweaty bodies, whose strong odors told her they probably hadn't showered in several days. She led with her recorder, forcing an arm out past several bemused bodies in spandex, latex, elf costumes, and gold bikinis. She reached the second row just in time to hear the blue woman pitch her mouth upon a rich, silky high note, mellow yet full-throated, sailing out into the cavernous ceilings of the convention hall.

Nita felt herself rooted to the floor, her arm and recorder extended outward desperately toward the hypnotic blue mouth, as if Nita was an anthropologist and the woman a newly discovered species.

Nita didn't know the song the woman was singing, but she didn't need to. The woman's lilting, sonorous cries felt to Nita like an act of pure devotion. She felt the song deep in her center, as if she was witnessing something miraculous. Something divine.

Apparently, not everyone felt this way, and certainly not the object of the blue woman's affections, who patted her on the head dismissively and began to walk away in one of the most spectacular rejections Nita had ever witnessed. "Stone cold," as her brother might have said.

The blue woman stopped singing. Her face, which only seconds before had been jubilant and light, was now a wall of pain. And Nita knew the worst was still to come. A mob of con-goers brandishing smartphones began to spray questions at her like artillery fire.

Nita watched the woman stutter and shrink further into herself. Her eyes darted in panic, looking for an escape route. Should she do something? She should do something, right? Nita was not the kind of person to intervene in others' affairs. She preferred to stay on the sidelines.

But then she questioned herself. Such a majestic creature should be the one rescuing Nita! From what? She couldn't say exactly. Perhaps the blue woman could save Nita from her writer's block.

The vloggers swarm thickened, and the woman attempted to shield herself with one of the many blue hoses attached to the sides of her face. Nita shored up her courage. She couldn't stand idly by.

She decided to play the journalist card and pushed herself into the small dense circle of air where the woman was kneeling. "There you are!" Nita said. "I've been looking all over for you."

The woman looked up from between her hands, confusion and panic muddling her.

Nita carried on, dialing up her voice and charm to its

most affable and agreeable levels. If someone had held a mirror to Nita's face just then, they may have seen her pupils replaced by tiny anime rainbows. "We have that interview at 4, remember?" She held out her hand.

The woman seemed to have caught on and took the hand Nita offered. "Right, yeah. I forgot."

"No trouble at all. I know that people as industrious and well-known as you have a lot of demands on their schedule. Come with me."

Nita's compliment had the intended effect, as the crowd now tittered with questions as to who the blue woman was and why she was so important, rather than focusing on the public rejection they had all just witnessed.

Nita pulled the woman up with one hand, and held the other out like an invisible shield as she pressed their bodies through the crush of elbows, foam, mesh, adhesives, and glitter. Once they were at a safe distance, Nita let go of the woman's arm, realizing too late that she felt reluctant to do so. From here Nita could smell the woman's scent, which was otherworldly but also effervescent, like a star fruit mimosa.

"You smell like brunch."

"What?"

"Sorry. Not important." Nita adjusted the orange wig she wore. It itched unbearably. She wasn't a cosplayer but didn't want to come off as an interloper, so decided to wear her Halloween costume from several years back. She still liked it, even though it had collected dust in her closet for ages. "Are you okay?"

"I don't know, but thank you ..." The woman held out her hand.

"Nita."

"Paula." They clasped hands and for a moment Paula

seemed to calm down a little, but then her hand began to shake. She shoved a black thumbnail between her teeth and started chewing. "Oh god, I'm so embarrassed. I can't believe that happened. Did you ... did you see everything?"

"I'm afraid so," Nita said.

"Oh god, oh god, oh god."

Paula's breaths came out in short, staggered bursts. Nita feared she might be on the verge of hyperventilating and steered her to a lounge chair. "Oh, okay, um–," she said, fumbling in her backpack for something–anything–that might soothe this panicked alien goddess. She pulled out a journal, several hair ties, $.85, and a phone charger she thought she'd lost, before she found a folded-up poster of Lucy Lawless dressed as Xena: Warrior Princess. She'd grabbed the promotional poster from one of the booths on her seemingly endless trips around the convention center floor, hunting for interviews.

She held the picture up to Paula's face. "Concentrate on Lucy Lawless. You are just like her: fearless, fierce, unstoppable. Be Xena. Be. Xena."

Find out what happens next at annapulley.com/books

acknowledgments

Thank you, dear reader!

If you enjoyed this book or it entertained you in some way, I'd love it if you left a review on Amazon. Even a line or two is great, as such reviews are invaluable for authors—and they're helpful to other readers, too.

Free bonus gift

As an additional thank you, head to this link to download *Transgressions: Erotic Stories* for free (https://dl.bookfun nel.com/qfqvtjgvhu)

Other thanks go to Cecily, for teaching me about chaos muppet theory, and to Kelly, Anni, Tori, and Lys, who provided insights and commentary on earlier drafts.

about the author

Anna Pulley is a queer, multiracial (white/Native American/Latinx), and hard-of-hearing author. She writes a syndicated sex and dating advice column for the Tribune Content Agency and has been published in *New York* magazine, *Mother Jones* magazine, *The Washington Post*, *San Francisco* magazine (the issue she contributed to won a National Magazine Award), Vice, Salon, BuzzFeed, and many others. She was also named a Top LGBTQ Writer on Medium. Her work has been quoted in Esther Perel's book, *The State of Affairs*. She's been a repeat guest on Dan Savage's podcast, Savage Love, on Daniel M. Lavery's "Dear Prudence" podcast, and on the 99% Invisible podcast, discussing flannel, appropriately.

For more books and updates, visit: https://annapul ley.com or sign up for her occasional, irreverent newsletter: https://annapulley.substack.com

THE LESBIAN SEX HAIKU BOOK (WITH CATS!)

Lesbian sex has been confounding people since the dawn of cucumbers.

Just what is it that two women do together in bed? Find out in this hilarious collection of haikus paired with cat illustrations.

Tegan and Sara said the book was "an adorable and hilarious way to start the day," Cheryl Strayed called it a "must-read," and *Bound* actress Jennifer Tilly said it was "thoroughly charming."

TRANSGRESSIONS: EROTIC STORIES

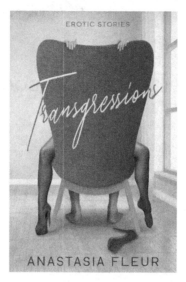

A man has a threesome with his bi girlfriend, her beautiful, occasional lover—and her strap-on. A woman goes on a second date in a public movie theater that turns taboo when the lights go down. Two young women lose their virginities—to each other. A submissive man searches for the "Holy Grail" (two women at once), but the actual quest they lead him on shocks, surprises, and changes him forever. In these sensual, explicit, hot—and, at times, surprisingly humorous—stories, anything goes. Playful BDSM scenes, pegging, public sex, queer characters, crossdressing, sexy consent, romance, and so much more. Throw the rule book away and unleash your wildest desires with this shameless, imaginative read.